THE CAMELOT CODE

CODE

Geeks and the Holy Grail

THE CAMELOT CODE

Book 2

Geeks and the Holy Grail

MARI MANCUSI

Disney • HYPERION
Los Angeles   New York

First Edition, October 2019
1 3 5 7 9 10 8 6 4 2
FAC-020093-19228
Printed in the United States of America

Text is set in Adobe Caslon Pro, Brandon Grotesque, Billy,
Penumbra Flare, Penumbra Sans, Eco Coding/Fontspring

Designed by Tyler Nevins

Library of Congress Cataloging-in-Publication Data
Names: Mancusi, Mari, author.
Title: Geeks and the Holy Grail / Mari Mancusi.
Description: First edition. • New York, New York : Disney • Hyperion, 2019. • Series:
The Camelot Code ; #2 • Summary: Twelve-year-old Sophie Sawyer's first assignment
as a Companion is to help Nimue, a young druid, and Emrys the Excellent, Merlin's
thirteen-year-old apprentice, protect the Holy Grail from the evil sorceress, Morgana.
Identifiers: LCCN 2018029853 • ISBN 9781368014779 (hardcover)
Subjects: • CYAC: Time travel—Fiction. • Magic—Fiction. • Grail—Fiction. •
Druids and druidism—Fiction. • Merlin (Legendary character)—Fiction. • Camelot
(Legendary place)—Fiction. • Arthur, King—Fiction. • Humorous stories.
Classification: LCC PZ7.M312178 Ge 2019 • DDC [Fic]—dc23
LC record available at https://lccn.loc.gov/2018029853

Reinforced binding

Visit www.DisneyBooks.com

To all my once and future readers! Your enthusiasm and passion for reading make being an author the best job in the world. I hope you enjoy the continued adventures of Sophie and Stu. Pepperoni pizza forever!

CHAPTER 1

"**D**on't let them get away!"

Nimue dove through the thick woods, forcing herself not to turn around as she clutched her precious cargo tightly to her chest. Her ears rang with the sounds of men shouting behind her. Women screaming. Her sisters surrounded by Morgana's men, fighting for their lives.

It was not supposed to go this way. Not at all.

Her heart pounded in her chest. She dared a glance down at the relic, wrapped securely in a gray woolen blanket and crushed against her. It looked so small. So insignificant. Yet somehow it had the power to change the future. And if it fell into the wrong hands . . .

She gripped the relic tighter. No. That was not going to happen. Not on her watch.

As the youngest druid on the island of Avalon, Nimue shouldn't have been on guard duty in the first place. At least not by herself. But Vivianne had been struck ill with a stomach sickness and needed to sleep it off. And the others had been tired; they'd already had their turns. So Nimue had volunteered, hoping to trade a sleepless night on watch for a future favor once they arrived in Camelot. Perhaps, if she were lucky, they would even allow her to attend the castle ball. Nimue had always wanted to go to a ball.

It was supposed to be dull work. Staying up all night, ensuring that the fire remained lit. That the relic was not tampered with or stolen. Which shouldn't have been a problem, seeing as no one should have had any idea the druids had it in their possession to begin with. Their mission was secret. Their true identities hidden by a combination of old rags and new magic. No passerby should have been able to observe anything beyond a group of peasant women, traveling to the capital city to attend a feast.

But someone had known. Someone who wanted the precious cargo all to herself.

That someone was the evil sorceress Morgana.

Nimue burst into a small clearing, nestled in the thick woods. She looked around, her ears pricked up for any sound, but all she heard was the grass, gently swishing in the night breeze.

She allowed herself a shaky breath, still clutching the relic like a newborn babe in her arms. Whatever happened to her, she could not allow it to fall into Morgana's hands. The entire future of Camelot depended on it.

It was then she heard the sound. A crashing through the woods, followed by a loud shout. She bit down on her tongue to stifle a scream as she dropped to her belly in the tall grass. Her mouth filled with the copper tang of blood, but she ignored it, her eyes locked on the knight clad in chain-mail armor, storming toward her, not ten paces away, brandishing a fiery torch.

"You think you can hide from me, girl?" he growled in a thick, ugly accent. He was tall, broad-shouldered, with a nasty scar slicing across his cheek. But it was the sharp-looking sword by his side that chilled Nimue to the bone. Swords were forbidden in Avalon, so she had never seen one close up. "Come out now and I will let you live."

But he would not let her live; she could tell from the eager flash in his eyes. And even if he did manage to surprise her, she would not trade her own miserable life for the relic. She'd made a pledge to protect it. She would not let her sisters down.

Nimue forced herself to still her breathing low and slow, even as her heart thumped maddeningly against her chest and her whole body trembled. Gathering her senses, she whispered a spell of distraction under her breath—one of the only spells she knew by heart, for she had unfortunately left her spell book back at the camp when she'd fled. It was a spell she'd learned with her best friend, Tamora, last year. They'd used it on their teacher to get out of a particularly boring lesson and had gotten three weeks of lugging well water as punishment for the deed.

But it might save her life now.

Save the entire world, in fact.

She finished the incantation—waited with bated breath. For a moment, nothing happened. Then...

Crash!

The knight jerked to attention. A cruel smile cut across his ugly face. "There you are, you blasted wench," he cried, taking off toward the sound.

Leaving Nimue alone.

It was all the advantage she needed. Scrambling to her feet, she dashed in the opposite direction, still clutching the artifact tightly in her arms. She knew the knight would circle back around once he realized he'd been tricked. She didn't have much time. But where should she go? What should she do? She couldn't keep running—some of the men had horses and would surely catch her eventually. Which meant she had to find somewhere to hide. Somewhere safe.

Nimue scanned the forest as she ran, desperate for some last-minute salvation. A deep hole, a large boulder, a particularly thick patch of foliage to hide behind until the men passed by. Something—anything—to—

She stopped short, her heels digging into the dirt. Heart thudding in her chest, she looked around, an odd feeling of familiarity suddenly rippling through her. A strange memory of those tangled vines, hanging just so off that craggy ledge. The odd pattern of stones at her feet. Had she been here before? But no, that was impossible. She'd only left the island of Avalon once, after all. When she'd been suffering from a wasting sickness and Vivianne had taken her to see...

Merlin.

She almost sobbed in relief as the memory came flooding back to her. Could it be? Had she actually stumbled upon the one man who could possibly save her? She ran to the familiar vines and carefully pulled them away, revealing the familiar glistening of multicolored gemstones. The entrance to the legendary Merlin the Great's Crystal Cave.

He had saved her life once. Could he do it again?

She ducked into the cave, feeling a little self-conscious. It was late at night—would the great wizard be asleep? She didn't want her intrusion to anger him. But she had very little choice in the matter if she wanted to survive.

"Lord Merlin?" she called out hesitantly when she stepped inside the cavern. It was lit by flickering torchlight, giving her hope he was still awake. "Lord Merlin, are you here? I am in desperate need of your assistance!"

She stopped short as her eyes caught a lone figure standing

in the shadows at the far end of the room. Her breath whooshed from her lungs in relief.

"Merlin," she whispered. "Thank the goddess."

"Uh, actually, Merlin's not here right now," the figure replied, stepping into the light. Nimue squinted at him, disappointment dropping like a stone in her stomach. The boy was tall, gangly, around her own age. Dressed in a long blue robe clearly meant for someone twice his girth and leaning on a wooden staff carved with the head of a dragon.

Definitely not Lord Merlin.

"What do you mean he's not here?" she cried, her voice cracking with dismay. Merlin was her only hope, she wanted to tell him. He had to be here. He just had to be! She stared at the boy. "And you . . ." she added. "Who are you?"

"My name is Emrys the Excellent," the boy replied with a sleepy shrug. "And as for Merlin? I'm sorry, but he's away on spring break."

CHAPTER 2

"**W**oo-hoo! Spring break!"

Twelve-year-old Sophie Sawyer laughed as her best friend, Stuart Mallory, danced out of Sacred Mary Junior High, throwing his backpack into the air and letting it land in the grass nearby.

"You are way too excited," she scolded as she watched him run to pick it up. "Are you even going anywhere for spring break?"

"Nope. I'm going to spend the entire week doing nothing but eating pepperoni pizza and playing video games," Stu declared. "In fact, I may not even put on pants."

"You're living the dream," she groaned, slumping down onto the grass. "Meanwhile I'll be living my own *Five Nights at Cammy's* wedding nightmare." She yanked off her backpack, setting it beside her. "You can't even imagine all the dress fittings and cake tastings and rehearsal dinners I have to get through this week before I can even think about loading up my PlayStation."

Stu gave her a pitying look. He knew better than anyone how much Sophie was dreading her father's upcoming wedding to Sacred Mary cheer coach and *Real Housewives* aficionado, Cammy Jones.

"I can't believe in one week Ashley Jones is going to be your stepsister," he remarked, looking down the hill at the school's football field, where the future stepsister in question was excitedly gesturing to her circle of minions, probably relating wild tales of thrilling new Snapchat filters.

"One week and two days," Sophie corrected as she watched Ashley jump in front of her group, holding out her phone to snap a selfie. Then another. And another. Sophie rolled her eyes. "Let's not rush this."

Stu plopped down beside her. "You sure there's no chance of your dad backing out?"

"Please. He's all in." She scrunched up her face. "I even caught him watching *Say Yes to the Dress* with the bridezilla-to-be when I came home from school the other day."

"Wow." Stu gave a low whistle. "That's actually kind of impressive."

Sophie turned away from the football field, trying to ignore the familiar sour feeling creeping into her stomach. After all, it wasn't as if she didn't want her dad to be happy. It was just that an actual wedding felt so final. Like the nail in the coffin of Sophie's fantasy of her mother returning home someday and the three of them being a family again. Of course, she knew this was impossible in real life. Her mother had *much* more important things to do. And, of course, she couldn't blame her dad for wanting to move on....

Still, the idea of soon sharing a bathroom with Ashley Jones made her want to throw up in her mouth a little. Or, you know, projectile vomit pea soup like the *Exorcist* girl.

Without thinking about it, Sophie pulled her phone from her backpack, glancing down at it with longing eyes. But, as always, there were no missed calls. No text messages.

No Camelot Code.

She sighed. "If only the Companions would call on me."

"You want to save the world on spring break?" Stu asked, raising an eyebrow.

"If it would get me out of dress fittings."

It had been three months since Sophie and Stu had left King Arthur's court and returned to modern-day America after saving the world from the evil sorceress Morgana. It had been the adventure of a lifetime, to say the least, and it had been tough to get readjusted to the real world. After all, it wasn't every day you traveled back in time, pulled the sword from the stone, and stood in for King Arthur like Stu had.

And then there was Sophie's mission—tracking down the missing monarch and convincing him to return home to fulfill his destiny. Which proved no easy task, especially once Arthur googled himself and found out what was in store for him back home—and decided he'd rather try out for the football team.

And to top it all off? There was the showdown with Morgana herself—and the rescue of Princess Guinevere. A total real-life video-game moment! Not to mention the day Sophie first learned she had magic stirring deep inside her. Just like her mom. The day she officially signed up to become a Companion—one of a secret sect of warriors dedicated to protecting the once and future king throughout the annals of time.

Sophie's mother was a Companion, which turned out to be why she'd left the family when Sophie was only seven. Sophie used to be mad at her mom for just taking off, and without even saying a proper good-bye. Now she understood her mother had her reasons—she had to save the world. Besides, how cool was it to have an actual time-traveling superhero as your mom? Not to mention having the chance to become a time-traveling super-hero yourself?

Except there had been no time traveling. And no superhero-ing, either. Her mother had said the Companions would call on her when they needed her, but evidently it had been smooth sailing through time for the last three months. Every day Sophie would wake up, hoping for a text message calling her into action. But at this point she wondered if the call would ever come.

She'd gotten one text, after they'd first returned. Sophie had been so excited, thinking she was being tapped for a real mission. But it turned out to be nothing more than a false alarm, the Companions testing the system to make sure it would work when the real emergency came. *Standard procedure*, they'd said. Like a fire drill at school.

Sophie had tried not to feel too disappointed. But still! It was tough to stay pumped for social studies and science class when she knew there was a time-traveling battle for the world going on, and she was stuck on the sidelines.

Stu patted her on the back. "They'll call," he assured her, then slung his backpack over his shoulder and stood up. "In the meantime, let's go grab a Slurpee. I hear 7-Eleven has the forty-four-ounce cups back in stock. And, as Lucas always says, nothing cures your troubles like a good old-fashioned brain freeze."

Sophie perked up. "Ooh. That sounds—"

"There you are! I've been looking *everywhere!*"

Ugh. Speaking of frozen brain cells...

Sophie's eyes fell on Ashley, marching up the hill, evidently finished with her series of selfies with her airheads-in-waiting. She was still wearing her cheerleading outfit—blue and white, the colors of the Sacred Mary Knights—along with an obnoxiously large matching bow on top of her auburn-colored head. Even though football season had ended months ago.

"Oh, hey, Ashley," Sophie said, trying to sound cheerful as she rose to her feet. Her dad had practically begged her to play nice—*She's going to be your sister, after all!* But at times it could be tougher than winning a *Fortnite* Battle Royale. "I was in the computer lab."

"Really? Did you get detention or something?" Ashley asked, looking horrified. As if she couldn't fathom any other reason someone would willingly hang out at school after school.

"Actually, she was hacking into the the principal's computer to change her grades," Stu said brightly. "How else do you think she gets all those As on her report card?"

Her future stepsister's eyes widened. "Really?"

"No." Sophie groaned. "Did you need something, Ashley?"

"Well, my history grade could use a boost. I'm pretty sure I bombed my last test." Ashley wrinkled her nose. "But seriously, who cares about ancient history, anyway? It has absolutely no effect on real life."

"Actually, you'd be surprised," Stu muttered.

Sophie bit back a giggle. "Do you need anything *else*?" she tried. "I mean, something I can actually help you with?"

"Um. I need you? In my mom's car? So we can get going?"

Sophie squinted at her, more confused than ever. "Going where?"

"Oh my gosh, do not tell me you forgot," Ashley burst out. "I sent you like twenty texts yesterday."

Right. Sophie vaguely remembered getting a series of texts from Ashley while she and Stu were knee-deep in a video-game dungeon, fighting vampires. It had gotten so annoying, she'd turned her phone to Do Not Disturb mode, promising she'd check them later. Which, she realized now, she hadn't.

But she couldn't let Ashley know that. In the cheerleader's mind, ignoring text messages was a capital offense, punishable by death. Or, you know, a lot more text messages. Sophie shuddered, still remembering the horror of that last group text she'd been stuck on for months. . . .

"Right," she said. "Of course. We were going to . . ."

"Buy avocados," Ashley finished, looking impatient.

"Avocados?"

"So we can glitter them."

"You want to *glitter* avocados?"

"So we can put them in the mason jars." Ashley crossed her arms in front of her. "For the tables at the reception?" She sighed. "Did you even look at the Pinterest board I sent you?"

Stu snickered. Sophie shot him a look, then attempted a smile for Ashley. "Of course! Right!" she tried. "Avocado glittering! So . . . Pinteresty."

Ashley beamed. "I know, right? Can you believe Mom tried to talk me out of it at first? Anyway, she's totally down now and she's even agreed to drive us to Michaels so we can pick up supplies. She's waiting in the parking lot. Come on!"

She grabbed Sophie's hand and started dragging her down toward the parking lot. Sophie shot Stu a "save me" look, but he only shrugged helplessly. In this dungeon, Princess Sophie would have to save herself.

She glanced down at her cell phone again.

No text messages. No Camelot Code.

Seriously, if the Companions didn't call soon, this spring break might truly break her.

CHAPTER 3

"Spring break? What on the Mother's great earth is spring break?"

Thirteen-year-old Emrys took a hesitant step backward as the strange girl stalked toward him, a desperate look on her face. She was tall—nearly half a foot taller than him, but slender. With long black hair braided down her back, brown skin, and piercing dark eyes. She wore a brown hooded cloak over a stained white robe cinched with a silver cord and clutched some kind of small bundle in her arms. She was perhaps the prettiest girl Emrys had ever laid eyes on.

Also, the most upset.

"I'm, uh, not entirely sure," he stammered. "I guess it's like a holiday?" He tried to remember Merlin's words before he left. "A...vacation, I think he called it?"

The girl stared at him blankly. He shuffled from foot to foot. "Well, he's not here," he spluttered. "And that's the end of it. If you want to leave a message, I'll put it with the others."

He gestured to the large array of sticky notes he'd affixed to the cave's wall. Messages left by uninvited guests who had wandered into the Crystal Cave, demanding Merlin magically heal their dying pig or help their wife give birth. The place was like a revolving door of need—with everyone wanting something—and he wondered how Merlin dealt with it on a daily basis without going mad.

The girl's gaze darted to the mouth of the cave and Emrys thought he caught a shimmer of fear wash across her face. "I don't need to leave a message. I need help now." She turned to him with an appraising eye. "Who are you again?"

Emrys puffed out his chest. "I am Emrys the Excellent," he repeated. "Lord Merlin's devoted apprentice."

She pursed her lips. "Do you know magic?"

"I wouldn't be a very good apprentice if I didn't."

"Yes, but how do I know you're a good apprentice?" she countered. "Perhaps you are terrible. Perhaps you are the worst apprentice ever."

"Perhaps *you* should be going," he shot back grumpily. After all, it was the middle of the night. He'd already been rudely awakened. He didn't need to be insulted to boot.

The girl's face softened. "I'm sorry," she said. "It's just... it's been quite a night. I'm sure you're an extremely talented wizard with plenty of powerful magic at your disposal."

"Uh... I don't know if I would go that—"

"So if you could just grab your spell book, we could get started." She glanced at the mouth of the cave again. "You see, I'm in a bit of a hurry, actually."

"Right." Emrys looked down at his hands. "I'm sorry, but I'm afraid that's not possible."

She scrunched up her face. "Why not?"

"It's just... I'm not exactly allowed to use magic at the moment."

"What kind of wizard isn't allowed to use magic?"

"The apprentice kind—when the master is away." He held up his hands helplessly. "I'm sorry, but Lord Merlin left very strict orders. No magic."

His mind flashed back to the endless list of rules Merlin had laid out before he left. No magic spells. No playing games on the magic box in the back chamber. No looking into the Well of Dreams portal. Not even to watch one of those splendid "Yankees games" Merlin had been viewing the day he arrived. In fact, about all Emrys was allowed to do while his master was away was mop the floor (by himself—definitely no conjuring up magic brooms!) and make batches of pea soup.

Emrys detested pea soup.

He started to turn away, but the girl grabbed his arm, pulling him back around. "You don't understand!" she protested. "The kingdom of Camelot is at stake!" She looked at him with dark, pleading eyes, her face a mask of desperation. "Please, Emrys the Excellent," she whispered. "You're the world's only hope."

Emrys froze, staring at the girl. The world's only hope? Did she just say *he* was the world's only hope? That was the kind of thing damsels in distress said to knights in shining armor in his mother's stories. Not to scrawny farm boys from backwater villages like himself.

But he wasn't a scrawny farm boy anymore, he suddenly realized. He was a wizard-in-training. The apprentice of Merlin the Great.

Something tugged inside him. He bit his lower lip, his mind racing. Clearly, this girl needed him. The *world* needed him. How could he turn the world away—simply because of a few silly rules? Surely, Merlin would want Emrys to help.

He cleared his throat, making up his mind. "What seems to be the trouble, m'lady?" he asked in the most gallant voice he could muster. Which, in truth, came off a bit more squeaky than gallant for his liking. He'd need to practice that.

In any case, it seemed to work. The girl practically drooped in relief. Emrys watched as she began to unwrap her parcel, revealing a small object beneath. A very familiar-looking object.

Emrys's eyes bulged. Could it be? But that was impossible! Though...

His mind flashed back to the stories his mother would tell him and his brothers by the fire after a hard day's work on the farm. Fantastical tales of dragons and evil knights and damsels in distress. (And sometimes damsels who saved themselves!) The stories had always sounded unbelievable to Emrys's ears. But his mother insisted each and every one of them was true.

Now he wondered if she had been right.

"Is that...?" he stammered. "Is that really...?"

The cup was small and plain. Hardly any ornamentation whatsoever. And yet, even in the dim light of the cave, it seemed to glow with an otherworldly shimmer, as if it was made of actual star fire.

"The Holy Grail," the girl said solemnly.

"But that's... that's just a story!"

"A *true* story," she amended. "The cup was brought to Britain a thousand years ago by a long-lost society that first colonized the land. It was hidden under a great hill, called the Tor, on the island of Avalon. And for the last millennium we have been its protectors."

"So you're... a Companion?"

Emrys's mother had also told tales of the Companions, a group of legendary warriors who served and protected Mother

Earth. They were noble, revered. He wondered, suddenly, if he should be bowing to this girl, but she quickly set him straight.

"No. I'm just a young druid-in-training," she said, and gave a small shrug. "An apprentice, like yourself. They call me Nimue."

"That's a beautiful name," he blurted out, before he could stop himself. His face heated in a blush. What was it Merlin had said? That he had "zero cool"? The girl was looking for help—not compliments, for goodness' sake.

"So, uh, if the Grail has been hidden all this time, why do you have it now?" he added hastily.

"It is needed in Camelot," she explained. "King Arthur has been struck down by a plague, and only the magic in this Grail can cure him. Without it, he will die, and the kingdom will be ripe for a takeover by Morgana."

Emrys's pulse quickened. Morgana? That was certainly a name he had heard before. In fact, she had been the evil sorceress in most of his mother's bedtime tales. He supposed if the Grail was real, she must be real, too.

He swallowed hard. "What do you want me to do?"

"I need you to hide the Grail, of course!"

"Right." He bit his lower lip, looking around the cave. "Maybe in the back room?"

"That's not good enough! They'll just ransack the place and find it! You need to use magic." She gave him an accusing look. "You said you knew magic!"

"Of course I know magic!" Emrys cried, trying to sound confident, even though he was now shaking with fear. This girl was counting on him. The world was counting on him. Merlin had put his entire life's work into Arthur and his rule. If he came back from spring break and learned Emrys had managed to muck it all up...?

Well, let's just say "zero cool" would be the least of his problems then.

"Let me look in Merlin's spell book!" he declared. "There's got to be something we can use."

He ran to the back chamber. Unlike most magicians, who kept their spells in an actual book, Merlin liked to store his on something he called an iPad—a magical glass rectangle he'd insisted Emrys never touch himself. Hopefully, the wizard would forgive him, considering the circumstances.

"Hurry!" Nimue cried, joining him. "I think I hear them approaching."

Emrys didn't answer, just tapped furiously on the iPad's glass surface. At least he'd watched Merlin enough times to know how to pick the proper picture under the glass. But once the spell app loaded up, he realized he was at a loss. All the spells were written in Latin. And Emrys hadn't really paid much attention in Latin class....

Fine. He hadn't even taken a Latin class.

"Um..." he said, his hands shaking so hard he nearly dropped the iPad. "Maybe I should pull up Google Translate...." He'd seen Merlin do that before when he was stuck on a strange word.

"I don't know what that is but there's no time for that!" Nimue cried. "I hear them outside. They'll be here any second!"

Emrys's gaze shot to the mouth of the cave. Sure enough, through the vines he could see a couple of men on horseback starting to dismount. They must have spotted the entrance—or maybe heard Nimue and Emrys speaking?

He had to cast the spell. Now.

He stared down at the cup. Then he drew in a deep breath.

Here goes nothing.

"*Transvorto Calix, Pullys!*" he muttered, probably murdering the pronunciation. "*Transvorto Calix, Pullys!*"

Poof!

The cup went up in a puff of smoke, electricity crackling in the air. Emrys leaped back so as not to be burned. Then a grin slid across his face. It had worked! His spell had actually—

BWAK!

What? He cocked his head at the strange sound, his eyes now locked on where the Grail had been a moment before.

The smoke had cleared. The cup was gone.

And in its place?

A big, fat chicken.

CHAPTER 4

"Wind and Rain!" Nimue cried in dismay. "Did you just turn the Holy Grail into a chicken?"

It was a stupid question. With an obvious answer. Because there, on the table in front of them, exactly where the Grail had been a moment before, now stood a large white-feathered fowl with beady eyes, red comb, and a sharp-looking beak.

"Cock-a-doodle-doo!" it crowed, as if in answer.

Nimue's heart sank in her chest, and fear spun down her spine. This was terrible. So, so terrible. And it was all her fault, too. What had she been thinking? To put the most precious relic in the world—the one she had sworn to protect with her life—in the hands of a complete stranger? Trusting that he would do right by it, just because he said he would?

She reached out to grab the Grail chicken. It gave her a hard peck on the hand.

"Ow!" she cried, jerking back, clutching her stinging palm. She glared at the chicken. "Was that really necessary?"

She turned back to Emrys, to demand that he give it another go. But then her eyes caught movement at the mouth of the cave. Blazes! They were already inside. The chicken would have to do—for now.

She glanced around the back chamber. Should she hide herself? None of the knights had seen her face, but they might recognize her robes and realize she was one of the druids they were looking for. But what else could she do? Short of having Emrys turn her into a chicken, too.

It was then she spied some kind of tunic hanging from a peg on the other side of the room. She ran to it, pulling it into her arms. It had a portrait on it—of a large castle and a strange-looking mouse with red trousers.

"That's Merlin's favorite shirt!" Emrys protested.

"And I'm borrowing it," she shot back, slipping the mouse tunic over her robe. It was too large for her, of course, and fell past her knees. But at least now they wouldn't recognize her.

She and Emrys headed back into the main cavern, Nimue in the lead. Two burly knights dressed in full chain mail and armed with swords strapped to their sides were rummaging through Merlin's things with rough hands. Nimue winced as a vase made of glass fell to the ground and shattered.

She cleared her throat, squared her shoulders, and forced a scolding expression onto her face. "Did your mothers not teach you to knock?" she demanded, stalking over to the men, hands on her hips. It was not proper, of course, to address knights with such disrespect. But these men were clearly working for Morgana and therefore deserved to be treated as traitors to the crown.

The men jumped; evidently they hadn't realized anyone was home. They turned to stare at Nimue and Emrys, ugly scowls on their faces. "And who might you be?" the first one demanded. He had a shock of black hair and an unkempt beard.

"I am Emrys the Excellent," Emrys declared before Nimue could reply. He stepped in front of her to face off with the men, his arms crossed over his chest. Which was pretty brave, Nimue had to grudgingly admit. "Apprentice to Lord Merlin. And you are intruding on his private residence."

"Lord Merlin, eh?" The second man raised a bushy eyebrow. He had bright orange hair and a pug nose. "And where might Lord Merlin be now?"

"He's away," Nimue broke in. "But we expect his return any moment now, and he'll be very cross if he finds you here, pawing through his private things. So I suggest you leave now if you don't want him to turn you into a toad."

"Or a chicken!" Emrys added staunchly. Nimue shot him a warning look. This was no time for jokes!

BWAK!

Speaking of... The chicken—otherwise known as the most precious relic in the world—chose that moment to strut into the cavern's main chamber, proudly parading itself in front of the two intruders, before stopping in front of the cave's eastern wall, observing the crystals embedded in the rock. Nimue cringed as it started to peck away at them, as if they were pieces of corn.

"What's that?" the knight demanded, narrowing his eyes.

"Lord Merlin's dinner," Nimue declared before Emrys could answer. She stalked over to the chicken and grabbed it by its feet. It yelped in apparent alarm and attempted to peck her again as she dragged it to the center of the cave and dropped it into the large black cauldron. Which thankfully wasn't heated yet. The chicken flapped around the bottom of the pot, squawking unhappily.

"And who might you be?" the second knight added, giving her a critical once-over. "And what in the blazes are you wearing?"

"She's just the cook. And she's very behind schedule," Emrys declared. He turned to Nimue. "Girl, go chop up those carrots! Make yourself useful for once!"

Nimue shot him a disgusted look. The cook? Really? That was the best he could do? Yes, it would be unusual for a girl to apprentice under a sorcerer. But then, Merlin was an unusual man! Was it so impossible to believe he could be open to the idea?

The men snorted, giving Emrys a knowing look. "Wenches!" the first one scoffed. "Gotta be firm with them. Or they'll walk all over you."

Of all the—! It was all Nimue could do not to walk all over *him*. Before punching him square in the jaw, that is. But then she caught Emrys's warning look. She sighed. *Right. Play along.* It did no good to defend one's honor if it led to one's body being run through by a sword.

She forced her hands back to her sides, but kept them clenched into fists just the same. It made her feel a little bit better.

"Now, good sirs, to what do we owe this honor?" Emrys asked the guards, evidently fully embracing his role as master of the manor. He pulled his robe tighter against him. "It is not every day we get visitors this deep in the forest. Especially fine knights like yourselves."

"We're looking for something. A very important relic was stolen from Camelot," the knight with the big nose explained. He was tall, but scrawny. Nimue felt she could probably take him in a fight, had he not been armed with a sword.

"I'm afraid you won't find any relic here," Emrys replied smoothly. "Besides those that belong to Lord Merlin, of course."

The first man eyed him suspiciously. "We'll be the judge of that."

Emrys shrugged, as if it made no difference to him. He made a sweeping gesture with his hands. "By all means, judge away."

The men got to work. They did more than "judge," of course. In fact, they pretty much destroyed the place before finally admitting defeat. Knocking over tables, upending shelves, spilling glass vials filled with foamy green liquid. They made a great investigation of everything—except, of course, the pot containing the chicken. From across the cave, Nimue gave Emrys an approving look. Maybe he'd had the right idea after all.

Finally, after what seemed like an eternity, the two men gave up. "I don't think it's here," the first one said.

The second one nodded. "We'd better circle back. Maybe one of the others has had better luck."

And with that, they headed out of the cave, not bothering even to say good-bye, let alone apologize for the disarray they had caused. Still, Nimue let out an uneasy breath of relief.

"That was close," she said.

"Aye. Too close," Emrys agreed, swiping his damp forehead with his hand. He looked around the ravaged cave. "What a mess. This is going to take weeks to set right."

Nimue gave him a rueful look. "Sorry about that."

He waved her off. "It's no bother. Gives me something to do while waiting for Merlin." He walked over to the table and pulled it upright.

Nimue watched him work. "Um..." she said hesitantly. "Aren't you forgetting something?"

He turned. "What?"

She nodded in the direction of the chicken, still strutting in circles inside the pot. "Our little feathered friend?"

"Oh, right. I suppose you want it grail-shaped again."

"Yes, please. I still need to get it to Camelot." She paused, then added, "Somehow..."

A sudden heaviness draped over her shoulders, blanketing her earlier panic. She'd been in full survival mode since she'd run from the camp, but now the reality of her situation was starting to seep in. Her sisters were dead. There was no one left to help her. She was alone.

She shook her head, trying to firm her resolve. She was a druid of Avalon and she had a mission. That had not changed. She would get the Grail to Camelot one way or another. And then she'd figure out what to do next.

If she made it. Her stomach wormed with uneasiness as she thought of the journey ahead of her. The roads were dangerous, even for a group. And Morgana would not give up looking for the Grail.

Perhaps she could ask Emrys to join her...? Having a wizard—even one who was only in training—could help. She nodded to herself, resolving to ask him, once he returned the

Grail to its rightful form. Surely he would be honored to assist in such a noble quest.

Emrys walked over and grabbed the chicken by the neck. It screeched and tried to peck his hand. For an ancient relic that had been living under a mountain for the last thousand years, it was pretty feisty, she thought. She'd be glad to see it return to its non-animal state.

The two of them headed back to Merlin's inner chamber, Emrys setting the chicken down on a table and grabbing the strange rectangle Merlin evidently used as a spell book. Emrys scanned the screen, then muttered something under his breath. A moment later, the chicken disappeared in a puff of white smoke.

Leaving behind... a slug?

"Um..." Nimue said.

Emrys scrunched up his face. "One moment."

He muttered some more words. Conjured up more smoke. Nimue had to admit, he was very good at the smoke-making thing. But when the air cleared...

"A loaf of bread?" she cried. "I admit, it does look delicious. But..."

Emrys groaned. His forehead was now drenched in sweat and his hands were shaking. His voice wobbled as he intoned yet another spell. This time producing an even larger plume of smoke—practically filling the back of the cave. And then...

BURP.

The smoke cleared. The bread was gone.

And in its place was... a baby dragon?

"What on earth?" Nimue cried in dismay.

It was about the size of a small dog, with shiny red scales, piercing green eyes, and a long swishy tail. And when it opened its mouth, it let out a large belch—and a tiny fireball shot through the air. Nimue backed away quickly to avoid having her hair go up in flames.

She turned to Emrys accusingly. "I said I needed it grail-shaped."

"I know! I'm sorry!" Emrys cried, collapsing onto a nearby chair. He raked a hand through his messy hair. "I can't do it. I can't change it back."

"What?" Nimue stared at him, horrified. "But you said—"

"I know what I said. But I... well, I might have been stretching the truth a bit," he admitted, his cheeks coloring a bright red. "I haven't been an apprentice very long, you see. In fact, I've only been an apprentice for three days."

"Three... *days?*"

He shrugged sheepishly. "I arrived early. I was too excited to wait. But Merlin was leaving for his trip two days later. So he told me I could stay here until he came back. Then we would start our training."

"So you have no training?" Nimue cried. "You don't know

magic?" This was unbelievable. She'd actually put the fate of the world in the hands of a total novice?

"I knew enough to save your precious Grail," he protested. "If it weren't for me, it'd be in the hands of Morgana's men right now!"

Nimue opened her mouth to speak, but a sudden horrible smell assaulted her nose. "Ew!" she cried, glaring at Emrys. "Did you just...?"

Emrys's jaw dropped. "No!" he cried. He paused, then wrinkled his brow. "Honestly, I think it was the Grail."

Nimue slowly turned to look at the dragon. It looked back at her, a guilty grin seeming to stretch across its reptilian face. It was then that she noticed the small puff of smoke trailing out from under its tail. She scrunched up her face in disgust, pinching her nose with her fingers.

"This is a disaster!" she exclaimed. "A true disaster."

"If you could just wait here for Merlin..."

"There's no time for that!" she protested. "Arthur is sick. I need to get the Grail to him or else he will die."

Emrys moaned. He rose to his feet and stalked across the cave, his steps eating up the distance between the walls. "What have I done?" he wailed, seeming to be talking to himself more than to Nimue. "Merlin's going to be furious with me. He might even refuse to train me. My whole life I've wanted nothing but to become a wizard! What if he sends me home?"

Nimue sighed. He looked so pathetic. It was hard to stay mad at him. And he *had* helped her keep the Grail from Morgana's men, she supposed. Better a stinky dragon here than a holy cup in the sorceress's hands.

"Look," she said. "There might be another way."

"Really?" Emrys's voice was filled with hope.

"You asked earlier if I was a Companion," she reminded him. "I'm not, of course. But I can summon them. I *think* I can, anyway. Vivianne taught me once. It's for emergencies only. But . . ."

The baby dragon enthusiastically launched itself off Merlin's table. It flapped its wings twice, then dropped like a stone to the floor, landing in a tangled heap. Nimue rolled her eyes.

"I think this qualifies," she finished.

Emrys looked like he wanted to hug her. "It definitely qualifies!" he cried instead, reaching down to scoop up the dragon and set it back on the table. "If anyone can help, it'll be the Companions."

Nimue nodded. "Well, then," she said. "Let's give it a try."

She reached under her tunic, finding the pocket of her robe, and pulled out the scrap of parchment paper containing the invocation to summon the Companions. Druids were required to keep it on them at all times, and thankfully, she'd not left it behind like her spell book.

Then, as Emrys and the dragon watched, she recited the Camelot Code.

CHAPTER 5

"You have got to be kidding me."

Sophie emerged from the dressing room Saturday morning, stepping in front of the large mirror and staring down in dismay at the bridesmaid dress she was wearing. It was literally the ugliest article of clothing she'd ever put on. For one thing, it was bright orangey-peach. It also had puffed sleeves and a high waist and waves of frothy chiffon ruffles poufing out the skirt. She looked like one of those creepy porcelain baby dolls that always seemed to come alive in horror movies.

"Orange," she muttered. "Who would actually pick orange on purpose?"

Maybe it was a joke? She glanced around the bridal shop,

praying to find a hidden camera. Like the ones you always saw on those reality shows on TV. A moment later a stylishly outfitted lady would bring her the actual dress she was to wear to her dad's wedding and say—

"You look GORGEOUS!"

She whirled around. Cammy stood behind her, clapping her hands in delight. Hands, Sophie couldn't help but notice, with fingernails painted the exact same color as her dress.

So much for a reality-TV miracle.

"Oh, honey," Cammy purred. "You are just *something* in that dress. It reminds me of—"

"A rotten pumpkin?" Sophie proposed.

"—peaches and cream!" Cammy finished proudly. "Like a Barbie doll come to life!" As if that were something people would actually strive to look like.

"Ta-da!" Ashley cried, whirling out of the other dressing room, her identical peaches-and-vomit dress swirling around her. She stopped in front of her mother. "Oh, Mom!" she gushed. "It's to die for!"

Sophie wrinkled her nose. Die of embarrassment wearing this in public, maybe....

"My two girls!" Cammy cooed, grabbing Sophie in a headlock and dragging her into a forced group hug with her soon-to-be stepsister. Sophie tried to squirm away, but Miss Cheetos-Colored Fingernails had a killer grip. All those Pilates classes, she supposed. "You guys are going to be superstars out there! You'll totally upstage the bride!"

"Uh, then maybe you should wear an orange dress, too?" Sophie suggested.

She could feel Ashley shoot her an annoyed look. "Don't be ridiculous, Mom," she scolded. "You are going to be the most beautiful bride ever! Hashtag-no-filter even!" She kissed her mom on the cheek. "Now let's see that dress!"

Cammy squealed—actually squealed—and Sophie almost ate it as she was dropped like a hot potato from the hug as her stepmother-to-be skipped over to the dressing room. "Okay," Cammy said, peeking out from behind the curtain, a mischievous grin spreading across her face. "Ready or not! Here comes the bride!"

She closed the curtain. Ashley turned to Sophie, her bright eyes narrowing into slits. "You know you could at least pretend to be into this," she scolded. "After all, my mom didn't *have* to make you a bridesmaid."

Sophie felt her hackles rise. It's not like she had asked to be one. In fact, the only reason she agreed to it in the first place was so as to not hurt her father's feelings. He'd been so excited when Cammy had made the suggestion that "both our girls" be by her side on their big day. Sophie didn't have the heart to say no.

She opened her mouth. Probably to say something she would regret. But before she could speak, her cell phone chimed, signaling a text message. *Saved by the iPhone.*

She ran over to her discarded backpack and pulled out her phone. She assumed, at first, it would be Stu, gloating that he'd just gotten the high score on *Plants vs. Zombies* or something. At least *he* was having a good spring break.

She looked down at the screen and her breath caught in her throat. The text wasn't from Stu at all. Her hands shook so hard she almost dropped the phone as she silently read the message.

Rex quondam, Rexque Futurus

"What is it?" Ashley asked, sounding curious despite herself. "Oh my gosh, is Stu having another video-game crisis? You tell that kid he needs to put it on pause. After all, we've got important things to—"

Sophie shoved the phone in her bag. "I've got to go."

"What? No way. You're not going anywhere!" Ashley cried. "You haven't even seen my mom's dress!"

"Text me a photo. This can't wait." Sophie glanced around the dress shop, heart pounding in her chest. Of all the times for the Camelot Code to arrive, it had to be now? When she was with Ashley? Wearing this hideous dress?

She bit her lower lip, wondering what she should do. Cammy was occupying the changing room. And who knew how long her stepmother's grand reveal was going to take? What if the code was only good for a limited time?

"Excuse me?" she called out to the shopkeeper. "Do you have a bathroom?" She could at least change in there. . . .

"Yes. In the back," the woman said.

"Great. Thanks." She turned to Ashley. "Tell your mom I'm sorry."

She grabbed her backpack and pile of clothes and dashed to the bathroom. Only when she got there did she realize she'd left her jeans in the dressing room. Great. She looked down at the dress. Guess she'd be saving the world in peaches and puke.

Pulling out her phone, she drew in a breath, then readied herself to say the words. Her mind raced with excitement and a little fear. What would the crisis be? How would she be able to help? Could it be another false alarm? Another test? Or were they really calling on her this time—needing her help on some valiant mission across time and space?

There was only one way to find out.

"On the count of three," she told herself. "One, two . . ." She cleared her throat. *"Rex quondam, Rexque Futurus!"*

"Sophie? Are you in here?"

She looked up, just in time to see Ashley barging into the bathroom. "My mom says she's supposed to take you home and—"

But she never got a chance to finish her sentence. Because at that very moment, the Code kicked in. And both Sophie and Ashley disappeared.

CHAPTER 6

I will never get used to time travel, thought Sophie, rubbing her aching head. She'd done it three times now and each time she was pretty sure she'd lost a few brain cells in the process. Every time she did it, she woke up dizzy and disoriented and sore all over. Her kingdom for a nice, cushy TARDIS like in *Doctor Who*.

She blinked twice, rubbing her eyes, trying to clear her head, which felt as if it had been stuffed with cotton candy. She forced herself to sit up, though her entire body protested the movement. Still, she couldn't risk waiting for the time-travel sickness to go away on its own. After all, the first time she'd traveled? She'd landed smack-dab in the middle of the road and had almost gotten run over by a pack of evil knights on horseback. If Arthur hadn't been there to save her, it would have been game over for sure.

This time, however…

Her vision cleared. Her eyes fell to glittering gemstones embedded in the wall. The rack of swords and shields. She sniffed, noting the lingering scent of oldish pea soup.

And something decidedly stinkier.

Ew. She wrinkled her nose. Next time she traveled through time? She was so bringing back a can of Glade. Or nose plugs at least. Her poor twenty-first-century nostrils were clearly not equipped to deal with the realities of a world without indoor plumbing and deodorant.

But in the end, even the stench couldn't squash the excitement rising inside her. Because she knew exactly where she was. Back in time. In Merlin's Crystal Cave. On an official Camelot Code assignment at long last.

She rose to her feet, her heart pounding with anticipation. And admittedly a little fear. This was not just some vacation, after all. This was a big deal. They might ask her to do something dangerous. Something possibly even deadly. Like infiltrating a band of outlaws. Outwitting a nasty troll. Descending into a deep cave to find a long-lost jewel. She and Stu had come up with all sorts of wild possibilities while waiting for the Code to come. And now she'd finally get to find out for real.

In her haste, she stepped over an upended table, heading toward Merlin's back room, where he usually hung out on his computer. "Merlin?" she called out, sure enough catching sight of a glowing blue light in the back. His monitor, she assumed. He was probably gaming. Or bingeing some new Netflix show. (He was super into the BBC *Merlin* show, go figure.) It was still a mystery to her how he was able to hijack Wi-Fi from the future and she wondered if he had his own account or had "borrowed" someone's password. "Are you—"

"GURG."

Sophie cried out in surprise as she accidentally tripped over a large lump on the floor, and grabbed on to a chair to keep her balance. A plume of dust burst into the air, causing her to sneeze.

"Wow. This place is even messier than usual," she said, marveling, looking around. "And that's saying something!" Merlin should seriously consider time-traveling a group of Merry Maids once in a while—or at least a Roomba. . . .

She leaned down to move whatever it was she'd tripped over. Her fingers brushed across something very . . . fluffy. And very . . . orange.

Or—perhaps more precisely—very peaches and cream . . .

Sophie's eyes widened in horror. "Oh no," she whispered.

Her mind flashed back to the scene in the dress shop, just as she'd been reciting the Code. She'd been so excited to get here, she'd almost forgotten how the door had swung open. How Ashley had burst in at the exact moment Sophie had finished the incantation.

"No, no, NO!"

Ashley poked her head up and squinted. "Sophie? What...? How...?" She shook her head, as if having difficulty forming words. She was still foggy from the trip. But it would only take her a moment to—

"AHHHHHH!" Ashley screeched, her eyes darting around the room. "Where am I? What is this? What—"

Sophie pounced on Ashley, covering her mouth with her hand. "Shh," she hushed her. "It's okay. Everything's okay!"

Well, sort of okay, anyway. Besides the obvious major issue of Ashley Jones having accidentally hitchhiked a ride through time on Sophie's Camelot Code. Which, in Sophie's opinion, wasn't okay at all. Stu was supposed to be her plus one. Not her stupid almost stepsister. How on earth was she going to explain this to Ashley in a way that made sense?

Or at least in a way that made her stop screaming for two seconds.

She met Ashley's eyes with her own, trying to make her expression as calming as possible. As if this wasn't the biggest disaster in the entire universe. "I'm going to take my hand away now. But do not scream, okay?"

Ashley managed to nod, her blue eyes bulging. Sophie sighed

and released her. Ashley collapsed onto the floor. "Is this a dream?" she demanded. "Tell me this is a dream."

For a moment, Sophie contemplated saying yes. No big deal, nothing to see here, just a big old fat dream. But then what if Ashley tried to do something crazy to wake herself up? Like jump off a cliff or something? That would be a tough one to explain to Dad.

"It's . . . not a dream," she said carefully. "We've just gone on a little trip, that's all."

"A trip . . . ?"

"You know. To another place . . ." Sophie bit her lower lip.

"And time?"

"Excuse me?"

This was not going well. Not that she'd expected it to. "Look, just chill for two seconds, okay?" Sophie begged. "We'll find Merlin and have him get you home."

"*Merlin?* Is that some new ride-share app?"

For the love of . . . "Just . . . trust me, okay?"

The look on Ashley's face told her she wouldn't trust Sophie to pick out the right shade of lip gloss at Sephora, but clearly she had no choice. Which made Sophie feel a teeny bit smug. After all, it wasn't every day one got to see Ashley Jones completely out of her element. For the first time ever, geek-girl Sophie had the upper hand.

She rose back to her feet and Ashley followed. The cheerleader looked around the cave, wrinkling her nose. "What is this place?" she asked. "It looks like a bomb went off in here. Also, it kind of stinks. And by 'kind of' I mean it totally reeks."

"Please excuse the mess. We ran into a little trouble earlier with some knights."

Sophie's gaze snapped to the back of the cave. In the doorway stood a boy and girl around her own age. One was dressed in wizard robes, much like the type Merlin would wear, but way too big. The other? Well, she wore a Disneyland Mickey Mouse T-shirt that hung to her knees.

Weird, Sophie thought. Even for Camelot Code standards . . .

The girl in the Mickey Mouse T-shirt stepped toward them. She was tall. Pretty. With brown skin and long black hair twisted into an intricate braid. The kind someone might get ten million views for if they posted the how-to on YouTube.

"It worked, Emrys!" the braid girl cried, her face lighting up with excitement. "It really worked."

The boy's gaze traveled from Ashley to Sophie. "Are you sure?" he asked, sounding suspicious. "They look a little young." He narrowed his eyes. "And what on earth are they wearing?" Which was a little rude, in Sophie's opinion. Especially seeing as he looked as if he had shrugged on his dad's bathrobe.

The girl stepped up to Ashley, who happened to be closer, giving her a small bow. "Thank you for coming," she said in an earnest voice. "We are in desperate need of your assistance."

Ashley stared at her. "My what? Who are you? What are you talking about?" She looked around the cave again, her eyes wild with panic. "Did you kidnap me? Have I been kidnapped?" She launched into a fighter's stance. "I know Zumba, you know. And I'm not afraid to use it!"

Sophie groaned. She ran over to Ashley, grabbing her soon-to-be stepsister's hands and lowering them to her sides again. "Will you relax?" she begged. "I told you, everything's okay. Also, I think you mean jujitsu. Unless you're hoping for a dance-off?"

Ashley's shoulders slumped—all the fight seeming to go out of her at once. She gave Sophie a helpless look. "I could totally win a dance off," she whimpered.

"I know, I know," Sophie said, patting her on the shoulder. "It's going to be okay, I promise."

"I don't understand! What happened to us? Where's the dress shop?" Ashley's voice cracked. "Where's my mom?"

For a moment, Sophie almost felt sorry for her. She looked so scared. Sophie hadn't forgotten the first time she'd traveled back in time and how freaked-out she had been. Though at least she'd had the common sense not to threaten a dance battle five minutes in.

"Just take a deep breath and let me handle this. I promise we'll get you home soon." She turned to their medieval hosts, who had been watching the entire exchange with doubtful eyes. So much for coming off like a professional. "So, uh, who are you? And where's Merlin?"

The girl stepped forward first. "I am Nimue," she said, pronouncing the name like ni-MU-ay. "A druid of Avalon. And this is Emrys. He's Merlin's apprentice."

"Merlin has an apprentice?" Sophie raised her eyebrows. "Since when?"

Nimue sighed. "Let's just say he's . . . new." She pressed her palms together. "Really new."

"And Merlin is . . . where exactly?"

The boy brightened. "That's actually what—"

"AHHH!" Ashley suddenly screamed. "What is THAT?"

Sophie whirled around, just in time to see Ashley back up into a corner of the cave. Unfortunately, this particular corner held a stack of pots and pans and dishes, all precariously piled to the ceiling. They crashed down on impact, burying Ashley in kitchenware. She screamed again.

Sophie closed her eyes, trying desperately to summon patience. She opened them again, giving Nimue and Emrys an apologetic look. "If you'll excuse me for one second . . ."

She turned and stalked toward the pile of pots and pans that had buried her almost stepsister, frustration rising inside her. It was like Ashley was determined to ruin everything in Sophie's life, piece by piece. She and Stu had been waiting for months for this first assignment. And now she was stuck with Ashley instead of him? She was pretty sure Ashley would be zero help when it came to saving the world. Unless the world was having a fashion crisis or needed to snap the perfect selfie.

Sophie pulled a pan off Ashley. Then another. Finally, the cheerleader managed to scramble back to her feet. She still looked terrified, though, and Sophie wondered what had her so freaked-out. Sure, the whole situation was beyond crazy, obviously. But she'd almost had it together a second ago.

"Are you okay?" Sophie asked.

Ashley didn't reply. Instead she raised a trembling hand, pointing to something behind Sophie. Sophie turned to look, wondering what on earth it could be. For a moment, she saw nothing. Then something red on a far table seemed to twitch. She stepped toward it, squinting to make out what it was.

She stopped short. Her mouth dropped open.

"Whoa," she whispered.

For there, sitting on a table at the other end of the cave, was a dragon. A baby dragon, to be precise, curled up and licking his paw, as if he were a tabby cat. His wings were folded against his body and his tail curled around him, long and spiky.

Sophie's mouth broke into a grin. Wow. A dragon. A real-life dragon!

Spring break had just taken an epic left turn.

CHAPTER 7

S ophie took a step toward the dragon, her heart pounding with excitement. "Since when does Merlin have a pet dragon?" she asked, marveling. She turned to Nimue and Emrys. "Or does this guy belong to one of you?"

"It's a rather long story," Emrys stammered.

"And actually the reason you're here," Nimue added.

Sophie's smile faltered a little. "Wait. You don't need me to slay him, do you?" She cringed at the thought. While she and Stu had certainly considered the possibility of slaying a dragon as one of their Camelot Quests, they hadn't taken into account that the dragon in question might be so adorable. And while, admittedly, it was probably easier to kill a fun-sized dragon than a full-grown one, she wasn't sure she'd have the heart to do it.

She tentatively reached out her hand toward the dragon. "It's okay," she said in a soft voice, trying to channel her inner Hiccup from *How to Train Your Dragon.* "I won't hurt you."

"Um, maybe you should be more worried about *him* hurting *you?*" Ashley reminded her. "*He* is the evil, fire-breathing monster in this scenario after all."

The dragon cocked his head at Sophie, looking at her with wide, curious eyes. She gave him a gentle smile. "Look at him," she cooed. "He's not evil. Are you, boy?"

The dragon's mouth creaked open, almost like a smile. Sophie felt something triumphant rise inside her. She was doing it! She was befriending a dragon! Wait till she told Stu!

She kept her eyes on the creature, smiling back at him. Any moment now he would take a step in her direction, going full Toothless. Nuzzling his head against her hand and—

Tooting like a trumpet.

EW! Sophie staggered backward, holding her nose as the smell cannonballed across the room. Guess that explained the mystery of the stinky cave....

"See?" Ashley pronounced, giving the dragon an affronted look. "Pure evil."

"He's not evil," Emrys corrected, running over to the dragon and scooping him into his arms. "At least we don't think so. He just has some . . . stomach issues."

"Possibly because he's not supposed to have a stomach to begin with," Nimue shot back, her hand over her own nose.

Sophie shook her head. "I think you need to start from the beginning."

And so they did, telling her about the Holy Grail and how the knights had attacked the druid caravan while trying to steal it. About Emrys's "oh-so-clever plan" (according to him) that had completely backfired (according to Nimue).

"Hang on a sec!" Ashley interrupted. "Let me get this straight. You're trying to tell me that we're back in time to the days of King Arthur? And Sir Stinksalot over there is the Holy Grail? Like, *the* Holy Grail from Indiana Jones part three?"

"You've seen Indiana Jones part three?" Sophie asked, surprised.

Ashley looked suddenly uncomfortable. "Um, maybe? It's the one with Han Solo in it, right? And old James Bond? My dad's a big fan."

"I do not know this Indiana Jones," Nimue interrupted. "But yes, the dragon is the Grail. And if we don't get him turned back to cup form soon, Arthur will die. And the kingdom of Camelot will be ripe for Morgana's takeover."

The air in the cave seemed to shift at the mention of the

sorceress's name and Sophie felt a small shiver trip down her spine. *Morgana.* She was back? Already? Sure, when they had defeated her the first time, she'd vowed revenge. But Sophie had been hoping that was just some bad-guy's-last-line-in-a-video-game type of thing. Not to be taken literally.

This was not good. Not good at all.

"Okay, just let me ask you one thing," Ashley broke in, holding out her hands, palms up. "Am I dead? Is this supposed to be my immortal punishment for living life as one of the cool kids? Trapped in Geeklandia Role-Play World for the rest of eternity?"

Sophie groaned. "Yeah, Ashley. You totally guessed it," she said dryly. "And the only way out is to not speak for three whole minutes." She turned to Emrys and Nimue, trying to sound businesslike. "So why can't you just turn the dragon back into the Grail and bring it to Arthur yourself?"

"I tried," Emrys admitted. "It didn't work out so well."

"We need Merlin," Nimue interjected. "But he's on...?"

"Spring break," his apprentice finished. "Whatever that is."

"Merlin's on spring break?" Sophie raised an eyebrow. "Seriously?" She tried to picture the magician partying it up on some tropical beach, wearing blue moon-and-stars swim trunks. "Where'd he go? Cabo? Cancún?"

Emrys wrinkled his forehead, as if trying to remember. "He said it was Lost Vegas."

"Wait, do you mean LAS Vegas?" Ashley broke in. Because clearly three minutes of silence in exchange for her immortal soul was not a bargain she was willing to make.

Nimue's face lit up. "You know the place?"

"I used to live there," Ashley informed her proudly. "Well, a suburb just outside. Before my mom decided to drag me to Massivelyboring-chusetts, that is."

Sophie pursed her lips. "But there is no Vegas here, in this time period," she mused, ignoring her almost stepsister. "There's not even an America. Which means he must have time-traveled." She ran a hand through her hair. "Though to what time period? That's the question."

"I don't know," Emrys confessed. "He didn't say."

"Are you sure?" Sophie urged him, not willing to give up. "I mean, maybe he mentioned something he was going to see? A certain sporting event? A historic casino heist?"

"A BOGO sale at Forever 21?" Ashley suggested.

Emrys shook his head. "I don't know," he moaned, staring down at the dragon, not meeting their eyes. "In truth, I wasn't paying much attention. I was busy trying not to add too much salt to the pea soup." He stuck out his tongue. "Merlin is obsessed with pea soup."

Sophie paced the cave, thinking hard. What would a Companion do in a case like this? she wondered. What would her mother do? Should she call her mother? No. She wanted to handle this by herself. She needed to. But where to even start?

She turned to Emrys. "Think hard. You must remember *something*."

"Actually, he did mention one name," Emrys said slowly. "But it didn't make much sense."

"What was it?" Sophie felt her hopes rise.

"Um...T-Swizzle?"

Her shoulders slumped. "That's doesn't ring a bell. Maybe it's some kind of candy he's looking for?"

"You aren't serious," Ashley broke in.

"What?"

"T-Swizzle? You don't know T-Swizzle? That's my girl Taylor Swift!" She beamed proudly. "I am a total Swiftie," she assured Nimue and Emrys.

"Um, congratulations?" Nimue said doubtfully.

"So wait. Merlin's friends with Taylor Swift?" Sophie stammered, trying to follow the conversation.

"Doubtful," Ashley sniffed. "She's very particular about her squad. But," she added, "she is on tour. And she performed in Las Vegas last night."

Sophie raised an eyebrow. "How do you know this again?"

"Um, because I'm alive and breathing?"

"Right." Sophie sighed. "So, fine. Let's say he went to Vegas to see Taylor Swift. But how are we going to find him? We don't even know what hotel he'd be staying in." Then a thought dawned on her. "Though we might be able to find out. If we check his computer."

"Computer?" Emrys questioned.

"His magic box?" she clarified, remembering the wizard's medieval term for his laptop.

His face lit up. "Oh! That's in the back room. Let me show you."

They walked to the back, where, sure enough, Merlin had a pretty sweet setup, especially for a time period in which electronics had yet to be invented. It was where he used to play the *Camelot's Honor* video game online with Sophie and Stu, back before they knew he was really an ancient wizard and not a surfer dude from SoCal.

Sophie leaned over the "magic box" and typed in Merlin's password. Thankfully, he hadn't changed it since the time Stu's stepbrother, Lucas, had hacked his e-mail. But then there probably wasn't a great need for Internet security in a time period that shouldn't even have Internet. Once his e-mail program opened, she typed "Vegas" into the search field. A moment later a hotel confirmation popped up.

She rose back to full height. "He's staying at some place called the Excalibur."

"Isn't that a sword?" Nimue asked.

"It's definitely a hotel," Ashley assured her. "It looks like a castle on the outside. It's pretty cool actually. And they have a big arcade."

"Sounds like Merlin's type of place," Sophie declared. "All right," she said. "I'll go and find him for you. Let him know he's needed back here." It wasn't the most exciting quest on earth, but she figured it would be doable.

"Great!" Emrys looked relieved. He strode over to Sophie and shoved the dragon in her direction. "Here you go! Good luck!"

"Wait, what?" Sophie held up her hands and shook her head. "I can't take a dragon to Vegas!"

"But you have to!" Emrys cried. "We can't keep him here. What if Morgana's men come back?"

"Or a dragon slayer decides to slay him for coin?" Nimue piped in. She gave Sophie a skeptical look. "Do you have dragon slayers in the future?"

"We don't even have dragons," Ashley assured her.

"Perfect!"

Sophie was clearly not going to win this fight.

"Okay, fine," she said. "Go ahead and zap me and Fire-Breath to Vegas. And zap this one back home." She nodded toward Ashley. "I think she's suffered enough." *Or at least I have*, she added to herself.

"I do not know how to zap anyone," Nimue confessed. "But here. These are the magic words of the Camelot Code. I believe they will transport you where you want to go." She handed Sophie the scrap of paper while Emrys held out the dragon again. Sophie reached to take him.

"C'mere, boy," she said, resigned to her fate. "Let's do this."

But to her surprise, the dragon refused to budge from Emrys's arms, instead burying his face in the apprentice's robes, whimpering. Sophie felt a shimmer of disappointment. Not that she'd wanted to take the dragon in the first place, but she'd thought the dragon would at least want to be taken.

"I'm not going to hurt you," she tried again. "I promise!"

The dragon stuck his head back out from Emrys's robes. Sophie started to smile at him. Then leaped back in alarm as he opened his mouth and shot a fireball in her direction, nearly setting her hair aflame.

"Okay, okay! You've made your point," she scolded the reptile. She turned to Nimue and Emrys. "Sorry. I don't think he likes—"

But she never finished her sentence. Because at that moment the dragon leaped out of Emrys's arms...

...and launched right for Ashley's shoulder.

"Ew!" Ashley cried, trying to shove him off with both hands. "Yuck! Yuck! Get it off me!"

But the dragon didn't take the hint. Instead he curled up on Ashley's shoulder, snuggling his head against her neck. He made a little chirping sound that sounded like a purr, then closed his eyes.

"He better not fart in my face," Ashley declared.

Sophie groaned and made another attempt to win over the dragon. "Come on," she said, reaching out. "She doesn't want you. Just come to me and I'll take good care of you."

But the dragon was having none of that. He'd clearly found his spot and wasn't about to leave it. Which was so annoying! Ashley didn't even like the dragon and yet she got to be besties with it. How was that even fair?

Nimue turned to Ashley. "It seems the fates have dealt their hands. If the dragon will only go with you, then you must go with the dragon."

"What? No!" Ashley spluttered. "I don't have time to go to Vegas."

"But the fate of the world depends on it!"

"Well, the world needs to get in line. My mom's wedding comes first."

Sophie approached Ashley, making sure to stay on her non-dragon side, just in case. "Look, it won't take any time at all," she pleaded. "We'll drop him off, then Merlin will zap us back to Massachusetts immediately. We won't even be missed."

Ashley seemed to mull this over. "I suppose there is that amazing craft shop just off the strip," she mused. "It carries the most incredible glitter you've ever seen. We could get some really cool colors for our avocado centerpieces...."

"Perfect!" Sophie cried, before she could rethink the matter. She did not want to take Ashley with her on the mission—and she certainly had no interest in glitter shopping while in Vegas—but she also didn't want to get mauled by a dragon days before her dad's wedding. Or fail her very first Companion quest, for that matter. She pulled out the Camelot Code paper. "Okay. How do we do this?"

Nimue pressed her lips together. "I think you just close your eyes," she instructed. "And think of where you need to go...."

Ashley beamed. "Oh, I'm thinking of it. Viva Las Vegas. Home sweet home."

Sophie closed her eyes. She thought of Vegas. All the bright lights. The castle hotel. Maybe this could actually be fun. Before now she'd never traveled anywhere outside New England. Not like Stu, who had been camping all over the country.

Oh, Stu, she thought, a heavy weight dropping to her stomach. She imagined him playing video games in his bedroom, not a care in the world—no idea that she was adventuring behind his back.

I'm so sorry, she thought. *Next time, I swear. I won't leave you behind.*

CHAPTER 8

"Dude. Your mom's here."

Stu looked up from his game, annoyed at the interruption. He'd just launched into the first fight of a super-hard *Camelot's Honor 2* solo dungeon, where Gawain takes on the Green Knight, and he had been planning to spend the entire afternoon fighting his way through. He turned to his stepbrother, Lucas, who was hovering at the doorway of their shared bedroom, and raised an eyebrow. "My mom?" he repeated. "Are you serious?"

It was a valid question. Mainly because Stu's mom made it a point to never step foot in his father and stepmother's house. Back when Stu was young, that meant meeting in a parking lot to do the whole kid-swap thing when it was her week to have him. These days he was expected to ride his bike between houses. Which was a super pain if he wanted to bring anything with him. Sometimes, if it was snowing hard, his dad would show mercy and drop him off or pick him up, but Mom never came here. Especially on a Saturday.

Which meant something big had to be up.

Reluctantly, Stu signed out of the game. So much for a drama-free spring break. Suddenly he was almost envious of Sophie and her dress fitting.

He rose to his feet and followed Lucas downstairs. Lucas pointed to the kitchen, where, sure enough, Stu's mom sat at the table with Stu's dad and stepmom. Stu's heart started beating a little faster. His mom was not only *here*, she was sharing airspace with the new Mrs. Mallory? Had the Apocalypse happened and he hadn't noticed?

"Stu!" his dad cried, looking up. He gestured for him to come over and join them. Stu glanced fleetingly at the front door, wondering if he could make a break for it. But that would only delay the inevitable. And, well, he was a little curious about what was going on.

He slunk into the kitchen. His stepmom pulled out a chair from the table for him and he sank into it. He looked from parental figure to parental figure. Then he sighed. "Am I in trouble?"

"Did you do something wrong?" his father shot back, raising his eyebrows.

"Um...I don't think so?" Stu racked his brain for something, but came up blank.

"Oh, stop teasing him," his mother scolded. She turned to Stu. "No, sweetie. You didn't do anything wrong. It's just...I've got news." A smile lit up her face. "*Great* news!"

Stu squirmed in his seat. There was something about that smile that concerned him. It looked almost...too happy. And his mom's eyes were a bit wild and panicked. Whatever this news was, he was guessing it wasn't necessarily great for everyone.

And by everyone...he meant himself.

"What is it?" he asked, fear creeping over him.

His mother clapped her hands. "I got the job!"

"What job?"

"Come on, Stu. You remember? The one I interviewed for. The marine biologist position at UCSD."

"Um, congratulations?" Stu said. He vaguely remembered her telling him something about this, but he'd been gaming at the time and admittedly hadn't paid much attention.

"Thank you! It really is a dream come true. And there were so many applicants." His mother shook her head. "I never thought they'd pick me."

"That's great, Mom," Stu said. She really did look happy. And he knew she'd been down in the dumps since she'd been laid off at the Boston Aquarium. "When do you start?"

"Well, that's sort of up to you."

"What?"

"The job is at *UCSD*, Stu," his father interjected. "University of California. San Diego."

Stu stared from his dad to his mom, not sure, at first, if he'd heard right. California? Like the state of California? Like, the state of California three thousand miles from his actual house?

"You're moving to California?" he blurted out.

His mom beamed. "No, Stu. *We* are."

"Wait, what?"

His heart started thudding in his chest as his mind raced to understand. Moving to California?

"I can't move to California!" he protested. "I'm—I'm...on the soccer team!"

It was the dumbest reason ever. But all he could think of at the moment.

His mother gave him a patronizing look. "They have soccer teams in California, Stu," she assured him. "Not to mention this amazing magnet school I've been looking into where you can actually study coding and video-game design. Isn't that cool?"

Okay, fine. A school where he could learn game design *would* be pretty awesome. But if it meant moving to California? No way.

"Dad," he tried, turning to his father. They'd had their

differences over the years. But surely he couldn't be agreeing to send his son away....

But the look on his dad's face told him it was already decided. "Sorry, kid," he said, staring down at his hands.

His stepmother broke in. "Don't worry, sweetie. You'll get to come back for the entire summer. And holidays, too! Spring break. You'll see us so much you're going to get sick of us," she declared.

Stu felt sick, all right. Sick to his stomach.

"Don't I even get a say in this?" he demanded. "I mean, it's my life here!"

His mother's smile faltered. "Look, I'm sorry, honey. I know it's not great timing, being in the middle of the school year and all. But this is a big deal for me. It's my dream job."

Stu looked up at his mom. At the pleading look on her face. As if she was begging him to understand. Something uncomfortable wormed in his stomach.

"I think it's great, Mom," he choked out. "I'm really happy for you. It's just...kind of a shock."

His mother reached out and squeezed his shoulder. "I know, sweetie. And I'm so sorry I had to spring it on you like this. It just all happened so fast. I'm freaking out a little, too!" She gave him a nervous laugh. "Look, I'll let you digest it all for a bit. Then, when you're ready, we can talk more."

He wanted to say he'd never be ready. But what good would

that do? Instead he rose woodenly from his chair and walked out of the kitchen. He could feel his parents' eyes on him, but he refused to turn around. Mostly so they wouldn't see the tears slipping down his cheeks.

California. Was he really moving to California? Away from his home, his stepbrother, the soccer team? And most importantly—Sophie?

Once outside his parents' view, he broke into a run, up the stairs, past Lucas. His stepbrother gave him a pitying look— evidently he'd overheard everything—but Stu would have to deal with him later.

Right now he needed his best friend.

CHAPTER 9

Sophie opened her eyes. She looked around, prepared to be awed. To see the bright lights and big city of Las Vegas as seen on TV. But, to her surprise, when her vision did finally clear, the view didn't look Vegas-y at all. In fact, it looked more outside-of-Stu's-house-y, if anything.

Uh-oh.

"What are we doing here? This isn't Vegas."

She whirled around to find Ashley storming in her direction, the dragon still perched on her shoulder. Sophie winced, realizing what must have happened.

"I . . . think I made a mistake," she stammered.

"You didn't think of Vegas?" Ashley looked like she wanted to murder her.

"I did!" Sophie protested. "And...then I...didn't. But only like for a microsecond."

"Evidently the right microsecond. We're back home. In Massachusetts," Ashley spluttered. "With a freaking dragon!"

The dragon lifted his head from her shoulder and emitted a large burp. Ashley glared at him. "Enough with the gas, dude! Seriously."

Sophie rubbed her face with one hand, trying to collect her wits. "Okay, don't panic," she said. "We'll figure this out."

"I don't have time to figure anything out! The wedding is in a week!" Ashley cried. "Avocados need glittering!"

"And the world needs saving," Sophie said wearily. "What do you want me to do?"

"I have no idea! You're supposed to be the saving-the-world expert here somehow. Though I still don't understand why."

Sophie groaned. "You sure you want to stick with her?" she asked the dragon. "'Cause I promise you I'd be a lot less annoying."

The dragon dug his claws into Ashley's shoulders. Guess that answered that.

"Ow!" Ashley protested, swatting at the tiny creature. "You so need a manicure, man. Also? I am not annoying. You can ask anyone. Well, except Stu. Stu probably thinks I'm annoying. But then he's pretty—"

Sophie stopped short. "Stu!" she exclaimed, hope rising in her. "That's it!"

"Huh?"

"Don't you get it? Stu is like the pet whisperer. You should see him at the park. The dogs flock to him. Practically knock him down they're so excited to see him. It's ridiculous. I have to stand like ten feet away just to avoid having an allergic reaction."

"I hate to break it to you, but this guy on my shoulder? So not a dog."

"Doesn't matter. Cat, rabbit, gerbil from Mrs. Wilkerson's first-grade class? They all love Stu. Maybe the dragon will, too."

Her heart started pumping with excitement. If the dragon would agree to go with Stu, then that would let Ashley off the hook. She could go glitter her avocados and Sophie and Stu could continue their excellent adventure as they should have been doing all along.

"Well, I guess we can try," Ashley said, looking surprisingly reluctant at the idea. She took a step toward Stu's house. Sophie jumped in front of her, holding out her hands.

"Are you crazy? You can't just walk in there with a dragon! His dad will see!"

"So what? He'll just assume it's some new kind of Hatchimal or something. No big deal."

"It will be if the dragon suddenly spits fire on the carpet," Sophie pointed out. "And the whole house goes up in flames."

"So what are we supposed to do, then? Just stand outside and wait for him to come out on his own? The dude's playing video games. That could take weeks."

Sophie considered this for a moment. "Why don't you take the dragon to my backyard? My dad should still be out bowling with the guys. I'll get Stu and we'll meet you there in a minute."

"Fine," Ashley replied. "But don't be long. I've got to get back to the dress shop. Mom's probably freaking out worried about us. I mean, we did just vanish into thin air. Which," she added, "would have been way more helpful if it had happened during my history test on Friday. Just saying."

"I'll be SUPER quick. I promise. Now go!"

And with that, Sophie turned back to Stu's door, giving Ashley a few moments to hurry down the street and turn the corner. But just as she was about to knock, Sophie felt her phone vibrate. She looked down at the caller ID and laughed. Of course. His timing was impeccable as always.

I'm at your front door, she texted back. *Come let me in! I've got amazing news!*

She waited for a moment, hearing Stu's footsteps clomp down the stairs, before the door swung open, revealing him on the other side. She raised an eyebrow when she caught sight of her friend's face. He looked . . . pale. And weirdly miserable.

"Dude, have you even left the house today?" she demanded, looking him up and down. "Too much gaming is bad for your health, you know. You need some sunshine, stat."

"And you need a new wardrobe consultant," he shot back, eyeing her from head to toe. It was only then that she realized she was still wearing the hideous orange bridesmaid dress. Ugh.

"Don't you worry, this is going right back to the store," she told him. "But first, grab your coat. We're going to my house." She grinned excitedly. "There's someone I need you to meet."

CHAPTER 10

Just tell her! Stu screamed silently as they walked toward Sophie's place to see whoever this mysterious stranger might be. Sophie had lived down the street from Stu for almost his entire life and he'd made the journey from house to house a thousand times over the years. But for some reason this time the trip felt incredibly long—each step painful— as if there were a green-skinned Creeper right on their heels, threatening to blow them to smithereens at a moment's notice.

He'd meant to tell her about his mom and the California move the second he opened the door. But she'd said she had amazing news, and she looked really happy for the first time since she found out her dad was getting married. He didn't have the heart to spoil whatever it was with his crappy announcement.

So Stu kept his mouth shut and tried to psych himself up for whatever it was Sophie planned to show him—mostly because he knew she would do the same for him were the situation reversed. She had always been there for him, ever since that fateful day in first grade when she'd found him sitting all alone on the swings after no one had picked him for dodgeball. She'd asked him if he'd like to play *Minecraft* on her iPad and he'd agreed. It had been a match made in gamer heaven ever since.

He felt a lump form in his throat. How could he just leave her to go to California? How could he leave any of this? His home, Lucas. Even he and his dad had been getting on a lot better since they had soccer to talk about now. But that would all go away when he moved to California, leaving his entire life behind.

Finally, they reached Sophie's house. But instead of bringing him inside, she stopped at the side gate to the backyard.

"Okay." Her blue eyes sparkled with excitement. "Are you ready for the most amazing sight in the history of sight?"

"Um, yes? I think so?" What on earth had her so excited? And why was it in the backyard? If she were anyone else, he might have guessed she'd brought home a dog or a cat. But Sophie had always been allergic to furry animals.

He watched as she practically danced over to the fence. She lifted the latch, then pulled the gate open, making a sweeping gesture in his direction. He stepped forward, a little doubtfully, and his nose caught something funny—some kind of smoky smell. Like a barbecue grill, before you added the meat. Then his ears picked up a small squawking sound. What on earth?

He stopped in his tracks, his eyes locking on movement in the back of the yard. Then he squinted, unable to comprehend what he was seeing. Mainly because it was impossible. Absolutely impossible.

And yet...

"Is that a...dragon?" he spluttered.

It was a dumb question. Because what else could it be? There, tied to Sophie's old playscape with a frayed jump rope, was an actual, literal, real-life baby dragon, trying and failing to climb up the slide.

Stu gaped, his mouth open like a cartoon character's, as his eyes roved over the tiny creature. It was about the size of a large pigeon, with shiny, crimson-colored scales, a long tail with a crook at the end, and a spiky ridge traveling down its back.

"What...Why...How?" he stammered, wondering for a moment if he'd ever be able to speak in full sentences again. But who could blame him? Sophie hadn't been exaggerating. This was the most amazing thing he'd ever seen in his twelve years on the planet. (And he'd once seen Diagon Alley at Universal Studios. So that was saying something!)

"Told you," Sophie declared, looking quite pleased with herself. She held up her phone. "Spring break has been saved by the Camelot Code."

"You finally got an assignment? A *dragon* assignment?"

She nodded and started running through the series of events that had led to this awesomeness of dragon proportions. Then she stopped—mid-story—to apologize. "I wasn't sure how long the Code would be good for," she explained. "So I had to act right then and there in the dress shop."

He shrugged. "Totally get it. When destiny comes knocking, you gotta answer."

"Yeah, well, destiny can totally bite me next time," a new voice chimed in. Stu whirled around to see none other than Ashley Jones herself coming out of Sophie's back door, holding a big plate of raw hamburger in her arms. Which was basically the second-most amazing thing he'd ever seen.

"Here you go, Spikey," Ashley cooed as she approached the dragon. "Get your din-din!"

"Spikey?" Sophie repeated, raising an eyebrow.

Ashley shrugged, looking down at the eager dragon, who was panting excitedly, his mouth wide open like a baby bird's. "Well, Spike, actually," she said. "After my favorite YouTuber. 'Cause they're both super hot." She looked at Sophie and Stu expectantly. "Get it? Dragon? Hot?"

"Um, clever," Stu managed to agree, his eyes still on the hotness in question as Ashley leaned down and presented the dragon with the plate of meat. In an instant, Spike was face-first in the food, gobbling it down like he'd never eaten before in his life.

"I grabbed it from your fridge," Ashley informed Sophie, as if it were no big deal. "I thought maybe he was hungry. And maybe it'll help with his...digestive issues."

Spike looked up and burped loudly.

"Or not." Sophie giggled.

"Okay, you guys really need to tell me what's going on," Stu demanded.

So Sophie, with a lot of help from Ashley, launched into the rest of the story. When they had finished, Stu let out a low whistle.

"So you're, like, literally on a quest for the Holy Grail," he realized aloud. "That's pretty much the most epic quest in Arthurian legend, you know."

"Actually, *we're* on the quest," Sophie corrected. "Assuming you're with me."

"And that Spike here won't burn you alive," Ashley added helpfully.

"What?"

"Let's just say he's not a Sophie superfan," she explained. "In fact, I'm pretty sure he'd rather cuddle Kylo Ren."

"You know me and animals," Sophie said, shrugging. "But I bet he'll love you." She gestured to the dragon, who had somehow already inhaled the entire plate of food and was staring longingly at Ashley, evidently ready for his second course. "Go ahead," Sophie urged. "See if he likes you."

Stu nodded, attempting to appear cool, calm, and collected as he took a step in the dragon's direction. As if this was just an everyday Saturday for him and not the craziest thing in his entire life. Which, seeing as he'd once stood in for a medieval British king, was saying something!

"Hiya, Spike," he said. "Nice to meet you, boy!"

As soon as the words left his mouth, he realized how lame they sounded. This was a magical beast of legends, after all! And here he was, some common human, basically saying, *What's up, dude?*

He tried again, bowing his head to the dragon, trying to show respect. "'Tis an honor and privilege to make your acquaintance, Sir Spike. I do hope you are finding our humble world to ye liking."

"And...we're back in Geeklandia," Ashley muttered under her breath.

"If forsooth there is anything you might require—"

Spike gave another juicy belch. A splotch of drool dribbled from the side of his mouth.

Stu burst out laughing. Well, okay, then. So much for formalities.

The dragon seemed to grin back at him, stretching out his little leathery wings and beating them a few times, as if testing them out. Then he leaped off the ground, going airborne. For a moment, he just hovered there, three feet off the earth, like a hummingbird.

Then he crashed to the ground with a heavy thump.

"Are you okay?" Stu cried, dashing to the dragon. To his relief, Spike lifted his head. He gave Stu a grumpy look and then shook his body. Glaring down at the grass, as if it had been to blame for his fall. Stu bit back another laugh.

"He's still working on the whole flying thing," Ashley explained. "After all, he's only been a dragon for a few hours."

Stu reached out, daring to stroke the dragon's scales with gentle fingers. He thought they would feel hard, like gemstones or steel. But instead they were as soft as satin—almost feathery. And when he pulled his hands away, Spike reached out and nudged him with his nose. As if to say, *That felt good—don't stop!*

"He likes you!" Sophie cried. "Thank goodness!" She took a step toward the dragon. Spike turned and growled. She groaned, backing away again.

"Maybe he doesn't like your perfume," Ashley suggested.

"I'm not wearing any perfume!"

"Maybe he wishes you were."

"Yeah, well, I wish he'd stop passing gas. So I guess we're even."

Stu ignored the girls, his focus on the dragon. "He's amazing," he murmured, stroking the creature under his chin. Spike made a throaty noise, almost like a purr. "Are you sure we have to turn him back into a grail? He'd make a pretty awesome pet."

Spike chirped in agreement, then snapped at a fly. He missed, so he opened his mouth and blasted it with a large burst of fire. Stu scrambled backward to avoid being flambéed. Whoa.

"Except he's not exactly house-trained," Sophie said drolly as she ran to stamp out the grass fire.

"Also, I doubt he'd stay baby-sized forever," Ashley pointed out. "And no way would our neighborhood association be cool with a giant, fire-breathing beast in the backyard. They don't even allow Rottweilers."

Stu sighed. "I suppose you're right."

"In any case, he's got an important job to do," Sophie added, watching the dragon once again try and fail to scramble up the playscape slide, in search of his next insect prey. He made it halfway up, then lost his traction and slid down. "Remember, Arthur needs the Grail medicine or he'll die and Morgana will take over the kingdom." She shuddered. "We already had to face her once. I don't want to do it again."

"I, like, really need to hear this whole story someday," Ashley muttered, grabbing Spike and pulling him off the slide. "Though . . . maybe it's best not to know." She wagged her finger at the dragon before setting him back on the ground. "We go *down* the slide, Spike. Not up."

Stu nodded in agreement. Morgana was bad news. And they didn't need her changing history all over again. Last time she made a complete scramble of their regular lives—not to mention a world without pepperoni pizza. What if this time there was no more chocolate ice cream? Or video games? Or it somehow sparked a zombie apocalypse? While a dragon would make a super-cool pet (and who said the homeowner association had to know?), he didn't want to be responsible for flesh-eating zombies on the loose, chasing down chocolate-ice-cream–deprived citizens who had no video-game skills to fall back on in a crisis.

"So, what's the plan?" he asked, trying not to laugh as Spike headed straight for the slide again. Ashley groaned and stalked after him.

Sophie watched the scene play out for a moment, then turned to Stu. "I've got it all worked out. I'm going to grab my mom's spell book and I'm going to teleport you, me, and Spike to Vegas. We'll go find Merlin at the Excalibur and he'll hocus-pocus Spike back into a cup." She beamed. "Easy peasy."

Spike burped a ball of fire, so hot it actually melted part of the plastic on the slide, warping it into a weird shape. The dragon grinned and started climbing up the slide again, this time making much better progress.

"Aww," Ashley proclaimed. "He's learning!"

"To destroy all my earthly posessions? Awesome." Sophie sighed. She turned back to Stu. "So what do you say? Are you up for a spring break adventure?"

"Will I have to put on pants?"

"Absolutely."

"You drive a hard bargain," Stu teased. "But sure. Let's do it. Let's save the world—once more, with feeling."

"Sweet! Well, then, Ashley, you're off the hook," Sophie informed her almost stepsister, smiling for the first time.

Ashley didn't smile back. "Um, great," she said instead, in a way that sounded anything but great. Stu caught her giving the dragon a weird look. Uh-oh.

"What's wrong?" he asked.

"Yeah," Sophie added. "I thought you'd be happy! I mean, now you can glitter overpriced produce to your heart's content!"

"Sure. It's just..." Ashley shuffled from foot to foot. "Remember I was going to go to that craft store in Vegas and stuff?"

"Yeah, but that was when you thought you had to come. Spike likes Stu. We don't need you anymore."

Ashley's face turned stony. "Wow," she said. "That's nice."

"Sorry. I didn't mean it that way." Sophie groaned. "I just... you don't *want* to come, do you?"

"Of course not. It's just... well, you guys don't know your way around Vegas. What if you got lost?"

"Uh, we'll use Google Maps?"

"Totally unreliable. And no substitute for a real guide." Ashley lifted her chin. "Look. I'll just pop over with you, help get you to Merlin, swing by the craft store for glitter, and then we'll come back. No big deal."

Sophie shot Stu an exasperated look. Clearly the last thing she wanted was her future stepsister along for their Camelot Code ride. But what could she do? Ashley was nothing if not persistent once she decided to do something.

Sophie tried one more time. "I really don't think—"

"You're taking me," Ashley said, cutting her off. "Or I'll tell your dad—"

"It's okay!" Stu broke in, jumping between the two girls. "Ashley, you can come. Sophie, I'll come, too. Two dragon whisperers are better than one, right?"

Sophie looked as if she wanted to claw someone's eyes out—namely, Ashley's. But in the end she gave a small shrug. "Fine," she said. "Let me go hit the bathroom and then we'll all recite the Camelot Code together."

"And make sure you think of Vegas this time," Ashley scolded. "I do not need to end up in Tahiti or something. Or back in that stinky cave."

"Yes, Mom," Sophie muttered, running into the house, leaving Ashley and Stu alone.

Ashley stubbed the ground with her toe. "Thanks," she said, so quietly it took Stu a moment to realize she was talking to him.

"Um, sure," he replied, turning his attention back to Spike, who was now contentedly crunching on all the dead bug-like things he'd found at the top of Sophie's playscape. Stu didn't want Ashley to get the idea that he liked her coming on this mission any more than Sophie did. After all, this was *their* thing—his and Sophie's. In fact, it might be their *last* thing before he had to move. And he certainly didn't need any distractions like Ashley Jones to ruin the potential epicness.

Which reminded him that he still had to tell Sophie his news. And he would, soon, he promised himself. But not now. She was mad enough about Ashley and he didn't want to make her even more upset. Not when they had a Camelot Code mission at long last.

He walked over to the ladder to retrieve the dragon. No. He'd keep silent for now. Not risk messing this up. He'd go to Vegas, find Merlin, turn Spike back into the Grail, and get him to Arthur in time to cure his sickness and stay on the right side of history. Once that was all done, then he could fill her in on the move.

After all, this might be his last mission. He was determined to make it awesome.

CHAPTER 11

"Well, that's that, I suppose," Emrys declared after he and Nimue had seen the Companions and the dragon off on their mission to find his master. He surveyed the ransacked cave, still a shambles from Morgana's men, and sighed. "I suppose I should start to clean up. I don't know when Merlin will return, and he will not be pleased to find such a mess. Not that it was all that clean to begin with, mind you. He's a terrible housekeeper." He paused, considering. "*Cave* keeper? In any case, now it looks positively—"

"Oh no you don't."

Surprised at the interruption, he turned back to the mouth

of the cave. Nimue stood there, her slim figure silhouetted by the rising sun behind her. She crossed her arms over her chest.

"I beg your pardon?" Emrys stammered. What did she want now?

"You can clean later. First you are escorting me to King Arthur's court."

"What? And why would I do that?"

She took a step into the cave. "Because I can't go alone," she explained. "Do you know how dangerous it is for a young girl to walk the king's roads by herself? Morgana's men are still looking for me. Along with all sorts of bandits and cutthroats who wander the paths, willing to maim and murder for a few copper coins."

"All the more reason for me to stay here," he declared, plopping down on a nearby chair. He didn't mean to be rude, but this was not his fight. He was Merlin's apprentice. And as Merlin's apprentice, he needed to serve Merlin. Which meant staying here, taking care of Merlin's cave until the magician got back.

Nimue scowled. "Coward," she spit out. "You're the reason we're in this situation to begin with. And yet you will not help?"

"Me?" He jerked up in his chair. "I was minding my own business, I'll have you know." He pointed in her direction. "*You* are the one who burst into the cave uninvited, demanding all sorts of magic."

"Only because you said you *knew* magic!"

"I do know magic!"

"Your magic turned the Holy Grail into a dragon!"

"Aye," he agreed, puffing out his chest. "And if it hadn't? Your precious cup would be in the hands of Morgana's men right now. And you would likely be dead. Which, I might add, makes me the hero of this story." He smiled sweetly at her. "So perhaps a little more gratitude is in order?"

Nimue sighed, stepping farther into the cave. "Fine," she said. "Have it your way." She grabbed a wooden chair off the floor and righted it. Then she sat down and stretched her arms over her head. Emrys watched her warily.

"What are you doing?" he asked.

"Making myself comfortable," she said matter-of-factly. "I don't suppose you have any tea?"

"Tea? But I thought you had to get to King Arthur's court."

"I do. Badly. But I can't very well go alone. So I suppose that leaves me stuck here." She let out a loud yawn. "Some cake would be lovely as well. It's been quite the day!"

Emrys raked a hand through his hair, exasperation rising inside him. "You can't stay here."

"Whyever not? There is plenty of room."

"Merlin wouldn't like it."

"Interesting that you would know Merlin's likes, considering you've only known him for three days," she observed calmly. "Much of which he's been in Lost Vegas."

That was it! Emrys rose to his feet, so fast he almost knocked his chair backward. "Can't you find someone else to take you to Arthur's court?" he demanded. "Your precious sisters, perhaps? A random stranger? Someone who *doesn't* think you're the most bothersome girl in the world?"

Nimue's smile fell. She stared at him for a moment, with a look of dismay, then dropped her gaze, staring down at her hands. A lone tear slid down her cheek. Emrys squeezed his eyes shut in exasperation. He hadn't meant it to come out like that. So harsh. And he certainly hadn't meant to make her cry.

"Look," he said, softening his voice. "I didn't mean—"

"They attacked our caravan," she interrupted. Her eyes stared down at her lap as if her gaze were holding the very world in place. "They killed my sisters. Morgana's men, I mean. Slaughtered them in cold blood." She looked up, staring into the distance, tears leaking from her brown eyes and splashing onto her hands. "There was so much blood," she added in a slow, dead voice. "So much screaming. My ears still ring with the sounds."

Emrys winced. "I'm sorry."

Her gaze snapped in his direction. "No. *I'm* sorry. I'm sorry I don't have anyone else to help me. That I'm trapped here, all by myself, throwing myself at your mercy. Everyone I have ever loved, whoever cared for me, is likely dead. And if I walk out of this cave now, I shall certainly meet a similar fate."

Emrys stared at her, horrified. He tried to imagine what it must have been like. To have your whole family struck down before your eyes. He thought of his own mother and his brothers and even his father. Imagined knowing he could never see them again. That he could never go home—because there was no home left.

Nimue gave him a hard look. "Long ago the druids of Avalon made a solemn vow," she said. "To guard the Holy Grail. And now I am the only one left to keep that vow." She cleared her throat, rising to her feet. Squared her shoulders and lifted her chin. "Arthur must be told the Grail is on its way. That he should hold on as best he can and guard against the approach of Morgana and her men. For if he does not, they will succeed in usurping his kingdom. Undoing all the good he has done."

Emrys watched as she stalked back to the entrance of the cave. When she reached it, she turned back to face him. "I apologize for putting you out," she said stiffly. "I will be leaving now. Do wish me luck that I am able to reach Camelot alive. If not for my own sake, for the sake of the world."

She turned to go, but before he realized what he was doing, Emrys ran after her. "Wait," he said.

She held her chin up as she gazed at him. He sighed. "Let

me just go grab some supplies," he told her. "It's a long journey. We'll need water. Some of that cake you mentioned, too. And, of course, Merlin's spell pad—in case we run into any danger."

He thought he saw a flash of hope in her eyes. "You are coming with me?"

"I suppose I am." He gave her an apologetic shrug.

A smile broke across her face, so wide and beaming it practically lit up the cave with its brilliance. "Oh, thank you!" she cried, throwing her arms around him in a boisterous hug. "Thank you so much! You don't know what this means!"

He grunted, patting her awkwardly on the back before working to untangle himself from her enthusiastic embrace. "Just don't expect me to turn into some big, brave knight in shining armor to protect you," he warned. "I'm shorter than you are."

"*But* you have magic."

"Oh yes. Because that worked so well the last time."

Something flickered at her jaw. "Just don't turn me into a chicken and it will all be fine."

"I promise nothing," he replied solemnly. Then he smiled. "But for you I will try."

Emrys grabbed a few things from the back room and stuffed them into a burlap sack. When he reached Merlin's private chamber, he grabbed the spell pad off the table. He felt a bit guilty pilfering it like that—after all, he wasn't even supposed to be looking at it, never mind stealing it. But he knew Merlin would understand, considering the circumstances. They were on a very important quest, after all.

He glanced back into the main cavern, where Nimue was waiting, a slow excitement beginning to build inside him. *An important quest.* He, young Emrys, was about to embark on an important quest. He'd never been big enough to be the knight he'd imagined himself becoming as a child. And he hadn't yet mastered enough magic to call himself an actual wizard. And yet, somehow, here he was. Serving as protector to a beautiful girl. Escorting her safely across a dangerous land. So they could save the king—and the kingdom. Just like in his mother's stories.

Now all I need to do, he told himself, *is to somehow find a way to live to tell the tale.*

CHAPTER 12

"Did you find it?"

Morgana urged her mare forward, stopping just in front of the two knights, her purple eyes scanning their saddlebags with failing hope. They had been gone a long time. She'd assumed they'd been killed. Though who would be left to kill them? Her mercenaries had all but slaughtered the druid caravan, and no thief or cutthroat in the forest would dare attack one of Arthur's knights.

She chuckled to herself. Well, the men Arthur considered his knights, anyway. Now loyal only to her.

It had been far too easy to bring them to her side. They were still resentful of a servant boy doing what they could not—pulling the sword from the stone and being pronounced king of England. And then there was Arthur's obsession with peace. He had united the tribes of Britain and all but eliminated war. Which was good for the peasants in the fields, perhaps, but true knights grew bored without an assignment or quest.

And she had been all too happy to give them one. The quest for the Holy Grail.

The first knight, Agravaine, pulled off his helmet, revealing a shock of unkempt black hair. "We found nothing," he admitted, looking a little sheepish. "We searched the druid camp thoroughly, but there was no cup to be found anywhere, besides those used for drinking."

"Then one of them must have slipped away with it," Morgana replied, feeling the irritation rise within her. These doltish dunces! Did she always have to do everything herself? "Did you not think to look for her?"

"We did!" the second knight, Sir Kay, replied in a sulky voice. He had once been Arthur's foster brother and had felt he should get special treatment because of it. But Arthur insisted on treating all his knights equally, much to Kay's chagrin. "We even searched Lord Merlin's Crystal Cave," he added. "But all we found were a couple of children cooking a chicken."

Morgana opened her mouth to speak, but paused. "A chicken?" she repeated. "Are you sure it was a chicken? In Merlin's cave?"

"Aye," Agravaine agreed, grinning. He was missing a few

teeth. "I almost stole it for dinner. But it was pretty scrawny. Not much meat on its bones."

"It was acting oddly as well," Sir Kay added. "Might have been sick, for all we know. Don't want to eat that."

Morgana considered this for a moment. The knights peered at her curiously. "If you're hungry we can snare a rabbit," Sir Agravaine told her. "Or bring down a deer."

She waved him off. "Why would there be a chicken in Lord Merlin's cave?" she pondered aloud.

"They said it was dinner."

"But it can't be. The Merlin I know has always been vegan."

The two knights stared at her dumbly. "A what?" Kay asked. Of course, they didn't know the futuristic term.

"He's a—" She groaned. "He doesn't eat meat!"

"Perhaps his apprentice does. Or his cook?"

"There was a cook?"

"Aye. A young girl. Wearing very strange clothes, I might add," Kay replied, scratching his head. "Like...a long tunic, bearing a portrait of a mouse standing on his hind legs and wearing trousers. Quite an odd choice for a cook, if you ask me."

Morgana frowned. "What did this cook look like?" For some reason her mind suddenly flashed to Sophie Sawyer, the miserable blond girl from the future who had once gotten the best of her. Could she be once again mixed up in this? Certainly the clothing sounded appropriate for the time period....

"She had dark skin and hair. Very pretty." The knight smirked. "Though a bit too surly for my tastes."

Morgana pursed her lips. Not Sophie, then. Maybe a Companion? Or someone else from the future, called in to aid the druids?

She slid off her horse and paced the forest floor, raking a hand through her long black hair. "I think there may be some magic afoot here," she said, looking up at the two knights. "I want you to go back and get a closer look at that cook. And that chicken."

Agravaine groaned. "It was a *chicken*!" he protested. "Wind and Rain, this is boring! Can't we return to Camelot and just attack Arthur? He's sick and weakened. We could sneak into the castle and stab him while he sleeps."

"A much better use of our time than going back for a chicken," Kay agreed.

Morgana groaned. Goddess Mother, save her from fools! "We can't kill him in his sleep," she informed the knights, who should by all rights already know this. "He's got the Pendragon scabbard to protect him."

She was still, admittedly, a little sore about that whole thing. She'd come so close to stealing the scabbard from Arthur, only to be defeated by Sophie and Merlin and that annoying boy with the sword who refused to die. Why, they'd attacked her in her own castle and she'd barely escaped with her life. It had taken her months to recover from it—months spent filling her head with plans for revenge. And then, when her spies had told her about Arthur's sickness ... about the druids secretly traveling to him, bringing the Holy Grail, she had seen her chance at last to turn the tide of fate.

But now ...

She stroked her chin with two fingers. A chicken. Could Merlin's apprentice have disguised the Grail somehow as a chicken? It seemed so preposterous.

Morgana dropped her hand. It was a slim chance, but the only one she had at the moment. She needed to find out for sure. Walking back to her black mare, she slipped her foot into the stirrup and mounted. Then she turned to the knights.

"I want you two to travel to the island of Avalon. Wait there in case any druids return. Capture anyone you find and ... convince them to tell you where they hid the Grail. By any means necessary."

The men saluted her, clearly happy to be given a task other than watching a chicken. Especially one that involved possible violence. Knights. They were all the same.

"And what will you do, m'lady?" Sir Kay asked.

"I need to pay a visit to this apprentice and his cook," she told them. "And see this chicken for myself."

CHAPTER 13

Sophie remembered being told, at some point, you should always get to the airport two hours early, but she'd never been clear on exactly why. Until today, that is, as they stood in a seemingly endless security line, waiting to get through to their gate and onto their plane to Las Vegas, while her skin crawled with nervousness.

The teleport spell hadn't worked. They'd tried reciting it a number of times to no avail. Forward, backward, each of them saying one word in turn. Every possible combination. But still nothing happened and they remained in Sophie's backyard with a dragon.

At first Sophie was baffled by this until she read the small print in mother's spell book and learned you couldn't just teleport willy-nilly from time to time, place to place, like you could in the TARDIS on *Doctor Who*. In real life, you needed a rest period before the magic would work again. According to the book, it would take three days for her recent round-trip teleport to wear off, which left them no choice but to purchase airline tickets. Thankfully, her mother had given Sophie a Companions credit card, for emergencies only. Sophie figured this counted.

At one point she'd actually considered calling her mother and asking what she should do. But in the end she'd decided against it. After all, this was her very first assignment. And she'd already accidentally managed to mess it up. To ask for help now? Well, that would ensure she never got an assignment number two.

She did try to call Merlin, to let him know they were coming. But the operator at the Excalibur had hung up on her after she asked to speak to Merlin the Magician—not sure of his last name.

And so they were headed to Vegas the Muggle way. If they could get through security, that is.

It had been easy to imagine tricking security last night, in the comfort of Sophie's bedroom when they'd bought the tickets. But now, surrounded by actual agents and police officers, she was, admittedly, starting to sweat it. What would the authorities do if they caught them? Scold them and send them back home to their parents in shame? Or was this something she could be arrested for?

Because yes, as a twelve-year-old, she could legally board a plane. But boarding it with a dragon in tow? That might just be another thing altogether.

Spike wasn't being much help in the matter, either. From the moment they arrived he'd been thrashing around his pet carrier, unable to settle into the confined space. Maybe Ashley had been right when she'd suggested they drug the dragon for the trip—like they used to do with her mother's old King Charles spaniel. At the time Sophie hadn't had the heart—or nerve—to do it. What if they gave him the wrong dosage? What if he was allergic to modern medication? It wasn't like they could call a vet if he got sick. And if he dropped dead on the way? Instamission failure, just add Benadryl. Not to mention, poor Spike!

They'd dressed him up, of course. An attempt to make him look more doglike than dragon. But what if Spike blew his cover the moment it counted? Like, literally blew it—by blowing fire at the TSA agents? They'd think the dragon was some kind of biological weapon of mass destruction. Part of a terrorist plot. Sophie's dad would pretty much kill her if she got sent to prison right before the wedding.

"Dude, I'm freaking out!" Ashley poked her in the shoulder for at least the fourteenth time since they'd gotten in line. "There's, like, all these guys with guns here. What if they see Spike?"

"Spike's fine. He's in his carrier. You can barely see him through the bars."

"You can see he has no fur."

"There are plenty of hairless dogs."

"But none of them look like dragons."

"Who wants to play I Spy?" Stu interrupted cheerfully. The two girls gave him a look. "What? It'd pass the time!"

"I prefer to spend my time in abject terror, thank you very much," Sophie said. "I mean, I told my dad I was going on a church field trip for goodness' sake. If he finds out I snuck off to Vegas..."

"Oh my gosh, I told my mom the exact same thing!" Ashley cried. She wrinkled her nose. "I hope they don't think we're together."

"Um, news flash. We *are* together."

"I know, but to, like, save the world. Not hang out."

"I also brought my Magic cards!" Stu added with an almost manic smile on his face. As if he were desperate to keep the peace. He reached into his bag and pulled out his deck. He pushed them at Sophie. "I'll even let you play my Spirit Dragon if you want."

Sophie forced a smile in his direction. She was glad he was so excited about the mission. And why shouldn't he be? This was what they'd been waiting for all this time and now it was finally happening! Who wouldn't be excited?

Besides, you know, someone stuck with their annoying future stepsister constantly blabbing in her ear.

What had she been thinking, agreeing to let Ashley come along? This was supposed to be Sophie and Stu against the world. The world didn't need a third wheel along for the ride.

But that wasn't Stu's fault.

She forced a smile. "I'll definitely play Magic with you," she assured him. "But you can keep your Spirit Dragon. I prefer to crush you with my Mog Fanatic."

"I think I'll stick to crushing candy," Ashley chimed in, as if anyone had asked her. "You know," she added. "On *Candy Crush*?"

Stu let out a loud laugh. Sophie rolled her eyes. And to think, most kids at school thought Ashley was so cool....

A squawk came from the pet carrier. Sophie dropped down to peer at Spike. The dragon had his snout pressed against the bars and was panting heavily, his black, very un-doglike tongue flopping out of the side of his mouth.

"Hang in there, buddy," she whispered to him. "We're almost there."

"Tickets and IDs, please," the agent at the desk called out.

Finally! Sophie rose back to her feet and reached into her pocket. She pulled out her passport and handed it to the agent. Stu and Ashley did the same.

The man looked down at the IDs and tickets, then up at them. He squinted suspiciously. "Where are your parents?" he asked.

Sophie's mouth went dry. Parents? Why was he asking about parents?

"Um..." she said. She shot a "save me" look at Stu.

"Um..." Stu repeated, which was not at all helpful or convincing. "They...um, they..."

"You can fly at age twelve!" Sophie blurted out, suddenly remembering. "It says so on the website!"

They'd done quite a bit of Internet research, in fact, before buying their tickets. Each airline had different policies when it came to letting minors on board by themselves. East Air seemed to be cool with it, which was why they chose to buy seats with them.

The agent's face clouded. "Well, there's the unaccompanied minor program," he said. "But usually that means the parents walk you to the gate."

Now Sophie's whole body was trembling. Had she gotten it all wrong? What if the guy didn't let them go? What if he demanded to see their parents? Could they convince some random adults in the airport to pretend to be their mom and dad? That seemed rather unlikely. Airports had strict warnings about strangers asking you to carry their bags. She was guessing there were even stricter warnings about leading strange children through security checkpoints.

She realized the agent was still waiting for an answer. "I know," she stumbled. "But...but..."

"But our dad is such a jerk!" Ashley broke in, pushing Sophie aside with such force she almost knocked her over.

The agent's gaze shot in her direction. "Excuse me?"

Ashley sauntered up to the desk, tossing her hair over her shoulder. "Yeah. So, like, when we got here, I just wanted to go to the bathroom, and he was like, 'We have to get to our gate.' And I was like, 'Look at the line, Dad. I'll pee my pants in that line! And I so do not want to sit on an airplane all the way to Vegas with pee-pee pants!'" She shook her head knowingly at the agent. "You know?"

The agent's face turned bright red.

"Anyway, he was like, 'Well, I'm going through. I'll meet you on the other side.' Which is super rude, don't you think? I mean, do you have kids?"

"I have a daughter...."

"Would you leave her alone in the airport if she had to pee?"

"Uh, she's three. So ... no."

"Oh my gosh, what a great father you are!" Ashley turned to Sophie and Stu. "Isn't he, like, the most amazing father ever?"

"Amazing," Sophie repeated, eyeing Ashley in awe.

"Anyway, we're going to go find him now. He's probably wondering where we are." Ashley smiled broadly. "Though I think I need to pee again first." She started to hop on one foot, as if to prove her point.

The guard shoved the passports in her direction. "Have a great trip!" he barked, looking very anxious to get rid of them.

Ashley took the passports, then danced over to the metal detector. She placed her large bright pink backpack on the conveyer belt.

"And . . . security is officially crushed," she pronounced. "No Spirit Dragons or Mog people necessary."

Sophie laid her bag on the belt, resisting the urge to glance back at the agent. She couldn't believe that Ashley's ploy had actually worked! It was like Ashley had literally used her annoyingness as a superpower. Which was annoying in and of itself.

"Dude, that was amazing," Stu said, coming up behind them and throwing his own backpack on the belt. Ashley beamed.

"Thanks!" she said. "It just came to me!"

"We're not through yet," Sophie reminded them, maybe a little too harshly. She knew it was ridiculous to feel resentful that Ashley had proven herself useful. But still! She was sure she could have figured it out if she'd just had a few more seconds to think.

She motioned to Stu and together they hefted the pet carrier up onto the belt. But before they could turn Spike in the right direction, a second security agent approached them, holding up a hand.

"You need to take that dog out," he instructed. "Walk him through the detector with you."

Uh-oh.

"You can carry him or use a leash," the man added helpfully.

This was not good. While Spike could maybe pass for a hairless dog behind the barred door of the carrier, there was no way he wouldn't look dragon-shaped out in the open. But what choice did they have?

She gestured to Stu. He reached down to open the cage. Spike's eyes lit up excitedly. She could see his wings moving from under his dog sweater. They had wrapped the wings tightly to his side using an ACE Bandage before they left the house, but what if they were coming loose? What if Spike decided to try to fly again in the middle of the checkpoint?

She bit her lower lip as Stu reached into the carrier and gently pulled the dragon out. As he set him down on the ground, Sophie could see the creature's eyes darting around the airport, his whole body tense with fear. Not surprising, she supposed, seeing as Spike had spent his formative years as a cup, deep underground in a cave with only a few druids to keep him company. A bustling airport was sure to be petrifying for the poor guy.

Keep it together, Spike, she urged him silently as Stu affixed the leash to the dragon's collar. *Just a little longer.*

Once the leash was fastened, Stu rose to his feet. He started walking toward the X-ray machine, tugging on Spike's leash. But Spike didn't move. Instead he dug his claws into the floor and made a terrified, very un-doglike squawk. His eyes were bulging from his head and he was panting with fear.

"Come on, Spike," Stu pleaded.

But Spike wouldn't move.

CHAPTER 14

"Will you hurry it up!" the person behind them growled. "Some of us have a plane to catch."

Stu gave another tug, but Spike wasn't having it. He had planted himself in his spot and he wasn't going anywhere willingly. Panic rose within Sophie. The longer they took, the more the guards would start paying attention. And if they realized the dragon was not a dog...

Suddenly Ashley pushed past her, leaning down and scooping Spike up in her arms. "Come on, you stubborn thing," she scolded, petting the dragon on his little head. She glanced over at the security agent. "He's super sweet, but super shy."

"What kind of dog is that?" the agent asked as Ashley waltzed through the X-ray machine. As if it was totally no big deal to be carrying a baby dragon dressed in a bright red Christmas sweater through airport security in the middle of March. Sophie had to admit, her future stepsister had guts.

"Oh! He's a rare breed," Ashley informed him, giving the gate agent her best fake smile. "A designer dog, imported from Tibet. In fact, he's one of a kind."

The agent's eyes locked on the dragon, his eyebrows furrowed. As if he were thinking really hard. Sophie sucked in a breath, adrenaline firing on all cylinders.

"Tibet, you say?" he asked, stepping closer. "Funny, I used to live there. I don't remember any dogs looking like that."

Uh-oh.

He didn't believe them. He didn't believe them and he was about to bust them. It would be game over. Mission failure. With possible world-ending consequences. What if the authorities took Spike away? What if they brought him to a government lab and wanted to do tests on him? Sophie and the others would never be able to get him back.

Sophie balled her hands into fists. No. She couldn't let that happen. She wouldn't! But what could she do?

It was then that she saw Stu, waving at her and Ashley on the other side of the metal detector. No. Not waving exactly. But making weird gestures with his hands, like he was playing charades. If Sophie didn't know better, she'd think he was miming pulling a rabbit from a hat. What on earth—? She shook her head at him, not understanding. He groaned.

"Wow!" he said overly loud. "This place is *magical*. I've never seen such a *magical*-looking airport before. . . ." Several people turned to stare at him, but he kept his eyes locked on Sophie.

Suddenly it hit her. Right! Her mother's magic. Of course! It had gotten them out of worse squeezes than this in the past. Maybe it could work now.

She turned back to the agent, drawing in a breath.

This is *a dog*, she pushed at him silently. Only *a dog*.

Suddenly her body prickled with electricity. The hairs on her arms stood on end. She shivered as magic seemed to rise up from inside her like water being drawn from a well. Would it work? Could she really change his mind?

It is not *a dragon*, she pushed again. *It's just a dog that* looks *like a dragon.*

She opened her eyes, scanning the agent's face. For a moment, he just stared back at her blankly. Then his frown vanished, replaced by a huge smile.

"Wow," he said. "That dog sure looks like a dragon! How cool is that?"

Sophie unclenched her fists, relieved. "I know, right?" she managed to squeak out. "People say that *all* the time!"

"Can I pet him?"

"Uh..."

Not waiting for an answer, the agent reached out to stroke Spike's head. Sophie bit her tongue, praying the little dragon wouldn't freak out and belch fire in the guy's face.

But thankfully Spike seemed to have calmed down now that he was in Ashley's arms. And he actually started purring as the man stroked his head. Sophie sighed. Seriously, did Spike like everyone on the planet more than he liked her?

Whatever. Spike could declare himself this guy's BFF for all she cared. As long it got them through security.

"He's very cool," the agent pronounced, thankfully backing away. He smiled at the girls. "You have a nice flight, okay?"

"Thanks!" Sophie cried. "You too!" She couldn't believe they had pulled this off. Between her magic and Ashley's fast talking they'd actually—

"Guys? Come with me."

She looked up. A third security agent had stepped into their path. Sophie's heart sank again.

"What is it, Officer?" she asked. "Did you...want to pet Spike, too?"

But the agent shook his head. "We need to check this bag," he said, holding up Ashley's overly bedazzled backpack.

Sophie frowned. "What did you put in there?" she hissed at her almost stepsister as they followed the agent to the bag-check area.

"Nothing!" Ashley insisted as Spike licked her hand. "Just . . . stuff I needed for the trip."

The agent put on a pair of clear plastic gloves before unzipping Ashley's backpack and rummaging through. Meanwhile Stu finally got through the metal detector and caught up to them, plucking Spike out of Ashley's arms. Time to get him back in his carrier.

"What's this?" the agent demanded, holding out an orange prescription bottle.

Ashley made a face. "Oh, geez. Those are my mother's antibiotics," she said with a groan. "She must have used my bag yesterday and left them in there. She's always borrowing my stuff. It's soooo annoying."

The agent tossed the pill bottle back into the backpack and resumed his search. Sophie turned her attention to Stu as he tried to wrangle Spike into his carrier. Unfortunately, it appeared the dragon was less than willing to go back behind bars. And the more Stu tugged on his collar, the more Spike planted his feet and refused to budge. It was then Sophie noticed his belly was starting to rumble. Uh-oh.

Please don't burp fire in front of security, she prayed. *Please, please, please!*

She'd already used her mother's magic. She wouldn't be able to recharge for hours. Which meant if the agents took a closer look at the dragon, they'd realize what he was. And they would all be—

The agent straightened as he pulled yet another item from Ashley's backpack. A full-sized bottle of what appeared to be glitter shampoo.

Sophie face-palmed.

"What?" Ashley asked defensively. "We're going to Vegas! A girl's got to look good when she goes to Vegas!"

"I'm sorry, but it is not permissible on a flight," the agent told them. "We only allow liquids of three ounces or less."

"But it *is* three ounces or less!" Ashley argued, unable to let it go. "I mean, look! There's barely anything left in the bottle. I practically used all of it last winter for the Snowflake Ball. I was going to be crowned Snowflake Queen, you know? And the Snowflake Queen has to have good hair. I'm pretty sure it's, like, a law or something."

Spike hiccuped. A spark of fire bounced off the floor.

Sophie leaped in front of the dragon, trying to hide him from the agent's view. Then she grabbed Ashley's arm, giving her a hard pinch.

"Ow!" Ashley cried, shooting her a dirty look. "What's your problem?"

"Come on, *sis*," Sophie ground out through clenched teeth. "You can buy new shampoo when we get there."

"This isn't just any shampoo! This is totally imported. Mail ordered. I can't just—"

Spike hiccuped again. This time the spark hit Sophie directly in the back of her calf. She bit down on her tongue to keep from screaming in pain and hopped on one foot.

"Are you okay?" The agent stared at her suspiciously.

"Totally fine!" she managed to squeak. She poked Ashley in the ribs. Hard. "Come on, *Elsa*. Let it go."

"Oh, fine!" Ashley pouted. "But if my hair is frizzy when we get to Vegas? I'm totally writing a letter to your boss!" She gave the agent an affronted look, grabbed the backpack from the counter, and stormed off in the direction of their gate. Sophie and Stu ran after her, dragging the carrier and Spike along with them.

Once they had turned the corner, Ashley stopped, turning to the two of them, her face lighting up with excitement. "We did it!" she squealed. "We totally tricked them!"

"Dude, you almost got us busted for shampoo!" Sophie protested.

"Yeah, but she did get us past the ID guy," Stu interjected. He turned to Ashley. "That was really cool, by the way."

Ashley beamed. "*And* I walked Spike through the metal detector thing, don't forget."

"Totally. I should have thought of that myself!" Stu raised his hand for a high five. Ashley slapped it with her own. "Go, Team Dragon!" he cheered.

"Don't forget my magic!" Sophie added, feeling a little left out.

"Your what?" Ashley turned, confused.

"Didn't you know?" Stu asked. "Sophie here is a powerful sorceress."

"That might be overstating it a bit," Sophie said, blushing.

"Please," Stu declared. "Don't be so modest." He turned to Ashley. "She helped me pull the sword from the stone. Defeat an evil knight. Now she's single-handedly taken on the TSA!" He grinned. "Honestly, I wouldn't be at all surprised if she started leaping tall buildings in a single bound at this point."

"Um, why would she want to do that?" Ashley asked, clearly missing the Superman joke. Because, of course.

"What I *want* to do is to get to our airplane," Sophie broke in. "We don't have much time before boarding."

Stu hedged. "About that," he said. "I was thinking…"

"Yeah?"

"Maybe we need to put Spike to sleep. Hook him up with some Benadryl from the gift shop or whatever. Just for the flight. He still seems a little nervous. And we do *not* need him setting our plane on fire."

"Oh my gosh, I said the *exact* same thing," Ashley replied. "But Sophie didn't want to do it."

"Really?" Stu looked at Sophie, surprised. "I mean, wouldn't it be safer that way? Even for Spike?"

Sophie shook her head. "We have no idea how he's going to react to Benadryl. Or what dosage to give. We can't risk it."

"What we can't risk is bringing a fire-breathing dragon on an airplane," Stu replied. He scratched his head. "Do you have a spell that might work?"

"If I did, I couldn't use it. I burned myself out back at security, getting the guy to believe Spike was a rare Tibetan dragon dog. I'm on magic time-out for at least another hour or two."

"Good thing you don't have to leap over any buildings right now," Ashley pointed out.

Stu's shoulders slumped. "What should we do?"

For a moment, they just stared at each other. Then Ashley squealed excitedly. "I know! I've got just the thing." She started rummaging through her bag. "It's somewhere in here...."

"Of course it is." At this point Sophie wouldn't have been shocked if she pulled out the entire land of Narnia from her sack.

Instead Ashley produced a single hair band. "Ta-da!"

"Um, we need him to stop breathing fire, Ashley," Sophie groaned. "Not get him ready for a beauty pageant." Seriously, if Spike had sported any sort of hair, he'd probably already have been doused with glitter shampoo.

Ashley waved her off, opening the pet carrier door and slipping the band over Spike's mouth. Sophie's eyes widened. Oh! That was actually a good idea.

"Sorry, little guy," Ashley cooed at the dragon. "But it's just temporary, okay?"

"Do you think it will hold?" Stu asked.

"It will if dragons are like other reptiles," Sophie mused. "Remember what that reptile guy showed us when he came to our school last year?"

"Oh yeah!" Stu snapped his fingers. "He said you can hold a crocodile's mouth shut with your bare hands."

"Right. All their strength is for snapping down. Not opening back up."

"And Spike's really little," added Ashley. "So I bet an elastic band will do it."

They looked down at the dragon. Sure enough, the elastic band was still intact. Spike glared down his snout at it, looking annoyed. He pawed at the elastic for a moment, then seemed to give up. He settled back down in his carrier with a sigh.

"We'll just have to check on him every so often," Ashley pronounced. "Make sure it's still on. In fact, I'll put a couple more bands on, just to be safe."

"Perfect," Stu declared. "I gotta say, the three of us make a good team." He held out both hands this time——for a double high five. Sophie and Ashley rolled their eyes in unison.

"If you suggest a group hug, I am going to smack you," Sophie declared. "Now come on. We need to catch our plane."

CHAPTER 15

"Wind and Rain, it is freezing out here!" Nimue declared, rubbing her hands together as she sank down on a nearby log. She and Emrys had been traveling all day on the road to Camelot and every bone in her body was aching with a mixture of exhaustion and cold.

The going had been slow without horses, not to mention the time it took to hide from view every time they heard another traveler approach from behind. She hadn't been exaggerating when she had told Emrys the roads were filled with thieves and cutthroats and they couldn't take a chance of running into either. Not if they wanted to make it to Arthur alive.

Nimue blew on her icy hands, a vain attempt to warm them.

"I don't suppose Merlin has a fire spell in that strange pad of his, does he?" She really wished she hadn't left her own spell book behind.

"I can look," Emrys said. He reached into his satchel and pulled out the book without pages. Nimue watched, anxious, as he pressed on the glass. But nothing seemed to happen.

"That's odd," he said.

"What is it?"

"It doesn't seem to be turning on."

With effort, Nimue rose to her feet, her sore muscles straining. She limped over to Emrys and tapped the glass with her own finger. The screen blinked once, a little white box flashing on the glass. Then it faded away and the glass was blank again.

"Is it broken?" she asked worriedly. That would be just their luck.

Emrys scratched his head. "I think it needs...energy?"

"Energy?"

"You know. Like after you've cast a lot of spells. Your magic depletes. You cannot cast again until after you rest."

Nimue nodded. She was well aware of that feeling.

"Well, the iPad is similar," Emrys explained. "Except instead of rest, it needs to be charged. Which can only be done by attaching it to Merlin's magic box."

"Well, that doesn't help us!" she cried, frustration rising inside her. "For Merlin's box is back at his cave." She glared at the useless iPad. "Why doesn't your master use a spell book like everyone else?"

"Merlin is not like everyone else."

Nimue shivered under her thin cloak. She sank back down onto the log, scrubbing her face with her hands. "What do you suggest we do, then?"

"I don't know. I'm new at this, remember?"

"As if I could forget," she muttered.

"Look," he said, his voice tightening. "It is you who asked me to come along. And here I am. What more do you want from me?"

"A fire, to start. So we don't freeze to death," Nimue retorted. "I don't think that's all that unreasonable...."

She trailed off as she caught the look on his face. Like that of a scolded dog. She sighed, pushing down her anger and frustration. It wasn't Emrys's fault they were in this situation, she reminded herself. And she couldn't expect him to fulfill her every need on demand.

She straightened her shoulders, firming her resolve. It wasn't as if she was some damsel in distress. She had been trained by the best druids in Avalon. And while she no longer had her spell book, she did have her training.

"Right," she said. "Well, then, I suppose we should try this the old way." She rose to her feet. "I'll gather some sticks and logs."

"I can help," Emrys replied eagerly, looking relieved to

discover a task he could actually complete. Nimue was tempted to tell him she didn't need his help—that she could do this all on her own—but in the end she decided against it. Together they could get the job done twice as fast—and that was worth more than her pride.

And so they wandered through the dark forest, collecting wood as they went. Some of the logs were far too damp from an earlier rain, but other pieces, found buried under thick piles of leaves, seemed to have potential. Nimue stacked the wood in her arms as high as she could before heading back to camp. There, she found Emrys had also returned, with a stack slightly taller than hers.

She nodded her approval. "Good. Now get me some small twigs and leaves and we'll see what I can do."

As Emrys went to do her bidding, she crouched by the log, creating a small fire pit with stones she'd found nearby. When he returned, she instructed him to dump the sticks into the middle of the circle. Then, finding two flat stones, she struck them together, working to create a spark. It took a few tries, but eventually they had a small fire going. Emrys gave a low whistle of approval.

"Very nice," he pronounced.

Nimue felt a smile flutter across her lips, pleased by the compliment. She straightened up and held her hands out to the fire. "At Avalon we are required to learn all sorts of skills," she told him proudly. "They say magic is only one branch in the tree of knowledge."

She thought back to those long, cold nights she'd endured with her fellow apprentices out in the woods when she was younger. They'd been dropped off by the elders with no supplies, no food, and no fire. They would either work together to find a way to survive, the elders told them, or they would perish in the cold.

At the time Nimue had thought the lesson ridiculous. After all, they had magic, why did they need anything else? But now she was grateful to her elders for having the foresight to teach them practical skills as well as the knowledge found in books.

"What made you want to become a druid, anyway?" Emrys asked, sitting down next to her in front of the now-roaring fire.

She shrugged. "I had very little choice in the matter," she admitted. "I was abandoned as a baby on the banks of a lake. Lady Vivianne found me when she came down to bathe. She asked around in the nearby villages but no one claimed me as their own, so she took me back to Avalon to foster me in her own house."

"That was nice of her."

"She was always kind," Nimue agreed. "As were my new sisters. And over the years we became as close as any true family." She poked the fire with a stick. "Though I still wonder, sometimes, where I came from. Who left me all alone by the lake?

Did they want me to die there? Or did they hope someone would find me? Did I ever have a family who loved me?"

"Well, if it makes you feel any better," Emrys said, clearing his throat, "some families aren't worth having."

"What do you mean?"

"Take me for example. I'm a constant disappointment to mine." He laughed bitterly and stretched out his arms toward her. "You may have noticed my skinny arms and sticklike legs, perhaps? Or the fact that I'm quite short, for a boy? My brothers are all strapping lads with bulging muscles." He made a face. "All my life they've called me Runt."

Nimue scowled. "That's absurd."

"Is it? My father always went out of his way to let me know how disappointed he was in me. No good on the farm, he'd say. Always had my nose in a book. If it wasn't for my mother..." He trailed off, looking wistful.

"So that is why you came to train under Lord Merlin?"

"Aye. It's my one chance to make something of myself. To prove to my father that I'm not worthless." Emrys kicked a small stone with his boot. "As long as Merlin doesn't cast me out for stealing his spell pad and running away with a druid girl my first days on the job, that is." He gave a wry grin.

"Such a bad apprentice," Nimue teased playfully. "And yet so noble!"

"I don't know about that."

"Come now!" she scolded, feeling suddenly generous. "Had you not turned the Grail into a chicken, it would be in Morgana's hands right now! Instead it is on its way to Lost Vegas—straight to Merlin. If anything, he should reward you for your service."

"I hope you are right."

"What a wondrous thing," Nimue said, marveling as she stared into the fire. "To be able to travel to the future on a whim. I wonder how Merlin spends his time there."

"I think he buys swords."

She cocked her head. "Swords? Really?"

"Sophie said he was going to a place called Excalibur. Which is the name of the sword Arthur pulled from the stone to become king."

"Right." Nimue nodded. "Well, I hope Sophie finds him quickly, and he's able to turn the Grail back into its rightful shape. I don't know how much time Arthur has left—"

She broke off suddenly, her ears pricking up at a rustling sound in the bushes. She glanced over at Emrys, putting a finger to her lips. Then she slowly rose to her feet, creeping in the direction of the sound while reaching for the knife at her belt.

She stopped at the edge of the brush, straining to listen. At first she heard nothing and was about to go back to the fire, dismissing the noise she heard as an animal or bird. Maybe an owl. Or a bat. Or—

It was then that she saw it. A pair of purple eyes, glowing out from behind a large bush. She let out a small gasp, her fingers gripping the knife so tightly her knuckles went white.

"You!" she whispered.

Before she could make a move, the figure turned and fled. Nimue dove after her, thrashing through the bushes, still gripping the knife tightly in her hands. Branches scratched at her arms and face, and roots threatened to trip her, but still she pressed on.

She could not let Morgana get away.

Her mind raced in horror as she ran, spinning through all they'd just spoken of by the fire. About the Grail, about the Companions, about Merlin himself and where he was. Why, she might as well have wrapped up the Grail in a fancy red ribbon and handed it to the sorceress herself!

"Morgana!" she cried as she ran. "Come back here, you coward! I thought you were a great sorceress. Yet you run from a helpless girl?"

Even as she spoke the words, she knew how foolish they were. Morgana *was* a great sorceress. While Nimue didn't even have her spell book and had to use flint to start a fire. What did she think she was doing, trying to goad her into a fight?

But there was no taking it back now. For Morgana had stopped running. She stood in front of her horse, a wicked grin slashing across her cold, hard face. She was terrifying—yet somehow still beautiful. With long black hair, high cheekbones, purple eyes, and full red lips with the power to whisper spells of death and destruction.

Nimue shrank back into the shadows, fear pounding at her heart. With a trembling hand, she raised her pitiful knife in front of her—a useless protection against a sorceress with so much power. But it was all she had.

Morgana lifted her palms. Lightning crackled from the tips of her bloodred fingernails. Nimue swallowed hard, her mind flashing back to her sisters, on the ground, their bodies blackened and burned.

She had escaped Morgana once.

But there was no escaping now.

CHAPTER 16

Emrys watched in horror from his hiding spot behind the thick brush, wincing as crackling sparks seemed to dance over the sorceress's fingers. For it could be no one but Morgana herself—the evil sorceress from his mother's stories—now standing before them in real life.

At first he hadn't understood what was happening. One moment Nimue was talking; the next she dove into the woods. What was she thinking? She was just an apprentice—without even her spell book to help her. While Morgana—at least according to the legends—was the most powerful sorceress in the land. How could Nimue even think about trying to best her in a one-on-one battle?

Was there any way he could possibly help?

"Silly girl," he heard Morgana purr. "Do you really think you have a chance against me? I am Morgana, rightful queen of Britain. Bow before me or I will take you down like I did your sisters."

Emrys shot a nervous look in Nimue's direction. *Do it*, he urged her silently. *You don't have to mean it. And you can take it back later. But for now—just bow!*

But Nimue didn't bow. Instead she seemed to push back her shoulders, standing as tall and straight as she could. "I am Nimue, servant of the Sacred Grove of Avalon," she declared, her voice defiant, though Emrys could detect a slight wobble just beneath the surface. She was scared, but trying to hide it. "And I serve only Arthur Pendragon, crowned king of all Britain." She pursed her lips. "I will never bow down to you, *witch*."

"Very well," Morgana said, with a sick smile. "Then you will join your sisters in death."

Fire flashed, seeming to come out of nowhere—flames barreling straight at Nimue. Emrys dove in her direction, managing to knock her down seconds before the fire blasted through, scorching the ground where she'd stood.

"No!" Nimue cried, struggling to get up. But Emrys held her down, shooting her a warning look.

"Stay down," he commanded as he staggered to his feet. He could see, out of the corner of his eye, Nimue trying to get up anyway—of course she wouldn't listen to him.

"Well, well," Morgana purred, her eyes lighting on him. "Whom do we have here?"

Emrys turned to Morgana, squaring his shoulders and puffing out his chest as best he could. He probably looked ridiculous to her. A pathetic runt of a knight without any shining armor to speak of. But Nimue had no one else, so the duty fell to him.

He drew in a breath. Here went nothing.

"I am Emrys the Excellent," he declared, meeting the sorceress's eyes with his own. She had beautiful eyes, he had to admit, though the pupils held a frightening darkness. He cleared his throat. "A wise and powerful wizard, trained under the great Merlin himself."

"I see." Morgana's gaze swept over him from head to toe. "And what do you want, little wizard?"

This was folly. Pure and utter folly. He wondered how his mother would feel when he didn't return to the farm. His father would likely say, *I told you so.* And he would be right.

But there was nothing to do about it now. "I want you to turn around and leave us and never come back," he said staunchly, trying to keep his voice from betraying his fear.

Morgana's mouth curled. A chuckle escaped her lips. "I must say, Emrys the Excellent," she drawled, "you are very brave. But also . . . well, I'm sorry to say . . . very foolish."

Emrys's heart beat faster in his chest. His whole body was

shaking like a leaf in the wind. But somehow he managed to stand his ground. "Three," he said. "Two..."

This had to be the stupidest thing he had done in his entire life. And it seemed likely it would be the last thing he would ever do. So much for studying to be a wizard. So much for showing his father he wasn't worthless. She would strike him down and then move on to Nimue and—

CRASH!

Morgana jumped. "What was that?" she cried, turning from him to address the sudden sound, coming from somewhere behind her. "Is someone there?"

Suddenly Emrys heard Nimue's voice. "Come on!" she cried. "Get on!"

Emrys looked up, shocked to see that while he'd been facing down Morgana, Nimue had managed to circle back and steal her horse. Now, with the sorceress momentarily distracted, she reached down and grabbed his hand. He climbed up behind her, gripping her shoulders to keep his balance.

"What are you doing?" Morgana demanded, turning back around. "You can't—"

"Go!" Emrys cried.

Nimue flicked the reins. The horse took off. From behind, Emrys could hear Morgana's shriek of rage, followed by firebolts blasting in their direction. Bushes went up in flames. The air began to thicken with smoke.

"Faster!" he begged Nimue. She flicked the reins again, and the horse, seeming to realize he, too, was in danger, picked up the pace.

They raced though the forest, not pausing for anything. Branches whipped at Emrys's face and arms, but he ignored them, holding tight to Nimue as if his life depended on it. Which, of course, it did.

Finally, after what seemed an eternity, they reached a clearing beside a small gurgling stream. Nimue pulled on the reins. The panting horse stopped and headed over to the water for a much-needed drink.

"I think we've lost her," she said, staring past him into the woods.

Emrys nodded, sliding off the horse, breathing heavily, as if he were the one to have run through the forest. His whole body felt limp; the heat of the moment had been the only thing keeping him upright before now. All he wanted to do was collapse, take a moment to breathe.

Instead he looked up at Nimue. "Are you okay?"

She nodded, though her face was still quite pale. "Thank you for rescuing me," she said. "I was sure I was done for."

"I'm not sure how good a rescue it was. If you hadn't grabbed the horse..."

She smiled. "What, you didn't have a great big plan for when you counted down to one?"

"Not exactly." He blushed.

"But it worked," she reminded him. "It gave me enough time to cast the distraction spell on her. And grab her horse." She patted the horse's neck.

"We make a good team," Emrys declared.

"Yes," she agreed. "Though..."

He cocked his head. "What's wrong? Are you worried she'll find us still?" He gave an uneasy glance toward the woods.

"No." Nimue shook her head. "Why would she bother to find us? What she really wants is the Grail. And thanks to my foolish tongue, she now knows exactly where to find it."

"Oh." Emrys winced. With all that had happened, he'd almost forgotten their earlier conversation. "What do we do?"

"There's nothing we *can* do. She's probably already on her way to Lost Vegas. Merlin and the others will have no warning!"

"Right." Emrys raked a hand through his hair. "Unless..."

Nimue gave him a sharp look. "Unless what?"

"What if we warned them?"

"How are we to do that?"

"We could travel through time, too. Using Merlin's Well of Dreams. It works as a portal to send people places. And since Merlin used it last, it should be able to lead us right to him." Excitement rose inside him as a plan formed in his mind. "Don't you see? We can find him and Sophie and the others before Morgana does. Warn them she is on her way."

For a moment Nimue didn't speak. And Emrys half wondered if she thought him insane. And maybe he was—to even think of traveling through time on such a crazy quest. But he could think of no alternative.

Finally, Nimue sat up. She lifted her chin. Met his eyes with her own.

"Well, then, what are we waiting for?" she asked. "Let's get back to the Crystal Cave."

CHAPTER 17

The good news? Spike made it through the flight, mouth elastic intact. In fact, he slept most of the way. The bad? When they landed, Stu's phone had about thirteen texts from his mother, each more urgent than the last. She wanted to talk to him. She *needed* to talk to him. He should come over tonight for dinner. They could talk more about the move. She wanted to make sure he was okay.

As the plane taxied to the gate, Stu's stomach crawled with nausea. What was he going to do? How was he going to answer her? And also, *was* he okay? He still wasn't sure, honestly. Mostly he'd been trying not to think about it—concentrating on their mission instead. But he couldn't exactly tell his mom to put all talks of moving on ice until he finished saving the world.

"Wow, your mom texts more than mine!"

Stu jerked his head in Ashley's direction. "What?" he stammered, quickly turning his phone over so she could no longer read the screen. Had she been peeking over his shoulder? Had she *read* his mom's texts? He glanced over at Sophie, who was thankfully leaning down to check on Spike, whom they'd stashed under the seat.

"Uh, she just...wanted to have dinner tonight," he blurted out, his heart beating furiously in his chest as he tried to remember if his mom had said anything about the move in her long series of texts. Something Ashley might have seen.

"Well, she looks like she's freaking out."

"Who's freaking out?" Sophie asked, peeking her head back up.

"Stu's mom," Ashley answered helpfully. Stu's face grew tomato red.

"I thought you were staying with your dad this week," Sophie said, puzzled. And for good reason. Stu's mom made it a rule never to text during Dad Week. Unless it was an emergency. "Is everything okay?"

"Everything's fine," Stu said, sweating bullets as he clutched his phone with white-knuckled fingers.

Sophie frowned. "You should at least text her back. You don't want her to start to suspect something and call your dad." She reached for his phone. "Here, I can do it for you—"

Stu leaped from his seat, jerking the phone out of her reach. One of the flight attendants gave him the evil eye. "Seat belt sign is still on," she barked at him.

Stu reluctantly slumped down in his seat, keeping his phone firmly in his hand, screen down. Sophie folded her hands in her lap.

"Sorry!" she said, sounding a little offended. "I was just trying to help."

His phone chimed again. He gritted his teeth.

"I know," he said. "I just—"

Thankfully, at that moment the plane's engines died. The seat belt sign blinked off.

"Finally!" Stu cried, leaping up again and shoving his phone into his pocket. He practically dove into the aisle, only to get stuck behind a dozen people doing the exact same thing. From behind him, he could feel Sophie watching him, puzzled.

"Don't forget you-know-who!" Ashley broke in, reaching under the seat to pull out the pet carrier and handing it to Stu. From behind the bars, Spike blinked at him sleepily.

The line of people started to move. Stu walked behind them, followed by Sophie, then Ashley. Hopefully Spike would stay sleepy until they got out of the airport and into the hotel. Then they could let him out—give him some food maybe. Did dragons really love tacos? He could go for a taco himself. Maybe it would even stop his stomach from churning.

As they stepped into the airport, his phone buzzed again.

"Argh!" he cried. "Leave me alone!"

Sophie put her hands on her hips. "Stuart Mallory, what is going on here?" she demanded. "Is everything okay?"

"Yes! Everything is *awesome!*" Stu blurted out, unwittingly channeling his inner Lego guy. From behind him, Ashley snickered.

"Are you sure?" Sophie pressed. "You look kind of pale. Was that your mom again?"

He sucked in a breath and turned to face her. "Actually," he declared, with as much bravado as he could muster, "it was the *fun police.* 'Cause we're about to have *too much fun!*"

"Um..."

"I mean, Vegas, baby!" he cried, shoving Spike's carrier at Ashley, then grabbing Sophie's hand and twirling her around. "Can you believe we're in Vegas? Just look at this place! Wild!"

Sophie looked around, a little bewildered. "We're still in the airport."

"And have you ever seen an airport like this? Look at the slot machines! Any of them could spit out a million dollars at any second!" He skipped over to a series of signs advertising the Vegas sights. "And check out this dolphin lagoon! How cool is that? And look at that *huge* Ferris wheel. We should totally ride that while we're here. Or I will anyway. I know you and heights."

"Um, sure? Maybe?" Sophie stammered, looking at him as

if he'd lost his mind. Still, Stu thought, at least she'd stopped asking about the texts. "But first we need to find Merlin. We're on a mission, remember? This is not some vacation."

"Speaking of fun police," Ashley muttered under her breath.

"What?"

"Oh, nothing! Last one to the cab stand is a rotten avocado!" She took off running. Sophie groaned and fell into pace behind her. Stu pulled his phone from his pocket, glancing at the screen.

"Sorry, Mom," he said with a sigh, then ran off to join the others.

Five minutes later they were in a cab, heading toward the famous Las Vegas "strip." Stu watched out the window as the driver pulled onto a street filled with bright lights and skyscraper hotels, many shaped like real places from around the world. There was an Eiffel Tower at the Paris hotel. A bunch of skyscrapers representing New York, New York. A Roman palace called Caesar's.

And then there were the people! Thousands of them crowding the streets. Many dressed very oddly indeed. "Look at him!" Stu exclaimed, pointing to a man half dressed in a Pikachu costume, the character's head sitting on his lap as he waited at the bus station, smoking a cigarette. "And them!" he added as they passed a couple of kids break-dancing on the sidewalk to a crowd of admirers who clapped and threw money into a hat.

"All these lights!" Sophie marveled, her nose pressed to the glass. "Can you imagine their electric bill?"

"They get their electricity from the Hoover Dam," Ashley informed them, not looking up from her phone. She'd been glued to the thing the whole time they'd been in the cab, clearly not impressed by the sights. Of course, this was her old neighborhood.

"I'd *love* to see the Hoover Dam!" Stu exclaimed. Then he glanced at Sophie. "After we save the world, of course."

She laughed. "I think you might need to hit up Merlin for a time-stopping spell," she teased. "To fit all this in."

As if on cue, Stu's phone buzzed again in his pocket. He groaned. A time-stopping spell could definitely be put to good use right about now.

"So you used to live here?" he asked Ashley as they drove by a giant pyramid-shaped hotel, complete with a replica of the Egyptian sphinx. He tried to imagine what it'd be like to grow up in a place like this.

"We actually lived outside of Vegas. In a regular neighborhood," Ashley explained. "But my mom worked on the strip and my dad would bring me in all the time to gam—uh . . . visit her and stuff." She set her phone in her lap, looking out the window. "He still lives here somewhere." She sounded weirdly sad.

"Did you want to meet up with him while you're here?" Stu asked.

Ashley turned from the window. "Nah. I'm good. I want to help you guys."

At that moment, the cab pulled off the main road and drove up a long driveway toward the Excalibur. Stu watched out the window, his breath caught in his throat as the castle hotel came into view. It was incredible! Much more amazing than he'd even imagined. With gleaming white and gray walls stretching into the sky and topped with brightly colored turrets of red, blue, and gold. Two towers rose on each side of the main building—presumably where the hotel rooms were. And all around were drawbridges, gates, and even a castle moat.

At the very front there was a large marquee sign with a giant depiction of the legendary sword for which the hotel was named. And underneath was an advertisement for some kind of show called the Tournament of Kings.

The cab pulled up to the entrance. After paying, they headed into the hotel, Stu dragging Spike's carrier along with him. For such a tiny little dragon, he was sure getting heavy. Stu could feel the small creature start to shift inside his cage, finally waking up. Stu picked up the pace, a little concerned about what Spike would do once he fully roused. The sooner they found Merlin the better.

But all thoughts of waking dragons fled his mind as he stepped through the front doors of the casino hotel and into another world. And here he'd thought the outside of the castle was over-the-top! Inside was something else altogether—with colorful stained-glass windows, stone walls, and mini-turrets that looked appropriately castle-esque right alongside rows upon rows of slot machines and bars and gaming tables that were decidedly less medieval themed. And then there were the people—hordes of them, milling about, talking and laughing and playing games.

"This place is huge!" Stu cried, having to shout over all the dinging and clanging of the slot machines. "How are we ever going to find Merlin?"

"I don't know," Sophie hedged. "I had no idea this place would be so crazy."

Stu set the carrier down and took a peek at Spike. The dragon was definitely awake now, his eyes darting from left to right as he began to claw at the front of the cage. He looked about as overwhelmed as Stu felt.

"Don't freak out, dude," he told the dragon. But if Spike understood him, he didn't give a sign. Thankfully, he still had his mouth strapped down.

Stu looked up at the girls. "We need to figure something out. Quick."

"What does Merlin look like?" Ashley asked.

"Well, he's old," Stu explained, rising back to his feet. "And he's got a beard."

"And he usually wears a long blue robe," Sophie added.

"You mean like that dude over there?" Ashley pointed across the casino.

Stu followed her finger. His eyes widened as they fell upon an old man with a beard, wearing long blue magician robes, just strolling through the casino. No way!

"Merlin!" he shouted, running across the casino floor, dragging Spike along with him. He couldn't believe that they'd found him so quickly amid all these people. Of course, he did kind of stick out. "Merlin! It's us!"

Merlin turned around at the sound of his name. "Children!" he exclaimed. "Welcome to Camelot!" He pushed a flyer into their hands. "I hope you will come see the show tonight. The Tournament of Kings! It's a magnificent jousting extravaganza. You'll love it!"

Stu's heart sank as he caught sight of the man's face for the first time close up. Not Merlin. At least not the real one. Just an actor playing the role. He took the flyer reluctantly, shoving it into his pocket. He should have known finding the magician wouldn't be that easy.

"We're actually looking for someone," he tried. "Someone named Merlin."

"*I* am Merlin!" the man announced in a grand voice, throwing out his arms. "Magician of Camelot." The crowd around him broke out in applause. Merlin gave a toothy grin, stepping away from Stu to strike a pose. Everyone held up their phones to take pictures.

Stu dove after him, accidentally photobombing what probably would have been a great shot. "I mean the real Merlin. No offense. He has a white beard. Sometimes has twigs in it? Blue eyes?"

Not-Merlin laughed heartily. "There is only one Merlin, lad!" he declared. Then he shoved Stu out of the way, preening for another picture. Stu noticed his fake beard was coming unglued from one side of his face; Stu had to resist the urge to rip it off altogether.

Finally, the crowd dispersed, leaving them alone. Not-Merlin turned to the three of them, his smile dipping into a frown. "Are you still here?" he sniffed, looking irritated.

Ashley reached into her purse. She pulled out a wad of bills and shoved it in his direction. "Merlin," she said in a voice that sounded as if she were talking to a three-year-old. "Do you know where the real Merlin is?"

The actor glanced from side to side, then grabbed the money quickly, shoving it into his robe. He nodded for them to follow him and led them over to a quiet corner. Or relatively quiet, anyway—it was Vegas after all. He gathered them around and spoke in a whisper. "I know exactly who you are talking about. And you can tell him to forget it!"

"Huh?" Stu cocked his head in confusion.

"That Merlin guy. The one with the twig-filled beard. He was here two days ago. Just wandering around as if he owned the place. Stealing my thunder, taking selfies with my tourists!" He huffed. "He even had the nerve to ask if he could fill in for me at the Tournament of Kings tonight! As if I would ever agree to such a thing! That's my show! My public expects me!" He fluffed up his fake beard.

Stu glanced at Sophie and Ashley, his heart beating a little faster. "Where is this Merlin now?"

"How am I supposed to know?" the man blustered. "I told him to get lost. That he wasn't welcome in my castle. I even had to call security! Guy wouldn't take a—" His eyes suddenly dropped to the pet carrier.

"What is that?" he demanded. "Is that a pet? We do not allow pets here at the Excalibur!"

Sophie leaped in front of Stu, attempting to block not-Merlin's view of Spike. "Thank you for your time," she told him. "Good luck with your show!"

And with that, the three kids turned, practically running out of the casino. Stu could hear not-Merlin shouting after them, but he and the girls ignored him, bursting through the doors and back outside. They ran halfway down the drawbridge, then stopped to catch their breath. Stu set Spike on the ground, his arm aching from carrying him.

"That was...interesting," he remarked. "You think he was talking about our Merlin?"

"How many Merlins could there be?" Sophie pointed out.

"True." Stu looked up at the huge castle. "So he's here. Somewhere."

"Yeah. But where?" Sophie scratched her chin. "That's the question."

"I don't know, but we need to figure it out fast," Ashley interjected. She had gotten down on her knees in front of the carrier and was looking worriedly at Spike. "Or at least get this guy to a quiet place where he can spread his wings and chill. He's totally flipping out."

Stu began to nod. But before he could speak, a loud roar suddenly echoed across the bridge, causing him nearly to jump out of his skin.

"What was that?" Sophie cried, sounding as alarmed as Stu looked. Her eyes darted from left to right, trying to locate the source of the sound.

"Look!" Ashley cried, pointing over the side of the bridge. "Down there!"

Stu peered down, surprised to see a mammoth green creature rise from the water.

A creature that looked a lot like a dragon.

CHAPTER 18

t wasn't a real dragon, of course. Stu could see that once it had
fully emerged from the moat. More like a giant animatronic
one you might find at a theme park. And it wasn't in the best
shape, either. Its plastic scales were flaking off in multiple
spots and its motions were jerky. Its eyes, however, glowed a
vivid green, and realistic puffs of smoke shot from its nostrils.
Stu imagined it probably looked pretty amazing at night.

"Oh my gosh, no way!" Ashley squealed.

Stu and Sophie turned to look at her. She pointed to the
dragon. "It was my mom's favorite show as a kid. This dragon
rises from the moat every hour and this wizard guy would come
out of his cottage to defeat it with his magic. I didn't know they
started it up again."

"Wizard? Do you mean like Merlin?" Sophie asked, her voice rising in excitement.

"Um, maybe? Anyway, he lived in that cottage down there." She pointed over the side wall.

Stu and Sophie scrambled to the side of the bridge to look down. Sure enough, they found a little cottage built into the side of the castle. It had a thatched roof and a wooden door and a small dock that led out to the moat, like a little hobbit house.

Stu studied the cottage. Could the real-life Merlin be staying down there? Hiding out from not-Merlin and his casino goons? If so, how would they ever get there to find him? He watched as the dragon "swam" closer to the castle and cottage. It must have been on some kind of rail. Its belly started to glow red. More steam shot from its nostrils.

"Now Merlin comes out," Ashley explained. "He fights the dragon with his magic and saves the—"

"SQUWAK!"

Stu almost fell over as Spike suddenly rammed the door of the pet carrier so hard it hit him in the back of the knees. He looked down, horrified to see the dragon going crazy, clawing at the cage, steam shooting from his nostrils.

"Uh, guys?" he said, trying to hold the carrier steady as Spike continued to freak out.

"Relax, Spike!" Ashley scolded, dropping to her knees to

attend to the dragon. "It's okay. It's not a real dragon. It's just pretend!"

But Spike didn't seem to care. He screeched angrily, butting his head against the wire door a second time. A few people on the bridge turned their attention from the show to the three of them, watching with curious eyes.

"What's wrong with him?" Sophie asked worriedly.

"I don't know!" Ashley cried, wrestling to keep the door shut. "Help me get him under—"

Spike charged the front of his cage, popping the door open like a cork from a bottle. He shot out into the air, his wings breaking through their bindings and sweater as he arced like a cannonball across the sky.

"Spike!" Sophie exclaimed. "No!"

Stu dove after the dragon, but it was no use. Spike had flown past the railing and was out of reach. The elastic bands they'd used to hold his mouth closed had finally snapped, allowing him to let out a burst of fire.

Not good.

Now everyone was watching. Even people who had just been walking past were crowding the railing, mesmerized by the spectacle. Many had their phones out, recording Spike as he flew in circles around the big fake dragon, screeching and blowing flames.

"Is this a new part of the show?" Stu heard one of them ask.

"How did they make that thing fly?"

"Maybe it's a dragon-shaped drone?"

Stu turned to Sophie. "Do something!" he begged. "Use your magic!"

Sophie nodded grimly, hands fumbling at the clasp of her bag. "Hang on. I need my spell book."

"Hurry!" he cried, turning back to the dragon. "Before he falls!"

Because, sure enough, Spike now seemed to remember he didn't know how to fly. Unfortunately, this realization came after he was already fifty feet in the air and nowhere near a good landing spot. Stu watched, horrified, as the dragon started flapping his wings desperately, eyes darting around, searching for a safe place to land.

"Spike!" he shouted, waving his arms madly at the dragon. "Over here! Come back here!"

Spike's head jerked in his direction. His eyes seemed to bulge in recognition. He started flapping toward Stu, trying to get closer.

Suddenly a large hawk seemed to come out of nowhere, swooping down through the skies, going straight for the tiny dragon. Spike let out a screech of horror and began flapping furiously, trying to get away. But he was losing elevation fast, dropping closer and closer to the moat.

Just before he hit the ground, the hawk plucked him up with

his talons, jolting him back into the air. The crowd gasped. Spike struggled, squealing with panic.

Just then there was a flash of light. Stu looked down just in time to see the cottage door swing open. An old man stepped out, cloaked in a cloud of smoke. He wore a full-length blue robe, accented with silver stars and moons, and . . . a Yankees cap?

"I am Merlin! Wizard of Camelot!" he declared loudly. "And, um, sorry I'm late. I ran into a little trouble with security and—"

He stopped short, clearly realizing no one was looking at him. Or at the big animatronic dragon, for that matter. His gaze lifted to the real spectacle in the sky—the hawk and the baby dragon. The hawk seemed to be having some trouble of his own, Stu realized suddenly. The dragon was fighting too hard, and the hawk was barely able to hang on. Stu didn't know what to root for. If the hawk dropped the dragon, Spike would crash to the ground and be flattened. But if the hawk managed to hold on—what would it do to Spike?

"Where'd Sophie go?" Ashley demanded. "Seriously, this is no time for a pee break!"

Stu turned, surprised. In all the craziness, he hadn't realized that Sophie had disappeared. For a moment, he was confused. Then it hit him.

He thought back to the fight they'd had with Morgana the first time they'd gone back in time. How Sophie had used her magic to turn into a bird.

Not just a bird. A hawk.

His eyes rose to the sky. Could it be? Could it really be her?

"Merlin!" he cried, waving frantically at the magician. "It's Sophie! You gotta help her!" He pointed up at the hawk.

Merlin cocked his head, looking confused. Which wasn't surprising. After all, Stu would be the last person he would expect to find in Vegas, interrupting his show.

"Stu?" Merlin stammered. "What in Excalibur's name are you doing in Vegas?" It was a valid question. But Stu didn't have time to answer. Hawk Sophie was struggling to keep elevation, and had started to flail. Stu didn't know how long she could hold on without dropping like a stone. If Merlin didn't do something quickly, they'd hit the ground too hard and too fast. It would be game over—for sure. A real-life one, with no do-overs.

"It's a long story. Just please help Sophie!"

Merlin nodded, then raised his hands above his head. He muttered something under his breath. To Stu's relief, the hawk and dragon stopped falling. For a moment, they seemed to hover in the air like they were weightless. Then they floated back toward the ground, slowly this time, as if being cradled by an invisible hand.

"Dude, how are they doing that?" demanded someone in the crowd.

"Wires," his friend decided. "Or mirrors. That's what magicians use."

The hawk and dragon landed on the ground. There was a puff of smoke. When it cleared, Sophie sat there, in human form again, cradling Spike in her arms.

The crowd went wild. Stu groaned. That was way too close.

"Wait, how did Sophie get down there?" Ashley cried. "And how did she get Spike away from that bird?"

Merlin looked up, his gaze trained intently on Stu and Ashley. *Meet us in the arcade*, he instructed Stu, though his lips never moved. *Right now.*

CHAPTER 19

"Wait here," Merlin instructed Sophie after they'd stepped through a small door on the side of the castle and into a tiny storage room filled with boxes. "I'll make sure the coast is clear." He slipped through a door, leaving her alone with Spike.

She sank down on a box, trying to catch her breath. She still couldn't believe she'd pulled off that stunt. One moment she'd been paging through her mom's spell book; the next she was launching herself into the sky, trying not to look down—or remember she was deathly afraid of heights.

She was lucky, she realized in hindsight, that Spike hadn't burned her to a crisp during the rescue. After all, he didn't even like the human version of her—never mind the predator who grabbed him out of the air and wouldn't let him go.

Thankfully, Merlin had been there to finish saving the day. Real Merlin. She'd never been so happy to see him.

She glanced over at Spike now, surprised to see the dragon was watching her. But not with the same suspicion she usually saw in his eyes. Instead he looked almost apologetic, as if he realized his mistake—and how she had saved him.

"Don't do that again," she scolded, shaking a finger at him.

He lowered his head meekly and let out a small sigh. Sophie felt her heart soften. *He doesn't know any better*, she told herself. The poor little guy had spent his entire life deep underground—as a cup. And now he'd been thrown into a new life, not to mention a new time period. And he had been caged and gagged for most of it without any explanation. She thought back to how terrified she'd been when she first got sent back to medieval times and Arthur had turned her into a bird!

"I know you were scared," she whispered to Spike. "I was scared, too."

Spike chirped miserably. He looked up at Sophie with soulful eyes. On instinct, she reached out—slowly, so as not to scare him. Then she dared to pet his wing. He let her do it, though he still looked a little nervous.

"There's a good boy," she said softly. "Sweet dragon."

Spike closed his eyes, letting out another small chirp. Not

exactly a purr, like he did when Ashley or Stu stroked him. And he didn't nudge his head against her hand, à la Toothless. But he also didn't try to burn her fingers off, so that was something. Maybe their shared near-death experience had brought them closer? Just a teeny bit?

The door burst open. Merlin poked his head inside. "Okay, we're good," he said. "Come quickly."

"Um . . ." She glanced over at Spike. "You might want to carry him." She didn't want to press her luck.

Merlin nodded, scooping the dragon up in his arms and tucking him under his robe so he wouldn't be seen. Sophie followed him through the door and down a long corridor, exiting into a huge arcade. The place was packed with video games of every kind—old and new. From an intense-looking *Star Wars: Battle Pod* to an oversized *Pac-Man* machine. There were carnival games, too. Horse racing and water-gun games and Skee-Ball, with a booth that gave out prizes in exchange for your tickets. There was even some kind of laser maze called the Quest for Excalibur, which looked like something she and Stu would love. A sign above read: WHERE PLAY SAVES THE DAY!

If only it were that simple.

"So," Merlin said, raising his voice to be heard over all the bings, bangs, and boops from the games. The place was packed with kids running all over, many without a parent in sight. "Perhaps now you might tell me what's going on?"

"Hey! Can we get a photo?"

A family of four ran up to Merlin, crowding around him, drowning out Sophie's answer. Merlin grinned, throwing up his hands. "Of course!" he cried. "I always have time for my fans!" He slung his arms around the mother and father as the father held out his camera in selfie mode.

"Say 'sword in the stone'!" the wizard cried cheerfully.

The father snapped the picture. Then he grabbed Merlin's hand and pumped it vigorously. "You look great. Really great. Straight out of Hogwarts!"

Merlin's smile dropped. "Hogwarts?"

"Of course! Dumbledore is our favorite!" the mother exclaimed. "House Gryffindor forever!"

"But I'm not—"

"Is that beard real?" asked the boy, who was probably around eight. He reached out and gave it a hard tug.

"Ow!" Merlin cried, now looking seriously offended. "Of course it's real! I am Merlin, wizard of Camelot!"

"No, no! We met Merlin upstairs a few minutes ago!" the father assured him. "Look! We even got a photo with him!" He held out his phone.

Merlin pushed it away. "What rubbish!" he grunted. "If you're going to pretend to be me, you should at least have the decency to grow a two-foot beard!" He huffed, fluffing out his own beard. "If I were you, I'd call management and complain about that phony baloney. See how he likes having security coming after *him* for a change."

The parents exchanged concerned looks. "Um, sure," said the mother. "We'll, uh, get right on that." She turned to her son. "Come along, Jake. Let's, uh, leave poor Dumbledore alone...."

And with that, they hustled away. A little faster than necessary, Sophie thought.

Merlin watched them go, a scowl on his face. "Dumbledore indeed!" he cried. "Come on! Anyone can see I am clearly a Ravenclaw."

Sophie rolled her eyes. "Now I see why you come here for spring break. You're like a legit celebrity."

"You're even trending on Twitter!" Ashley exclaimed as she and Stu ran down the stairs to meet them. She held out her phone for Sophie to see. Sure enough, #HawkVsDragon was trending, along with several close-ups of her and Spike wrestling in the air. She didn't know whether to be excited or horrified.

She glanced over at Merlin. "Uh, maybe we should talk somewhere quieter?" she suggested. "I mean, not that I want to disappoint your public or anything. But we really need your help."

Merlin nodded. "Of course. And my apologies," he said. "I get a little excited being around all these people. It gets lonely back home, deep in the woods. Though I did recently take on an apprentice."

"Yeah," Sophie deadpanned. "We know."

Merlin gave her a puzzled look, but waved his hand for them to follow. "This way," he said.

Sophie, Stu, and Ashley stepped in line as Merlin led them through the casino arcade, past all the cool carnival and video games. Under other circumstances Sophie would have totally challenged Stu to a round (or ten) of *Dance Dance Revolution*. Instead they followed Merlin down another set of stairs into a place that, according to its signs, held the Tournament of Kings. A moment later they emerged inside a large indoor jousting arena.

"Hey! This is just like Medieval Manor!" Stu exclaimed, looking around. "But way bigger."

Sophie nodded, impressed. Just like the famed dinner show back home, there was a large tilt yard for jousting down in the pit, surrounded by rows of benches and tables for the audience. Each section of seats was labeled for a different country except the one immediately across from them—which was the Dragon section, go figure. Down on the field, men wearing full suits of chain-mail armor were practicing their moves, presumably for the evening's show.

Merlin gestured for Stu, Sophie, and Ashley to take a seat in the back, out of earshot of any of the men on the field. Once they were seated, he reached into his robes and pulled out Spike. "Now," he said, "will you please tell me why you're here? And why you have a baby dragon in your possession? And, also, who *are* you?"

He tilted his head, looking at Ashley.

"Oh! I'm Ashley Jones. So good to meet you!" She beamed at him, holding up her pink backpack and pointing to a large button with Taylor Swift's face on it. "Swiftie for life!"

Merlin's eyes lit up. "A fellow Swiftie! Wonderful! Were you here for the concert last night? I had front row seats!"

"Tragically no. Was she amazing?" Ashley asked. Then she held up her hands. "No, don't even answer. I know she was. She always is."

Stu scrunched up his face. "Er, what on earth are they talking about?"

"Don't ask," Sophie muttered. "Ashley is my soon-to-be stepsister," she informed Merlin.

"How lovely! And what about this little guy?" Merlin asked, gesturing to the dragon. "Will he be joining your family as well?"

Sophie snorted. "No way. We could never afford the fire insurance premiums."

Spike chirped, leaping out of Merlin's arms and settling onto Ashley's shoulder, clearly his preferred perch. Sophie fought a wave of disappointment. She and Spike may have shared a moment—but Ashley was clearly still his favorite.

"Merlin, meet Spike," Ashley introduced. "You might know him as the Holy Grail."

Merlin's bushy eyebrows shot up. "Holy Grail?" he repeated. "That's a joke, right?"

"I wish," Sophie replied, eyeing the dragon.

Spike belched in response. A small fireball shot from his mouth, landing nearby. Stu ran to stomp it out. Sophie sighed. Hopefully Ashley had more of those hair elastics in her bag. . . .

"So remember that new apprentice you mentioned?" she continued. "Well, let's just say he might need a little more instruction." She quickly related everything that had happened in the Crystal Cave.

"That boy!" Merlin swore under his breath. "I told him to leave my iPad alone!"

"Yeah, well, if he had left it alone, the Grail would be in Morgana's hands right now," Stu pointed out. "Which would be way worse, right?"

"*That* would be catastrophic," Merlin agreed miserably. He looked down at the dragon. "Though this isn't much better. Without the Grail in its proper form, we can't get Arthur the medicine he needs. And his reign, as well as the kingdom of Camelot, will be doomed." He raked a hand through his thick silver hair. "This is what I get for trying to take a teensy little vacation. I leave for one moment and the entire realm falls apart!"

"Relax, Merlin," Sophie told him. "We're still fine. The Grail is here. You can just change it back to a cup and deliver it to Arthur. Easy peasy."

But to her surprise, Merlin shook his head. "I wish it were," he said. "But alas, from what you say, it may already be too late."

"Too late? What do you mean, too late?" Sophie demanded, alarm flaring inside her. This, she was not expecting. Getting to Merlin was supposed to be the hard part of the mission. He was supposed to take care of everything from here on out. After all, they needed to get zapped back home before it got dark and their parents started to worry.

Merlin gave her a regretful look. "Transmogrification—the spell used to turn things into other things—well, that is quite simple. Even a foolish apprentice can make it happen," he added. "But to change something back to its original form? That is another matter altogether. Sure, I could change the dragon back into something cup-shaped. But it would no longer be the Holy Grail. And it would no longer have the magical properties needed to heal Arthur. It would just be a fancy cup that held water."

Sophie stared at him, wondering at first if he might be kidding. After all, he was Merlin. He could do anything, couldn't he?

But the look on his face told her he wasn't joking. Her heart sank in her chest. She glanced over at Stu and Ashley, who looked just as devastated as she felt. After all they'd done to get here—all the risk taken at the airport to smuggle the dragon through. Was it all for nothing?

She opened her mouth to reply, but was interrupted by a loud buzzing sound. She looked over, realizing Spike was curled up in Ashley's arms, fast asleep, snoring like a trooper. Guess his little adventure had worn him out.

"Isn't there anything you can do?" Stu broke in, evidently not willing to take no for an answer. "I mean, you're Merlin the Magician, for goodness' sake! Surely your powers go far beyond trending on Twitter."

Merlin lowered himself down onto one of the benches, his hand toying with his long beard.

"There may be something," he said in a low voice. "But it would be very dangerous. And you are only children. I would hate to willingly send you into harm's way."

Sophie cleared her throat. "In case you forgot, I am an official Camelot Companion, commissioned by the great Tracey Sawyer—my mother—to serve and protect the once and future king throughout the annals of history. Which," she added, "I will do. Without hesitation. Despite any risk."

Wow. That was pretty good if she did say so herself. She glanced over at Stu. He smiled back.

"And I once fought a knight ten times my size," he added staunchly. "And won."

"And I..." Ashley began. She frowned, silent for a second. Then a big grin spread across her face. "I once faced down Saint Francis's entire cheer squad in the Halftime Challenge Competition. And I totally stuck the landing of my round-off back handspring."

Sophie wasn't sure how that specific skill set would prove

useful at a time like this, but she did appreciate Ashley's swagger, so she let it go.

"What do we need to do?" she asked Merlin.

Merlin steepled his fingers, thinking for a moment. "For a spell like reverse transmogrification to work, we'd need a very specific ingredient. A rare herb called Agrimony. But it is not found in this world."

"So where is it, then?" Stu asked.

"In the land of Faerie."

"Excuse me?" Ashley broke in. "*Fairyland?* Are you for real?"

"As real as the beard on my face, I'm afraid," Merlin said, giving them a grim look.

Ashley shook her head. "I swear, by the end of this week I'm going to start believing in Batman and Steel Man as well," she muttered.

"Um, do you mean Iron Man?" Stu interjected. "Or the Man of Steel?"

"Is there a difference?"

"So where is this place again?" Sophie broke in, before Stu could go on a ten-hour-long rant about the differences between Marvel and DC characters.

Merlin stroked his beard. "The land of Faerie is not easy to get to. It lies beyond the mists on the island of Avalon. In another dimension outside our world."

Sophie wrinkled her nose. "I was afraid you were going to say something like that...."

"It is a long journey and a dangerous destination. Ruled by Queen Morgan le Fay, cousin to Morgana herself."

Ugh. Morgana had a cousin? Really? And she was queen of the fairies? Sophie suppressed a shiver, her earlier bravado all but extinguished. "So... not your typical Tinker Bell," she said.

"Absolutely not. The land of Faerie is far from some kind of Pixie Hollow. It's a dangerous place with goblins and other vile creatures who love nothing more than to trick mortals like yourselves. They may act quite welcoming, offering you food and drink and hospitality. But one drop of nectar or one bite of food and they will make you their prisoner for eternity."

"So... don't eat strange food. No problem," Ashley broke in. "I think we can handle that. I have tons of protein bars in my backpack."

"Is there anything you don't have in your backpack?" Sophie said, marveling.

Stu leaned forward. "So, we go to Fairyland. Then what?"

"You must seek an audience with the queen. And you must bring her a gift. It is the faerie way. A gift in exchange for a favor."

"What kind of gift?"

A smile flittered across Merlin's face. "The queen has a

weakness for expensive skin-care products. Specifically a certain facial cream from Dr. Brandt."

"A woman of discernment," Ashley declared. "I like her already."

"She used to be able to get this product by mail order," Merlin continued. "But after a few couriers went missing while passing through the mists, Amazon stopped delivering. She'll likely be desperate, at this point, for more."

"Well, that sounds easy enough," Sophie said. "We can hit the drugstore before we head out. Piece of cake."

"Except…" Stu interjected. "What about our parents? They're going to freak out if we don't come home tonight." Sophie watched as his hand went to the cell phone in his pocket again. Her brow wrinkled. Was his mom still texting him? What on earth could she want that was making him so stressed out?

"Allow me to take care of the parental units," Merlin assured him. "A simple spell, implanting a memory of a school-sanctioned, overnight spring break trip they'd forgotten about should do the trick."

"Cool," Ashley declared. "Can you also change my history grade while you're at it?"

"I'm a magician, not a hacker," Merlin said, patting her on the arm. "Anyway, you just worry about the fairies. I'll take care of things back home."

"Wait—aren't you coming with us?" Sophie asked. She'd just assumed they'd be doing this together, like last time.

Merlin shook his head. "I can take you as far as the gateway to Fairyland," he told them. "But I am not welcome through the mists."

Sophie expected there was more to this story, but if there was, Merlin didn't offer it.

"Okay," she said, trying to put together a plan. "So let's say this Morgan le Fay lady agrees to hand over the goods. What then?"

"I will prepare you a potion that will transport you back to the human realm," Merlin said. "We'll turn the dragon back into the Grail and we'll deliver it to Arthur, as promised."

His gaze shifted to the entrance of the arena. Two security guards had entered and were looking around. Merlin hastily rose to his feet. "I shall begin work on the potion immediately," he said, keeping his voice low. "It will take a few hours to brew. In the meantime, I would be happy to provide you with a couple of hotel rooms to freshen up in, as well as tickets to tonight's Tournament of Kings. It's a wonderful show." He made a face. "Even if they do use a subpar Merlin who can't even be bothered to grow a proper beard."

"Sweet!" Stu declared. "I love a good joust." He turned to the girls. "Should we hit the drugstore for our skin cream first?"

"Actually, you take Spike and hide him," Ashley said, pushing the dragon in his direction. "I'll take care of the face cream. And the glitter, of course." She turned to Sophie. "You want to come?"

"I'd better not," Sophie said apologetically, surprised that Ashley would even think to invite her. "I've got to review my mom's spells. We may need them when we're in Fairyland."

Ashley nodded. "Take good care of Spike while I'm gone," she said, reaching out to pat the dragon on the head. "Not going to lie, I'll be a little sad to say good-bye to him when this is all over."

"Right?" Sophie agreed, feeling a little wistful. "He may be smelly, but he's pretty cute."

Spike grinned up at the girls, then let out a proud belch. They laughed, pinching their noses and waving their hands to blow the odor away.

"Spike!" they cried in unison.

And for once they were in agreement.

CHAPTER 20

"Is this it? Are we in Lost Vegas?"

Emrys blinked, trying to adjust his eyes to the sudden light. To figure out where they were. *When* they were. The last thing he remembered was himself and Nimue diving headfirst into the Well of Dreams.

Now they were in another world. A world with so much light it looked as if it were on fire.

His gaze darted from sight to sight, jaw slack. He'd never seen anything like this place. Everywhere he looked, there were windowed structures, impossibly tall and lit up brighter than the very sun. Many had moving pictures dancing across them. People, places, words—all larger than life. And then there were the strange horseless carriages. Bright white lights, chasing brilliant red tails, each carrying one or more people in its belly.

In fact, there were people everywhere, spilling out of buildings, stumbling down the streets. More people than Emrys had ever seen in his entire life. A man shoved by them, without apologizing, while a woman passed from the other side, singing at the top of her lungs.

But what was really astonishing was what the people were wearing. Or... not wearing, as the case might be. Emrys had never seen so many bare legs and arms in his entire life—and many of the women were wearing trousers. He shuddered, averting his eyes. Did no one in the future have any sense of decency?

He turned to Nimue. To his surprise, she was twirling in a circle, her robes swirling around her and her eyes lit up with excitement.

"It's so beautiful!" she said in a breathless voice. "The most beautiful place I have ever seen! As if the very stars have fallen from the sky and scattered around the earth."

Emrys wasn't sure about that. At first glance, yes, it all looked shiny and bright. But if you looked closer, you realized there was a lot of dirt and decay as well. Like the pile of large black sacks abandoned on the side of the road that smelled worse than dragon gas. And when you got close to the shiny buildings, you realized many of them were caked in grime. Even the ground was littered with cups and paper, blowing around in mini-whirlwinds by their feet.

The sooner they got out of here, the better.

"Come on," he said to Nimue. "We don't have time to waste. We must find Merlin and the Companions before Morgana does."

"But how will we find them?" Nimue asked, scrunching up her face. "This place is huge! Larger than an entire kingdom. And there are so many people!"

"You kids lost or something?"

Emrys startled at the sound of a sudden voice. He looked down to see an older man with slicked black hair sitting on the side of the road, his back against a stone building. He was dressed in white from head to toe, accented with a wide gold belt, and wore dark glasses over his eyes, like the ones Merlin had in his cave, even though it was night. By his side was an odd-looking guitar and a white dog dressed exactly like his owner, complete with the glasses.

"Who are you?" Emrys couldn't help but stammer.

The man looked a little offended. "Don't you know?" he asked, gesturing to his outfit. "I'm the king, baby!"

Nimue's eyes widened. She quickly dropped to her knees in a low bow. "Your Majesty," she said. "I'm so sorry. We had no idea." She grabbed Emrys, forcing him down with her. He reluctantly got to his knees, though he felt a little suspicious of the man's claims. If he were really king, why wasn't he at the Excalibur castle? And why did he look so dirty?

The man's eyebrows rose, as if he hadn't expected this reaction. Then he chuckled. "And who might you be?" he asked. Then he held up a hand. "No. Let me guess. You are playing Merlin," he said, pointing to Emrys. "And you, my lady, are Queen Guinevere."

"Oh no! I am no queen!" Nimue exclaimed, shaking her head. "I am only Nimue. A simple druid of Avalon."

The man tapped his chin with his finger. "Nimue," he said, pondering. "Right. I remember now. That's the girl who traps Merlin in a tree for a thousand years."

"What? No! I would never do something like that!" Nimue cried, horrified.

"Don't worry. I'm sure he deserved it." The man chuckled. "Anyway, you both look great. I had no idea Comic-Con was this week."

Emrys scrambled to his feet. This was too strange. "We should probably get going," he said warily.

But Nimue refused to budge. "Do you know Merlin?" she asked the king. "We need to find him. It's very important. And I promise I won't trap him in a tree."

The man's dog made a move toward her. She stuck out her hand, palm up. The dog sniffed her for a moment, then licked her palm. She smiled. "What a lovely dog!"

"Eh." The king waved her off. "Ain't nothing but a hound dog. Barking all the time." He paused, giving them a pointed look. Then he shook his head. "What do parents teach kids these days?" he muttered. Then he shrugged. "In any case, if you're really looking for Merlin, your best bet is the Excalibur Hotel."

Emrys's heart leaped in his chest. Excalibur! Now they were getting somewhere. Maybe this strange king could help them after all. "We're trying to get to Excalibur," he said eagerly. "Do you know the way?"

The man nodded. With effort, he attempted to rise to his feet. Nimue grasped his arm, helping him stand. Once upright, he raised a hand and pointed into the distance. "Do you see that castle?" he asked. "That's the Excalibur."

Emrys followed his finger until his eyes fell upon the most beautiful castle he'd ever seen. Not that he'd seen a lot of castles, but even if he had, he was sure that this one would stand above the rest. It was so colorful—with bright blues and reds glowing in the night sky. It looked like something out of a dream.

"It's pretty far from here," the man added. "You might want to take a cab."

"What is a cab?" Nimue asked.

The man chuckled. "Staying in character, eh? I like it. I'm just sorry I don't have a pink Cadillac to offer you, m'lady. I can hail you a cab, though. Do you have any money?"

Nimue shook her head. "I was never allowed to carry coin," she said apologetically.

Emrys hesitated for a moment. Then he reached into his robe's pockets, pulling out a small gold coin. The one his mother had given him at the start of his journey to apprentice under Merlin. It was meant to last all year and provide him with food and lodging in Merlin's cave. He wasn't sure what he'd do without it. But what choice did he have?

He held out the coin to the old man. "Will this do?" he asked.

The man plucked the coin from his hand. He turned it over, squinting at it closely, then looked up at Emrys, his blue eyes wide with astonishment. "Love me tender!" he exclaimed. "Where did you get this?"

Emrys felt hollow. "My mother gave it to me."

"Will it pay for a cab?" Nimue asked.

"It might pay for an entire car," the man replied. "Are you sure you want to cash this in, son?"

Emrys shrugged, not sure what he meant by "cash." "We need to get to Excalibur. If this can help..."

"Money always helps," the man declared, then broke out into a coughing fit. When finished, he gestured to a small, squat building behind them. "I can go exchange it for you, if you like," he said. "I know the owner. But I don't think he'll deal with kids."

Emrys bit his lower lip. The building's windows were covered in bars, as if it were a dungeon. Above the door there was a glowing sign that read CASH 4 GOLD with a picture of a jewel above it. Ah! Perhaps "cash" was another word for "jewel" in this world, and perhaps jewels were what they used for money.

"Thank you," Nimue said before Emrys could speak. "We will watch your dog for you while you're gone."

The man looked a little taken aback by this, but finally nodded. He shuffled over to the store and rang a bell. A moment later, Emrys heard a strange buzzing sound and the man opened the door, disappearing inside.

Suddenly a worried feeling began to worm inside him. What had they just done? Given all their money to a complete stranger! What if he left the building by the back door, taking their only hope with him?

Panicked, he ran to the door, grabbing the handle and trying to yank it open, but to his dismay, it seemed to be locked. He tried ringing the bell, as he'd seen the king do, but there was no buzz back this time, and the door remained closed.

"Let me in!" he cried, kicking the door repeatedly. "Give me my money!"

A few people walking by stopped to watch him with amused expressions on their faces. "Viva Las Vegas," one of them muttered, while another handed him a piece of paper that read

Gambler's hotline followed by an odd string of numbers. A third man tried to offer him what looked like a loaf of bread with some meat inside it—which admittedly did look pretty tasty.

Still, he pushed it away. "I don't need food!" he cried. "I need money!"

The man shook his head pityingly and walked away. Emrys turned back to the door. There had to be some way to break it down.

Suddenly Nimue was by his side. "What are you doing?" she demanded, looking annoyed.

"He's taken our money!"

"Yes. To trade it for what we need."

"What if he robs us?" Nimue had spoken of bandits on the road to Camelot. Why couldn't she see there could be bandits in this world, too?

Nimue walked over to the dog, dropping to her knees to pet his head. "Why would he do that?" she asked in a quiet voice.

"Did you look at him? He said he was a king! But he was clearly a peasant," Emrys declared. "He's made his home on the streets."

"So? Does the fact he has no home mean he also has no virtue?" she demanded, looking offended. "Look at me! I have no coin. And no home to go back to. Do you think I would steal from you?"

"No. Of course not!"

"And what of Morgana? She is rich beyond belief and yet hungers for power."

He sighed. She had a point. "I hope you're right," he said. "Because if you're not, I don't know what we're going to do."

Nimue didn't answer. Instead she picked up the man's guitar, turning it over in her hands. After a moment, she started strumming it softly, then began to sing under her breath. It was a song Emrys had never heard before and Nimue had a beautiful voice. It wasn't long before a few people stopped to listen to her. And when she finished her song? Much to Emrys's amazement, they clapped and left coins at her feet. He quickly gathered them up.

"Silver!" he cried, turning one of the coins over in his hands. On one side was a portrait of an older man with long hair, tied back with a ribbon. On the other was a building, underneath which was written *five cents*. "What a world this is! That they give money to you for singing on the streets!"

Nimue also looked impressed. "I have always loved to sing. But I have never gotten paid to do it."

"Sing another!" Emrys suggested. "This way if the king does not return we can still pay for the cab."

"Good idea," Nimue agreed. She started singing again. A few more people threw coins. Soon they had quite a pile of copper and silver. Emrys scooped it all up and placed it in his lap.

"Look at all of this!" he said, marveling. "We're rich!" He

held out the pile of coins to a woman in a short red dress who happened to be walking by. "Lady! How much money do I hold in my hands?"

The woman eyed the coins. "Uh, you've got like a buck seventy-five there."

"Will that get me a cab?"

She snorted. "It won't even get you a hot dog in this town."

"Oh." Emrys's excitement sank as she walked away. He dropped back to the ground. "Well, we already have one of those," he muttered as the dog in question (who did look quite heated, the way he was panting and all) licked his hand.

He stared up at the buildings, which were still alive with lights and pictures, and missed the forest back home and Merlin's simple Crystal Cave. What had they been thinking, coming here without a plan? And what if they couldn't find Merlin? Would they be stuck here forever?

"Don't worry," Nimue said, placing a hand on his arm. "He will be back. A man will never leave his dog, even for all the money in the world."

As if on cue, the door to the Cash 4 Gold shop suddenly opened and their friend hobbled outside, a large wad of paper in his hand.

Emrys frowned. "What is that?" he asked, gesturing to the paper. "Those aren't jewels." He glanced back up at the sign, puzzled. "It's just paper."

"It's your cash," the man said, handing it to him. "Sorry it took so long. Turns out your coin is very old and rare. They had to e-mail a picture of it to an expert to verify its authenticity." He grinned, flashing white teeth. "You should thank your mama, boy. That was quite the gift."

Emrys stared down at the paper in horror. "I gave you gold," he reminded the man. "You traded it for paper?" He thumbed through the small pieces, confusion and anger rising inside him. What had he been thinking? He knew he shouldn't have trusted this man!

"But look, Emrys. This isn't normal paper!" Nimue exclaimed, taking the stack from him and flipping through it herself. "Each piece has a picture on it. Like a portrait." She looked up at the man. "They are quite exquisite. Are they valuable in your world?"

The man laughed, giving her a mock bow. "Yes, m'lady. Why, men have sold their very souls for this paper. For when one has it, one can buy anything one's heart desires."

The dog barked. He smiled down at the dog. "Even dog food," he said, ruffling the beast's head.

Nimue seemed to consider this. "How many pieces of this paper would it take to get to Excalibur?"

"Probably twenty bucks. That's one of these," the king said, pulling out one of the papers from the stack. Sure enough, upon closer examination, Emrys saw the number twenty written several times on it.

Nimue plucked the twenty from the stack. "And how many pieces of paper will it take to get you a good meal and a place to sleep tonight?"

The man shook his head. "Oh, I couldn't take your money."

"You did us a good deed," she insisted. "Surely you deserve something in return!"

The man's face brightened. "Well, then thank you. Thank you very much," he said with a grin. He ruffled the dog's head again. "Come on, Elvis. Let's get these fine young people a cab."

CHAPTER 21

The hotel Excalibur might have looked like a castle on the outside. But thankfully, the rooms Merlin set them up in were simply furnished and had modern plumbing, much to Stu's relief. Let's just say he was still a little scarred from his bathroom adventures in medieval England when filling in for King Arthur.

Their adjoining rooms (one for him and one for the girls) also had a terrific view of the Las Vegas strip. It was just beginning to get dark and the neon lights were coming on, giving the world outside a vibrant, electric glow. Below them was the giant Sphinx that led to the pyramid hotel, and in the distance he could see the replica of the Eiffel Tower. There was also this weird glowing emerald-colored hotel across the street straight out of *The Wizard of Oz*.

"I can't believe we're here!" he cried, pressing his hand against the glass window. "This is so cool."

"Totally," Sophie agreed, barely looking up from her mother's spell book, which she'd been thumbing through since they'd gotten to the room.

Stu longingly watched the people milling up and down the streets, all looking as if they had somewhere awesome to go. He and Sophie had been sitting here, waiting for Ashley to get back with the face cream for what felt like forever, and he was starting to climb the walls with boredom.

"Do you want to do something while we're waiting?" he asked. "We could try to find that huge Ferris wheel thing. Or go explore that pyramid next door?"

"Dude, we can't leave. We're waiting for Ashley. And Merlin, remember?"

"Fine. Then let's go back to that arcade downstairs. We can text Ashley and let her know where we are."

"Maybe in a bit," Sophie said with a yawn.

Stu frowned. "Come on, Sophie! We're in Vegas! By ourselves! We should be... doing something! Something crazy."

"Um, we're preparing to travel to another dimension to trade skin-care products with the fairy queen," Sophie reminded him. "That's pretty crazy. Just saying."

"Sure. But that's later. We're just sitting here now!"

He knew he probably sounded a little desperate, but who

could blame him? This might be the last chance he and Sophie had to hang out for a very long time. He didn't want to waste it in a hotel room!

Sophie set down her spell book. "*You're* just sitting here," she reminded him. "I'm trying to study. Merlin said Fairyland is dangerous, right? I want to be prepared. Also"—Sophie waved a hand at Spike, who was curled up sleeping on a small pillow on the other bed—"we can't exactly leave Mr. Fire Hazard unattended."

Stu hung his head. "Right. Sorry."

She tossed a pillow in his direction. "Look, I promise I will whip your butt in Skee-Ball a gazillion times once we get home. But for now? I gotta focus." She picked up her spell book again.

Ugh. Her words made Stu's stomach twist into knots. Because of course Sophie would think that. To her they had all the time in the world. She didn't know that in just weeks they'd be living three thousand miles apart. Their days of casual Skee-Ball and everything else would be over. Forever.

He slumped to the floor, his earlier enthusiasm deflating. He tried to remind himself that at least Merlin had bought them more time with the whole Fairyland trip. Otherwise they'd be zapping back right this very second. But try as he might, he just felt depressed.

"Are you okay, dude?"

He looked up to see Sophie staring down at him. "Yeah?" he tried. Probably not sounding super okay.

"No offense, but you've been acting weird this whole trip." She squinted at him. "Is it Ashley? Because trust me, I didn't want her to come along, either."

"No." He shook his head. "Ashley's fine. She's actually been helpful, weirdly enough."

Sophie snorted. "I know, right? Who would have thought?"

Stu tried to laugh. It came out more like a sigh.

"Come on. I can totally tell something's bugging you," Sophie pressed. "Can you just tell me what it is? Did I do something to make you mad?"

"No! Of course not!"

"Then why are you acting all weird? Is it your mom? Is she still texting you? What does she want, anyway? It's not even her week to have you."

Her question hung in the air as silence fell over the room. Stu swallowed hard, not sure how to answer. Because this, he realized, was it. The opening he'd been waiting for since they started this whole thing. The perfect opportunity to confess everything. She was going to be furious at him for not telling her sooner. But that couldn't be helped. Better to just get it out in the open and—

"GLITTER BOMB!"

Ashley burst through the door, dancing across the room, tossing handfuls of gold sparkles everywhere. A good portion of which landed directly on Sophie's head. Ashley giggled. "Oops!"

Stu groaned. And . . . there went his chance to confess. No

way was he going to break such big news in front of Princess Sparkle.

A weird sense of relief rushed through him. Yup, this was definitely not the time—or the place. Which was no big deal, of course. Because he could just tell Sophie later tonight. After the show. Or just before bed. Though then she might not sleep well. And she needed a good night's sleep before going to Fairyland. Maybe he'd wait until the morning....

He could feel Sophie's questioning eyes on him; she was clearly not ready to drop the conversation. He needed to distract her somehow. Like he had in the airport. Make her forget anything was up until he was ready to explain.

He forced himsef to scramble to his feet, his heart pounding a mile a minute. "Whoo-hoo!" he cheered. "Now, *this* is Vegas!"

He danced around the room, grabbing fistfuls of fallen glitter and tossing them up in the air. From the bed, Spike squawked with excitement, sticking out his little black tongue, trying to catch glitter flakes as if they were snow.

"Isn't this stuff great?" Ashley gushed. "It's from the craft store I told you about. They have the best glitter ever." She grinned. "Our avocados are going to be epic."

"The Epic Avocados," Stu pronounced. "That sounds like a great band name." He could feel Sophie still looking at him, but refused to turn around. He knew he was being kind of obnoxious, but desperate times and all that.

"Please tell me you got the face cream, too," she said.

Ashley gave a dismissive nod. "Obviously. I got everything we could possibly need. Including genuine unicorn poop!" She presented Stu with a large tub of glitter that did, indeed, claim to be the excrement of a certain horned horse of legends.

Sophie jerked to her feet. "Glitterific," she muttered. "I'll go let Merlin know we're set," she said stiffly. "Stu, do you want to come with?" She shot him a meaningful look.

Stu swallowed hard, his heart pounding in his chest all over again. Everything inside him told him he should go with her.

Though . . . hadn't he just determined it would be better to tell her tomorrow? Tomorrow would be a way better time. Or maybe when they got back from Fairyland?

Because, he realized with dread, when he finally did tell her? It would change everything. And he wasn't ready for that just yet.

"I'm good," he said, waving her off, refusing to meet her eyes. "I . . . need to keep an eye on Spike. Um, like you said."

He waited for her to argue. To remind him that Ashley would easily watch Spike in his stead. But instead she just stood there, in the doorway, silent. Then she turned and walked out the door, letting it slam a little too loud behind her.

Stu's shoulders slumped. *Good going, dude.* First he'd worried her. Now he'd made her mad. This adventure was going just about as well as the first one they'd had together—when she'd thought he was ditching her for the soccer team. And now he really *was* ditching her—for California. Even though that was so not his fault.

"What's wrong with her?"

He looked up to see Ashley. She'd put the glitter back into the bags on the table and was now watching him with a curious expression on her glittery face.

"Nothing," he said with a shrug. He walked over to the bed and flopped down on it.

"You two have a fight?"

"Not exactly."

"Uh-huh," Ashley said, not sounding at all like she believed him. Probably for good reason. She sat down next to him on the bed, where Sophie had left her mother's spell book. She picked it up and flipped through a couple of pages. "Whoa. There are some legit spells in here. Can Sophie actually do all of these?"

"I think so," Stu replied, wondering if there might be a make-someone-not-mad-at-you spell in there. Because that would be super useful right about now. He wondered if he should go after Sophie—try to catch up with her. But try as he might, he couldn't get his cowardly legs to move.

Ashley stopped on a page. "Ooh! An invisibility spell!" she cried, her eyes sparkling along with the rest of her. "How useful would that be?" She grabbed her phone and took a photo of the page. Then she grinned at Stu. "For emergencies only, of course."

"Don't let Sophie see you do that."

Ashley groaned. "Ah yes. Our lovely fun police."

"She's really not that bad," Stu protested, not knowing why he bothered. "It's just . . . this is important to her."

"Isn't it important to all of us? I mean, we're all part of the team here, right?"

"Right. It's just . . ." Stu didn't know how to explain. Especially since Ashley was kind of making sense. Still, Sophie was the official Companion here. They were just her helpers.

Though, in truth, he hadn't been very helpful so far.

"Whatever. I don't even care," Ashley declared. She threw the spell book back on the mattress. "Now where's that Nintendo thing you had on the plane?"

Stu raised an eyebrow. "*You* want to play Switch?"

"You have a problem with that?"

"Of course not. It's just—"

"That I'm a cheerleader? Insanely popular?" Ashley made a face. "Way to stereotype, dude." She fiddled with the ring on her right finger. "Anyway, I play when I visit my dad, okay? It's, like, the one thing we can do together without fighting."

Stu nodded, thinking of his own dad and soccer. "Sure, I'll play," he said. Anything to get his mind off Sophie and the move.

They propped up the screen with a pillow and loaded up *Mario Kart*, choosing their characters and cars. Ashley surprised Stu by picking Toad over Princess Peach. He picked Dry Bones for himself and the game loaded at the starting line.

"Prepare for a butt whipping of epic proportions," Ashley declared, her eyes glued to the screen.

"You think so, huh?" Stu shot back. "Well, it's on, gamer girl. It's so on!"

And with that, they were off, racing down the track for the first loop. Stu gripped his controller tightly, swerving right to grab an early power-up, then zooming forward, leaving Ashley in his dust. He flashed her a triumphant grin, only to slam straight into Mario and lose his momentum. Ashley laughed, zipping past him. Stu watched in dismay as his character spun out of control.

"Lucky break," he muttered.

Out of the corner of his eye he could see Spike watching them with curious eyes. He was about to suggest they pause to check on him, when his cell phone buzzed loudly.

Mom. Again.

He gritted his teeth, narrowly avoiding crashing into Luigi's car. Didn't Merlin say he was going to take care of the parental units? Well, he needed to get on that, stat. At this point his mom had sent a billion text messages and he hadn't answered more than two of them. Mostly because he had no idea what to say. Like, *Sorry, Mom, I can't talk about your new job and our big move because I'm busy saving the world. Also playing Nintendo. In Vegas.*

She would so not understand.

"Your mom still harassing you?" Ashley asked, her car

launching off a jump, collecting coins in its wake. She was still in the lead, though not by much. Stu was sure he could catch her on the next corner.

"What can I say? The woman has a gift."

Ashley snorted. "By the way. I'm sorry you have to move. That really stinks."

Wait, what?

BAM! Stu slammed his car straight into a wall. Dry Bones flipped from the track and fell into the abyss. Stu dropped his controller, turning to Ashley.

"How do you know that?" he demanded. "Did you read my texts?"

"Of course not!" she said, sounding offended. She sent her car leaping over a jump, grabbing at least seven coins in the process. "Lucas texted me and I told him I was hanging out with you. He asked how you were taking the move. I guess you didn't answer his texts, either, and he was starting to worry."

Dry Bones appeared back on the track. Stu grabbed his controller and tried to keep going, but his heart was racing faster than his car. How could Lucas tell Ashley—when Stu hadn't even told Sophie yet? But then, of course his stepbrother would have no idea he hadn't told Sophie. Because normally Stu told Sophie everything. Immediately.

This was not good. And yet, at the same time, he felt a weird sense of relief. The secret had been bottled up inside him this whole time. Now he could finally talk about it to someone. Someone who already knew. (And didn't care one way or the other.)

"My mom got a job in California," he explained. "She wants me to live there with her and only go back to my dad's for summer and holidays."

"Ugh." Ashley made a face as she hit a power-up and zoomed into the second lap. "I'm sorry. Believe me, I know how much that blows."

"You do?"

"Uh, yeah. My mom did the exact same thing to me. We were living here in Vegas. I had tons of friends. I was on the Pop Warner cheer team, about to start a new football season. But then my mom, out of nowhere, decides to up and move us clear across the country, just to get away from my dad."

"What did you do?" Stu asked.

"When you're nine, there's not much you *can* do. I begged her not to go. I asked if I could stay with my dad. But he was . . . having difficulties," she said hesitantly. "He gambled a lot. He wasn't really home enough to deal with a nine-year-old."

"I'm sorry," he said, glancing over at her. "That must have stunk."

"It wasn't a day at the spa," she said. She hit another speed power-up, sending her blasting over the finish line. She raised her fist in triumph. "Take that, gamer boy!"

"Argh!" Stu fell back on the bed, clutching his heart with his hand. "Defeated by a cheerleader! There goes all my geek cred."

"Don't worry." Ashley smirked. "I'll never tell."

She tossed her controller onto the nightstand and lay back on the bed, staring up at the ceiling. "Anyway, don't sweat it too much. It'll all work out in the end. In fact, don't tell anyone, but I actually like Massachusetts now," she confessed. "Except the snow. I will never like the snow."

"True. They don't get much snow in Southern California," Stu mused. "And there's a beach, of course."

Ashley poked him playfully in the arm. "See? California has everything you need!"

"Yeah," Stu said. "Everything except my best friend."

The ache rose inside him again, so strong he felt a little like he was going to throw up. He'd been trying not to think of it all this time, but now reality was crashing over him like a tidal wave. For almost his entire life he'd had Sophie as a neighbor. Anytime anything happened—a bad day at school, a humiliating defeat in the Math Pentathlon, the time he'd accidentally deleted his *Minecraft* world, whatever—she would be there. To make him laugh, to make him forget. To make him realize everything was going to be okay.

But now she would be living across the country. And that was never going to be okay.

Ashley's face clouded with sympathy. "Leaving friends is

tough. Not gonna lie." She propped herself up on her side with her elbow. "What did she say when you told her?"

Stu winced. "Uh, I haven't told her."

"Wait, what?"

"I know, I know." He sat up, scrubbing his face with his hands. "I was totally going to. But then this whole quest thing came up and she was so excited. I didn't want to ruin it for her." He rose from the bed, then paced the floor. "I figured I'd tell her the second we got home from Vegas. But now we're going to Fairyland first and it's getting really awkward. Like, I need to tell her. But if I tell her now, she's going to know I didn't tell her earlier and . . ."

He kicked the bedpost in frustration. Spike squawked, looking alarmed. Stu sighed. "Sorry, boy," he said, scooping the dragon up into his arms. "It's not your fault I've made such a mess of things."

Spike looked up at him with big dragon eyes, cooing softly, as if trying to comfort him. Stu felt a small smile flutter at his lips. He scratched the dragon under the chin. "You think she's going to forgive me?" he asked.

"She's your BFF. Of course she will," Ashley assured him, stepping off the bed and joining him in petting Spike. "And if she doesn't? She's not much of a friend."

"Yeah, well, I haven't been much of a friend, either, keeping it a secret." Stu pushed the dragon into Ashley's arms. "She's going to kill me if she finds out you knew before she did."

"Your secret is safe with us," she assured him, holding Spike out. "I mean look at this guy. Does he look like a snitch to you?"

Spike farted happily—the gas hitting Ashley square in the face. She screeched, dropping the dragon on the bed.

"Gross, gross, gross!" She hopped up and down, pinching her nose.

Stu started laughing. "Come on! In the bathroom! Quick!"

They ran to the bathroom, slamming the door behind them. Stu grabbed a towel, sticking it in the crack under the door to try to block the smell. When he rose back to full height, he realized Ashley was giggling like crazy. He started laughing, too. He couldn't help it.

"So gross!" Ashley cried. "So, so gross!"

"Seriously, what does he eat to make it smell so bad?" Stu asked.

Suddenly they heard the hotel room door open. Then Sophie's voice.

"Hello? Where is everyone?"

Stu kicked the towel aside and headed out the door, Ashley behind him. Sophie gave the two of them a weird look as they emerged from the bathroom together.

"What were you doing in there?" she asked.

The two exchanged glances. Ashley started to giggle. Stu tried to keep a serious face, but then another wave of stink rose in the air and he couldn't help laughing.

"Sorry!" he cried. "It's just…" But he couldn't get the words out he was laughing so hard.

Sophie looked less amused. In fact, she looked kind of hurt. As if they had some private joke they weren't sharing with her. She walked into the room and sat down on the bed, staring down at her hands. Stu stopped laughing. He shot a helpless look at Ashley. She patted him on the shoulder and nodded in Sophie's direction.

"Go talk to her," she mouthed. "I'll wait in the other room."

She made a move to leave. Stu sucked in a breath, trying to steel his nerves. Time to come clean. "Look, Sophie," he began.

But he never got a chance to finish, because at that moment there was a knock on the door. Ashley pulled it open to reveal Merlin, standing on the other side. The wizard had changed out of his robes and was wearing an *I <3 T. S.* T-shirt paired with some dark-rinse jeans. He had a trucker cap on his head that read *I am not weird, I am limited edition* and a pair of Ray-Ban sunglasses over his eyes.

"Well, *that's* quite the fashion statement," Ashley said, wide-eyed.

"I'm in disguise, obviously," Merlin explained, looking a little offended. "So I can take you to the show. Can you believe that

Merlin wannabe with the fake beard put up a 'wanted' poster with my picture on it backstage at the arena?" He huffed. "I mean, really! Because of one little mistake! And how was I supposed to know that random door I walked through led onstage just as he was about to perform his grand finale?"

"Well, you definitely look disguised," Ashley assured him, patting him on the arm. When Merlin turned away, she shot Stu a horrified look. He stifled another laugh.

The wizard stepped through the door. "So let's see this face cream," he said. "I want to make sure you have the right thing. The fairy queen is very particular."

"Oh yes!" Ashley said, scrambling over to her bag. "Actually, I picked out a whole skin-care regimen. Cleanser, toner, some exfoliator. And this amazing magnetic mask." She held up a small tub. "My mom swears by the stuff."

Merlin took the bottle and scanned the ingredients. "Not this. It has iron particles in it. Fairies are very allergic to iron." He handed it back to her and looked over the rest of the products. "But everything else is perfect. I even use this one myself! Works great on faces with real beards. And, uh, others." He put all the products back in the bag. "Good work, fellow Swiftie. We might just charm the fairy queen yet."

Then he clapped his hands. "Now, who's ready for the show?"

CHAPTER 22

Walking behind the rest of the group, Sophie dragged her feet, watching Stu with miserable eyes. What was his deal? Why had he been acting so weird this entire trip? All she wanted was to get him alone, to ask him what was wrong. She was sure he was about to tell her before Ashley had barged in. But now she'd lost her chance again. If only she could get him alone for five minutes to demand some answers.

But no. That was impossible with Miss Glitter Giggles around. Ashley had barged her way into their special adventure, just as she'd barged her way into Sophie's everyday life. Sure, she'd proven herself useful a time or two. But that didn't mean Sophie and Stu couldn't have figured things out without her.

Sophie and Stu against the world. That was how it had always been. That was how it should always be.

But it wasn't how it was. And that hurt.

She felt a weight in her stomach as her mind involuntarily rehashed the previous scene. Stu and Ashley hiding in the bathroom, laughing and joking—thick as thieves. And as they came out, sheepish smiles on their faces, something rotten had risen in her chest. Something that felt a lot like jealousy.

A horrifying thought struck her. Did Stu like Ashley? Like, *like* her like her? Was that why he was acting so weird? He clearly wanted to tell Sophie something. Something he seemed to think would make her mad. This would certainly qualify.

Her gut churned. Not that she would mind if Stu found a girlfriend in general. It was certainly going to happen eventually—he was an awesome guy, even if no one in school noticed but her. But still! Ashley Jones? Of all the girls in the world *not* worthy of her awesome best friend? Ashley Jones pretty much topped the very long list.

"Is everything okay, Sophie?" Merlin asked, dropping back to check on her. Up ahead, Ashley and Stu were talking and laughing and playing hide-and-seek with the dragon under Ashley's jacket. Like they were best friends. Or something more . . . ?

"Tell them they need to keep the dragon under wraps!" she snapped. "This isn't some kind of game. If someone sees him . . ."

Merlin gave her a pitying look. As if he could read her mind.

He patted her on the shoulder. "It's going to be okay," he said in the kindest voice, which made Sophie want to burst into frustrated tears. Then he nodded at Stu and Ashley. "Leave those two knuckleheads to me."

He ran to catch up with them and a moment later she heard his scolding voice. Stu turned around and gave her a guilty look. But he didn't come back to talk to her. More frustration rose inside her.

After the show, she swore. *I am getting you alone and you are going to tell me everything.*

When they arrived at the auditorium, there was already a long line. They waited patiently until it was their turn, then handed over their tickets and found their seats. Once they were settled in, Merlin leaned on their shared table. "All right," he said. "Someone will be over to serve you dinner shortly. And when the show is over, I'll come and collect you." He glanced over his shoulder at two nearby security guards who were eyeing him suspiciously. "In the meantime, I've, uh, got a potion to finish."

And with that, he dashed back up the steps, making a hasty retreat to the exit.

Ashley looked down at her place setting. "Where's the silverware?" she asked, lifting up her plate.

"There was no silverware in medieval times," Stu told her. "They all ate with their hands. It was super messy, too. If I wasn't worried about changing history, I totally would have invented the fork while I was there."

"No worries. I think I might have one in my bag." Ashley started digging into her bottomless pink backpack, which clearly did contain everything.

Stu turned to Sophie, poking her in the side. "This place is amazing, huh?" he cried. "Way bigger than Medieval Manor back home. Look at all the weapons they have lined up on the side. Do you think they use all those in every show? 'Cause that spiked mace is way cool."

He was talking a mile a minute. Pretending nothing was wrong. Sophie suddenly wanted to strangle him.

"Congratulations," she spit out. "Guess you got your Vegas adventure after all. Despite the best efforts of the fun police."

Stu's face fell. He sat back in his seat, looking stunned. Sophie immediately felt bad. "Look," she said. "I just—"

He waved her off. "I have to go to the bathroom," he said, ducking under the table before she could protest. "Don't worry. I promise not to have any fun while I'm gone."

"Stu..."

But he just shook his head, pushing his way down the aisle, past the arriving tourists, and up the stairs. Sophie sank back in her seat, squirming with misery. Awesome. This was getting better and better.

"Dude, what is your problem?"

And ... even better.

Sophie turned to find Ashley watching her. Eyes flashing with displeasure. "What?" she asked tiredly.

"I mean, no offense? But you're acting like a total jerk."

"Excuse me?" Sophie sat up in her seat, anger igniting inside her. How dare Ashley pass judgment on her? She wasn't even supposed to be here!

Ashley sniffed. "I think you heard me just fine."

"Oh, I heard you all right," Sophie shot back. "Because for some random reason, you're still here."

"What?"

"Come on, Ashley," she said. "You've got your stupid glitter. Why are you still hanging around? Wouldn't you rather go home and update your precious Pinterest board? Get fitted for a foofy dress?" She narrowed her eyes, shooting daggers in Ashley's direction. "Or are you trying to stick around for Stu?"

For a moment, Ashley said nothing. Then she burst out laughing. "For Stu?" she spluttered. "Oh my gosh, you don't think ..."

Confusion flared through Sophie. Had she been wrong? Was there nothing going on between them after all? Her face flushed bright red. "I just thought—"

"Please. I have a boyfriend back home. Not that you'd ever pay five seconds of attention to me to notice," Ashley huffed. "I am so not interested in Stu."

"Oh." Sophie's entire body was now on fire with embarrassment.

She stared down into the arena. A few men were sweeping the dirt, filling in the potholes, getting ready for the show as all the spectators took their seats. Could she crawl into one of those holes and die of embarrassment alone?

"Then I don't understand," she said instead, forcing herself to turn her attention back to her almost stepsister. "Why are you here?"

"Clearly because I'm an idiot," Ashley muttered, turning away from her to stare out into the crowd.

"What?"

For a moment, Ashley was silent, watching the men place flags in each corner of the jousting pit. "I just thought..." She wrinkled her nose. "I thought we could do something together. You know. Something... sister-like before the wedding. Something you were into—since you're clearly too cool for bridesmaid dresses and Pinterest projects."

Sophie's stomach dropped. "I never said that."

"You didn't have to. You made it quite clear. My poor mom thinks you hate her."

"What? I don't hate her!" Sophie protested. "I just... I don't know."

"What?"

"I just don't want my dad to get remarried, okay?" she blurted out before she could stop herself. "Not to your mom. Not to anyone!"

"Oh." Ashley sank back into her seat. "Okay..."

"I mean, come on!" Sophie cried, now on a roll and unable to stop. "Do you really want your *mom* to get remarried? Do you want to move into my house?"

Ashley's forehead creased. She stared down into the arena. The workers had finished sweeping and a few men on horseback were galloping up and down the field, checking it over. She watched them for a moment. Then she turned to back to Sophie, her expression oddly serious.

"Yes," she said. "I mean—I don't want to move, really. I like our house. I like my room. But my mom? Well, she's been so unhappy for so long. My dad..." She chewed on her bottom lip. "He wasn't always a nice guy. And your dad? Well, he's pretty great. In fact, I've never seen her so happy."

Sophie stared down at her hands, guilt flooding her inside. Her dad had been sad for a long time, too. And who could blame him? His wife had up and disappeared, without ever saying good-bye. And though she had good reason—and little choice— he didn't know that. It had been rough for him, and he had been lonely all those years since. And Cammy? She brought a new sparkle to his eyes. For the first time in forever, he talked about the future as if it was a good thing. Something he was looking forward to.

And all he wanted was his daughter to understand...like

Ashley seemed to understand her mom. Sophie had always thought Ashley was so shallow and full of herself. Had she misjudged her completely?

"Anyway, you don't have to worry," Ashley added quietly. "I'm not going to crash your Fairyland party. I'll give you the skin cream—you can send me home. I'll get the avocados done before you get back." She shrugged and averted her eyes, pretending to be interested in the line of horses prancing out onto the field below. "I know you never wanted to decorate them anyway."

Her voice was soft on the last part, and Sophie felt a second round of guilt bearing down on her. While Ashley wasn't completely wrong about her lack of interest in glittering avocados, she could tell it meant something to her future stepsister—a chance for them to bond—and Sophie had basically laughed at her for it.

It was amazing Ashley even wanted her to be her stepsister at this point.

"Don't be ridiculous," she said, placing a hand on Ashley's shoulder. "You can come to Fairyland. You're part of the team now. You've saved our butts a ton already. We can't do this without you."

Ashley's face flashed with hope before she could hide it. "Are you sure?" she asked. "'Cause you and Stu—"

"I'm sure," Sophie cut her off. Mostly because she wasn't sure at all—but it seemed the right thing to say. "I want you to come. And I'm sure Stu does, too." She glanced off in the direction of the bathroom. What was taking him so long?

"About Stu..." Ashley added hesitantly.

"What?"

"Just...don't be too hard on him, okay? He's...going through a lot, and...well, I'm not sure he really knows how to tell you about it."

Sophie shrank back, Ashley's words like a knife to the gut. So there *was* something going on with Stu. She knew it!

Except...she didn't know it. But Ashley did? How would *Ashley* know? She and Stu weren't even friends!

She sat up in her seat. "What did he say to you?" she demanded. It took everything inside her to ask the question. To admit she didn't have the first clue as to what was going on with her best friend.

But Ashley only shook her head. "You're going to have to ask him yourself," she said. "Just...try to be nice, okay?"

Before Sophie could say anything else, a waiter dressed in a tunic and tights, and with a floppy hat on his head, arrived at their row, asking what they'd like to drink.

"I'll take a Diet Coke," Ashley declared. "No ice."

"Um..." the man said, squinting at Ashley, looking puzzled.

"They probably don't have Diet Coke," Sophie whispered, trying to save her. "Just like they don't have silverware."

"Oh. We have Diet Coke," the man corrected. "It's just...
are you okay, miss? There's something...moving...in your
shirt."

Ashley's eyes widened. She looked down at her jacket, which
was, indeed, wiggling. Uh-oh. Spike must have woken up.
Sophie's heart beat faster in her chest. *Please don't poke your head
out!* she silently begged the dragon.

Ashley leaped up from her seat, shaking her entire body. "I'm
just excited!" she cried. "And I just can't hide it! I'm a cheerleader,
you know! We really like to root for our team!" She raised a hand
in the air. "Go, team...?"

"Dragon," Sophie suggested, trying not to laugh.

"Go, Team Dragon!" Ashley whooped. The man gave her a
weird look and retreated quickly.

Ashley smirked, dropping back down to her seat. Sophie
shook her head, impressed. "Wow," she said. "That was some
quick thinking."

"I know, right?" Ashley agreed. She stole a peek down her
shirt. "The last thing we need is for this little guy to show his
face again. After all, he's only just stopped trending on Twitter."

Sophie laughed. "Well, I appreciate you taking care of him.
I know he's not your favorite accessory."

"Eh, he's not so bad," Ashley said with a small smile, reaching under her jacket to give the dragon a little pat on the back.
"In fact, he's kind of cute."

At that moment a trumpet echoed through the arena. The lights flickered, indicating the start of the show. Stu returned to his seat—just in time. But not in time to talk. Sophie wondered, for a moment, if this was intentional.

She turned her attention to the pit. The guy they'd met earlier—real Merlin's nemesis—had stepped out into the middle. His beard had been fixed, thankfully, and his robes looked freshly washed—which was very unrealistic, when it came to real Merlin. On his head he wore a pointy sorcerer's hat and he carried a large, ornate gold staff.

"Ladies and gentlemen!" he declared, the microphone amplifying his voice. "Welcome to Camelot!"

As the crowd went wild, Sophie leaned back in her seat, stealing a glance over at Stu. Seeing Merlin down there—even a fake one—had brought back that moment in medieval times when Stu had pulled the sword from the stone. She remembered how nervous he had been about filling in for Arthur. And how she'd used her magic to help him—without even realizing she'd done it. She remembered the look on his face as he held the sword high above his head while the crowd cheered him on and bowed before him. And as his gaze swung to her, they'd shared a smile, knowing it had been a team effort. They'd done it together.

But now? Stu was still here. Yet she felt more alone than ever.

CHAPTER 23

The horse gave an uneasy whinny, swishing its tail from side to side as Morgana snuck up behind it. She peered around its hind flank, trying to catch a glimpse of something—anything—to give her a clue as to the Grail's whereabouts. It had to be here somewhere. All signs pointed to this castle—to this tournament—starring none other than Merlin himself.

She chuckled to herself. It had been almost too easy. Those ridiculous children had given her all she needed to know about the Grail's whereabouts with their casual conversation by the fire. They may have outwitted her in the end and stolen her horse, but that was of little consequence. She could always get a new horse. But the Grail? This was a once-in-a-lifetime opportunity.

And she planned to make the most of it.

It had been simple after that. Travel to Merlin's Crystal Cave and cast the spell to activate the waters of the wizard's Well of Dreams. And soon she found herself on her second trip forward in time, to a land of dazzling lights and colors and sounds. At first she'd been, admittedly, a bit lost—and rather overwhelmed by all the people and buildings rising high to the sky. But a simple tracking spell showed the way. To the castle Excalibur. To this very show.

The Grail was here. In this building. She was certain of it. She just had to find it.

"Places, everyone! The show starts in three minutes!" a man to her left, carrying an armful of swords, barked at the crew.

She watched as the knights around her fastened their armor and secured their swords while ladies donned colorful skirts and applied thick paint to their faces. This was evidently going to be quite a tournament. Her eyes lifted to the throne, sitting high on a platform above. There sat a bearded man—the king, she assumed—drinking a cup of bubbly brown liquid and eating some kind of chicken.

They were all eating chicken, she suddenly realized with dismay. Everyone in the entire arena. Oh dear. What if someone accidentally ate the Holy Grail?

No. Merlin would not let that happen.

Where was Merlin, anyway? And did he have the Grail? The

wizard was always messing with things that were none of his business. Morgana would never forget the day he broke into her family's castle when she was just a child. She had been playing with her little brother, Arthur, when Merlin ripped the baby from her arms.

It was then Morgana had learned the truth. That Arthur was the son of High King Uther Pendragon and the destined heir to the throne of the kingdom of Camelot. And Merlin was determined to raise him to reflect his own twisted image, making Arthur his puppet before putting him on the throne. Turning her own brother into her worst enemy.

She started to move forward, to continue her search. But a voice stopped her dead in her tracks. "I am Merlin," the man called. "Wizard of Camelot. Welcome to the Tournament of Kings."

Morgana's ears pricked up. Speak of the wizard. She peeked out into the tilt yard, where, sure enough, a man with long silver hair sat astride a tall horse. He had flashing blue robes and seemed to be holding something. She squinted, unable to see him very well with his back to her. But there could be no mistaking it. She had found Merlin at last!

Merlin continued. "Tonight you will see feats of bravery and daring stunts, performed in the name of chivalry," he went on. "All to win this prize. The Holy Grail itself!"

Morgana's eyes lit up as he lifted the silver cup to the sky. For a moment, it seemed to shine with an otherworldly glow, before settling back to silver. The crowd roared its enthusiasm.

"Hey! What are you doing back here? No one's allowed backstage besides the performers."

She whirled around, seeing a knight approaching her. Great. She'd been spotted. For a moment, she wondered if she should tell him she was part of the court. But as he came closer she saw the sword hanging at his side. Not worth risking it. She raised a hand, summoning a brief wind. It struck him hard in the chest, knocking him backward.

"What are you doing?" he cried. A little too loudly. Suddenly all eyes were on him. Then her.

Time to make her move.

She leaped onto the horse, urging it forward, galloping into the main arena. As she emerged from the tunnel, she was blinded for a moment by all the lights. But she gritted her teeth and dug her heels into the horse's flanks, increasing her speed, eyes locked on Merlin and his cup.

"Merlin!" she cried. "Give me the Grail. Now!"

The wizard turned. His jaw dropped as he caught sight of her. She frowned, for the first time getting a good glimpse of his face.

It wasn't Merlin at all.

At least not *the* Merlin. This imposter's beard wasn't even real. And the cup he held in his hand?

Definitely not the Holy Grail.

A furious growl escaped her throat. She reined in her horse, scanning the arena. All around her people were cheering and jeering. Clapping and waving their fists. Where was the Grail? It had to be here somewhere! And where was the real Merlin? Had she been tricked into coming here? Were those children in the woods cleverer than she'd thought?

But no. The tracking spell could not lie. The Grail had to be here. Somewhere.

"Get her!"

Men poured through the tunnel. Some dressed as knights. Others in some kind of official-looking blue outfit with a matching hat. In a moment she would be surrounded. They would take her captive. They would lock her up.

Giving the real Merlin time to steal the Grail away again.

Desperate, she reached out, grabbed the imposter Merlin by the collar, and yanked him up onto her horse. He cried in protest, thrashing around to fight her. She pulled a knife from her belt and pressed it against his side.

"Quiet," she told him in a low voice. "Or I will gut you and feed your entrails to the dogs."

His face drained of color and he stopped struggling. The rampaging soldiers stopped, too, giving one another wary looks, as if to say, *What now?*

Morgana smiled. This was more like it. She turned to the audience, lifting her voice. "I seek the Holy Grail," she called out. "I know it is here somewhere, in this room. Whether it be cup or chicken—I care not. Bring it to me, or this man will die."

CHAPTER 24

Stu stared down into the pit, a big bite of chicken stuck in his mouth. Until this moment he hadn't been paying a ton of attention to the show; he'd been too stressed out about Sophie. But suddenly his eyes were glued to the field below. A terrified shiver tripping down his spine.

"Is that...?" he whispered. "No. It couldn't be."

But it was, of course. He would never forget that face. Those purple eyes. Those red lips.

Morgana.

His mind flashed back to the last time he'd laid eyes on the sorceress. The two of them battling to the death in the depths of her dark castle. She'd struck him down with a mere wave of her hand. If it hadn't been for Merlin's healing, he would have died then and there.

Instead he had killed her. Though by the looks of her now, it hadn't exactly stuck.

Morgana galloped around the arena, not-Merlin held tightly in her grip. The rest of the audience, of course, thought this was all part of the act. They leaned forward in their seats, rapt expressions on their faces. Some were booing. Some were actually cheering. Stu turned to Sophie and Ashley.

"What are we going to do?"

"There you are!"

Stu's head whipped around to find a boy and a girl around his own age running down the stairs in their direction. They were dressed in long robes and looked as if they could have been part of the show as well.

"Nimue!" Sophie cried, rising to her feet, clearly recognizing them. "Emrys! What are you doing here?"

Wait. Nimue and Emrys? Stu squinted at the pair. From Merlin's cave? How did they get here? This was getting crazier and crazier by the second.

"It's a long story," the girl—Nimue—told her. "Where is the Grail?"

Ashley pointed to herself. "He's in here," she said, motioning to the little dragon snout peeking out from her jacket.

"You didn't turn it back yet?" Nimue cried, looking horrified.

"Also a long story," Sophie said. "But we're working on it."

"Maybe it's for the best," Stu pointed out. "Morgana clearly thinks she's looking for a cup. Or a . . . chicken, for some reason?"

"Don't ask," muttered Nimue.

The five of them looked down into the arena. Morgana still had not-Merlin by the throat. A knife pressed to his side. She'd stopped at the front of the castle set at the far end of the tilt yard, where the "king" and his daughter were looking down in concern. Clearly they knew, if no one else did, that this was not part of the show.

"Give me the Grail!" Morgana screamed, sounding less patient this time. "Or I will kill him!"

The audience booed excitedly. "We have to help him!" Stu cried.

"*And* protect the Grail," Nimue added.

Sophie turned to Ashley. "Take Spike back to the room and lock the door. I'll text you when it's safe."

Thankfully, Ashley didn't argue. She zipped the dragon into her jacket and ran out of the arena, not looking back.

"Okay. Now what?" Sophie said.

"You go find real Merlin," Stu told her. "We'll try to hold her off until you get back."

"But if she sees you, she'll kill you!" Sophie protested.

"If she doesn't, she may kill fake Merlin. We can't let that happen! No matter how annoying he might be." He clapped her on the shoulder. "We're Companions, remember? Or at least one of us is."

Sophie gave him an anguished look, but in the end, she did as he said. He watched her go, his heart pounding in his chest. Sure, he had put on a brave front for her, but inside he was shaking like a leaf.

He turned to Nimue and Emrys. "Does either of you have any magic?" he asked, crossing his fingers for a yes. "Emrys? You're Merlin's apprentice, right? Any spells that might work?"

Emrys was clearly distraught. "Merlin's spell book is out of energy."

"What does that mean?" Stu demanded. He watched as Emrys pulled out an iPad from his satchel. "Wait, Merlin keeps his spells on an iPad? There's an app for that?"

"It needs to be attached to Merlin's magic box!" Nimue explained. "To recharge."

Stu reached into his own backpack, unplugged his phone from its portable charger, and grabbed the iPad from Emrys's hands. With shaky fingers, he somehow managed to plug it in. The iPad blinked, indicating it had started to charge.

"Man, you guys really drained this thing," Stu noted in dismay.

"How long will it take to wake up?" Nimue asked.

"A few minutes."

"You have ten seconds!" Morgana screamed, as if she had heard them. "Or I will break his neck!"

Okay, that wasn't good. Stu looked down at the iPad. "Come on, come on!" He shook it. As if that would speed things up.

"We need to do something," Nimue cried. "Distract her, like you said."

Stu thought back to the first fight they'd had with Morgana. At the time *he* had been that distraction. Could he do it again?

He shoved the iPad in Emrys's direction. "When it wakes up, do your thing."

"Wait. Where are you—"

But Stu had already dived under the table. Sprinting down the aisle, he waved his hands above his head to get Morgana's attention. "Hey, witch!" he cried. "Remember me?"

Even as he called her out, he knew how stupid he was to do it. She could blast him with a single shot of fire and he had no armor, this time, to protect him. No healer, either.

Guess that was one way to get out of going to California....

Morgana's head snapped in his direction. Her purple eyes narrowed in recognition. "You!" she cried. "I should have known."

She shoved not-Merlin off the horse. He hit the ground hard, collapsing into a crumpled heap. Stu watched, relieved, as a moment later the actor scrambled to his feet and limped to the sidelines. At least he was safe.

Stu, on the other hand, was now in mortal danger. But there was no turning back. He vaulted over the barrier that separated the audience from the pit, grabbing a discarded sword from the sidelines. It wasn't real, of course. Just a prop sword that hadn't even been sharpened. But he had a feeling Morgana wouldn't know that. And maybe that would buy them some time. He held it up in front of his face, as if it were a deadly weapon.

"Come and get me if you can!" he called out.

The crowd was on its feet now. Everyone was freaking out—cheering, screaming, applauding. Some were rooting for him. Some actually seemed to be rooting for Morgana. Many had their phones held up. He was bound to end up on YouTube after this. Maybe he'd even go viral like Sophie had. He just hoped his parents didn't click on the link.

Morgana yanked on the horse's reins, turning to face Stu. Then she dropped the reins, raising her hands menacingly in his direction. Sparks seemed to crackle over her fingertips. Stu sucked in a shaky breath, willing himself not to look back up at Emrys and Nimue—to see how they were doing with the iPad. If he did, Morgana would spot them for sure.

"Stop," he told Morgana, making his voice sound as brave as he could, under the circumstances. "Kill me now and you'll never find your precious Grail."

She stopped. Set her lips in a straight line. He could practically see the gears turning in her head. She knew he was right. Thank goodness. "Where is the Grail?" she demanded.

He forced a cocky grin. "That's for me to know," he said.

"And for you to never find out." Childish, he knew. But kind of satisfying at the same time.

A storm cloud flashed over Morgana's face. "Take care, child. I may not be able to kill you," she ground out, "but I can make you wish you were dead."

Stu swallowed hard, his bravado fading. She had a point. A not-deadly but likely very painful point.

He squeezed his hands into fists, trying to stop his whole body from convulsing with fear. What was he going to do? How was he going to hold her off? If only Sophie were here. Like when he faced down King Lot. It had been her magic that had turned the tides in his favor. But now...

Don't back down, he scolded himself. *Everyone's counting on you. Time to channel your inner King Arthur.*

He squared his shoulders. Lifted his chin. Looked Morgana in the eyes. "Go for it," he spit out. "Give me your best shot. Just make sure you don't knock me out. It would be a real shame for me to go into a coma and take the Grail's whereabouts with me."

Or, you know, to go into a coma in general. And maybe never wake up....

Oh man, what was he doing? What if she called his bluff? What if she—

Morgana's face twisted. She flicked the reins of the horse, charging in his direction. Stu stumbled backward, horrified at the deadly look he saw on her face. All his words had meant nothing. She would kill him and figure out how to get the Grail later. He wouldn't be moving to California, because he would be dead. Maybe his mother would bury him in California. Or scatter his ashes in the sea—

BOOM!

Purple smoke exploded through the arena. Everyone screamed. And the lights went out.

CHAPTER 25

Emrys groaned, clutching his head in his hands. His eyes fluttered open and he looked around, no idea where he was. Last he remembered he was scrolling frantically through Merlin's iPad after it had finally loaded up, looking for a spell. Something—anything—to defeat Morgana. Or at least make her temporarily disappear.

At last he'd stumbled upon a banish spell, which would cast her out of this world. It wouldn't be a permanent fix—she'd be sure to figure out a way back. But at least it would give them some time.

He'd uttered the Latin words, probably not very well. There had been a flash of light. A loud popping sound, and then—

"He's awake!"

Emrys's head snapped in the direction of Nimue's voice. He hadn't realized anyone else was in the room. But there she was, standing by his bedside, her hands clasped so tightly her knuckles had turned white.

"Are you all right?" she asked.

He blinked and ran his hands over his body. He was sore all over—and his head was throbbing—but nothing felt out of place. "I think so."

Her shoulders slumped in relief. "I was so worried! You looked like you were dead. We had to drag you out of the arena. You've been out for some time."

He swallowed hard. "And . . . Morgana?"

"Gone," Nimue declared. "As if she had never been here to begin with." She squeezed his shoulder. "All thanks to you."

Emrys felt a warm feeling rise inside him. *All thanks to him.* Which meant he'd done it. He'd actually done something good for once in his life. His magic had worked—in the way it was supposed to. He'd stood up to a great sorceress and he'd lived to tell the tale. Just like the heroes in his mother's stories.

Maybe he wasn't so useless after all. . . .

"You useless, blithering dolt!"

Or . . . maybe not. He looked up, his heart pounding in his chest, to see Merlin storm into the room, blue robes flying out behind him. The wizard's eyebrows were furrowed and a dark frown slashed across his face. As his heavy steps ate up the distance between them Emrys shrank back in bed.

"Hey...Merlin," he cried, trying to keep his voice from trembling. "Um, it's good to see you?"

But it was not good. Not good at all. His mind flashed back to all he had done. All the rules he'd broken. The stuff he'd touched that he'd promised to leave alone. Sure, he may have saved the day just now. But the day wouldn't have needed saving in the first place had it not been for him.

And Merlin clearly knew it.

His mouth went dry. What if Merlin wouldn't accept his apology? What if he refused to keep him on as an apprentice and sent him home in shame? Emrys cringed at the thought of returning to the farm. To see his mother's disappointed face. His father's smug grin. Having to admit to his brothers that he'd failed yet again.

Not such a hero after all.

Merlin crossed his arms over his chest, staring him down. "Do you have something to say to me, boy?" he demanded.

Emrys's face was now burning hot. "I'm sorry," he blurted out. "I never meant to disobey your orders. I just—just—"

"Turned the Holy Grail into a Holy Dragon! That's not exactly adding too much salt to the soup."

Emrys bowed his head in shame. "But I thought..." Then he trailed off. Because what good would it do? All the explanations in all the world wouldn't excuse what he'd done. He didn't deserve Merlin's forgiveness.

The wizard gave an exasperated sigh. "This is exactly why I told you to stay away from magic to begin with, you know."

"I know."

"Come on, Merl. Give the dude a break."

Emrys startled at the sound of the new voice. In his humiliation, he hadn't realized their audience had grown. Now he realized that Sophie and Ashley and the boy who had faced down Morgana—Stu?—stood by the door watching them. Wonderful. His fall from grace would happen for all to view.

"A break?" Merlin blustered, turning to Stu. "A break, you say?"

"Uh, yeah," Stu replied. "I mean, come on, man. We all mess up. Remember that time I jumped in the river to save Elaine from drowning and my King Arthur illusion wore off?"

"And remember when I told Arthur to go play *Camelot's Honor*," Sophie piped in, "thinking it would convince him to go back home? Instead it made him want to move to the twenty-first century full-time."

"Yes, yes," Merlin grumbled. "But those were honest mistakes. This—"

"Also, he did just kind of save my life out there," Stu added, walking over to Emrys's side. He slapped him on the shoulder. "Thanks for that, by the way."

"You're welcome," Emrys mumbled, staring down at his lap.

Merlin threw up his hands. "Yes, it worked out this time! And I'm glad it did! But what if it hadn't?" His eyes locked on Emrys. "Is it so wrong that I don't want you to get hurt?"

Emrys folded his hands in his lap. "No," he said quietly. "I don't want to get hurt, either. And I don't want to get anyone else hurt. No more spells," he said, and looked up at the group. "Not until I learn how to use them properly." His eyes locked on Merlin. "Not until you say it's okay."

Merlin's stern face vanished, replaced by a toothy smile. He slapped Emrys on the back, with a little too much force. "That's my boy!" he cried.

Emrys felt relief wash over him. Merlin would forgive him. He wouldn't send him back home. As long as he didn't manage to muddle anything else up, all would be okay.

No more magic, he told himself. *No matter what happens.*

Merlin cleared his throat. "Now I need to finish that potion. If you'll excuse me . . ." And with that, he exited the room, leaving the four of them alone.

Nimue turned to Sophie and Stu. "Now," she said, "back to the real problem at hand. Why is the Grail still dragon-shaped?" She gestured to Spike, who was sitting on the other bed, clawing at a dirty spot on the blanket. His mouth was tied up with some kind of string, Emrys realized. Probably to keep him from breathing fire?

"Yeah, about that," Sophie said. "Turns out your little mission was a bit more complicated than we thought." She filled them in on the latest, ending with their planned trip to the land of Faerie. Emrys listened to it all, his chest sinking when she came to the part where they'd have to risk their lives again. All because of him.

Maybe Merlin *should* have sent him home. He didn't deserve to be a wizard.

Nimue listened solemnly. When Sophie had finished, she nodded. "You are very brave to do this for us. Most would turn their backs."

Sophie looked embarrassed. "It's my job," she said. "I am a Companion, after all."

"And we're her loyal followers!" Stu declared, patting himself on the chest. Emrys caught Sophie giving him a weird look, and wondered if there was something else going on between them. Not that it was any of his concern.

"Well, I am a druid of Avalon," Nimue chimed in, making the symbol of the Great Mother—an open cup—with her hands. "I have sworn to protect the Grail with my life. I would be honored to aid you in your quest." She looked down at Emrys. "Are you with us?"

He shifted on the bed, feeling all sorts of uncomfortable. Did they really want him? Or were they just trying to be nice? He couldn't bear it if this was a pity invite.

"Are you sure you want me?" he asked quietly. "After all I've done?"

Nimue's eyes grew stern. "I would not ask if I did not." She slipped her hand into his and squeezed lightly. "We need you, Emrys. You are as much a part of this as the rest of us."

"Yeah, dude. Come with us! It'll be fun!" Stu added encouragingly. "Or at the very least, an adventure."

Something in Emrys's heart tugged. He looked up at the group—at their encouraging faces.

"Very well," he said. "I'm in."

CHAPTER 26

Using Merlin's magic, they traveled back to medieval times, abandoning the bright lights and big city of Vegas for a thick dark wood. It should have been comforting, Nimue thought, to return to the familiar sounds and smells of the world back home. But in truth, she wished she could have explored Vegas just a little longer. If only to taste another one of those "ice-cream sundaes" Sophie had ordered from a magic box she called "room service" before they left.

But all that regret faded away when Nimue stepped into the familiar clearing. Her breath caught in her throat.

Avalon. She was home.

She dropped to her knees, her hand clasping at her chest.

She'd run ahead of the rest of the group when she started recognizing landmarks. The oddly shaped tree at the fork in the path that had twisted itself into a knot. The giant boulder she and her best friend, Tamora, used to hide behind when trying to avoid their chores. The white stone path leading up the hill to the altar of the Great Mother.

And now...she took in the familiar sights of her village. The tiny huts made of mud with thatched roofs and red-painted doors. Old stumps, serving as stools, circling a giant fire pit where they would make their meals. It all seemed so small and crude compared to the wonders she'd witnessed in Vegas.

But to her, Avalon had been everything.

"Hello?" she cried out, heart pounding in her chest as she ran to the first hut—the one belonging to Vivianne. "My lady, are you here? Is anyone here?"

With shaky hands, she pushed open the door and stepped inside. The cottage looked exactly as she remembered it. The same simple wooden table and chairs, the plain straw mattress on the floor. But now every surface was covered with a thick layer of dust.

It was the same in the next hut. And in the small dormitory she and her sisters had shared. Silent. Empty, save for the ghosts of her memory. She felt the tears well in her eyes.

So it was true. They were all gone.

She staggered back out to the fire pit, ran down the path, and dropped to her knees before the sacred spring. Her mind flashed back to all the times she'd been ordered to fill buckets with water to drag up the hill to the altar. She'd complained about it then, yet what she wouldn't give for such an order now.

But there was no one left to give it.

A sob choked from her lungs. All this time she'd been so focused on her quest—to get the Grail to Arthur—that she hadn't fully grasped her own fate. Her sisters were gone. Her world was gone. And she was all alone.

"All right, everyone. Gather round!"

Well, not totally alone. At least not for the moment. She looked up through tear-blurred eyes to see Merlin standing by the fire pit, gesturing for everyone to join him. A moment later Stu, Sophie, and Emrys emerged from the forest. Ashley came last, with the dragon on her shoulder.

"Sorry," Ashley said. "I had to give him a potty break. I so do not need dragon pee on this shirt! Especially not here—in a world with no Tide Pods."

Merlin scanned the group. "Is everyone here?" he asked. "Where's Nimue?"

She sighed, struggling to her feet. "I'm here," she called out. They all turned to look at her. She knew she must look a mess. Maybe they'd blame it on the time travel. She could feel Emrys shooting her a worried glance, but she refused to meet his eyes.

"Very well," Merlin said. "Let's go over the plan once again. We don't have any time to waste."

Back in Vegas, Merlin had sent a message to King Arthur using something he called "e-mail." Nimue wasn't clear on what it was, but Sophie and Stu had been very impressed that the wizard had set up something called "Wi-Fi" at Camelot.

In any case, the news from Guinevere had not been good. They had tried everything, she told them, and Arthur was still sick. He needed the Grail. If he did not get it, he would likely die within a week.

After assuring her that they would not let that happen, they made their plan. Merlin would accompany the Companions to the gates of Faerie while Nimue and Emrys stood guard with the dragon deep underground, in the secret spot under the Tor, where he had once been stored in the shape of a cup. They'd stay hidden there until Merlin returned. Safe from any potential attack from Morgana or her men.

They still didn't know what had happened to Morgana after Emrys had cast his spell—a fact that seemed to worry Merlin quite a bit. She could be anywhere, he warned, meaning nowhere was completely safe.

After going over the plan once again, they broke from the group to get ready to go. Nimue sank down on one of the stumps, scrubbing her face with her hands, exhaustion washing over her.

"Are you okay?"

She looked up to see that Sophie had come up beside her. The Companion peered at her with questioning eyes. "Are you worried we won't be able to do it?" Sophie asked.

Nimue shook her head. "It's not that," she confessed. "It's just . . . this place."

"This is where you lived, right? Before . . ." Sophie trailed off, but Nimue knew all too well what she didn't want to say.

"I had hoped . . ." Tears welled in her eyes. "I had hoped that some of my sisters might still be here. That they might have escaped somehow. When Morgana and her men attacked, I took the Grail and ran. That was what I'd been instructed to do. But what if I'd stayed?" she asked, her voice cracking on the words. "Maybe I could have helped them."

"Or maybe Morgana would have killed you, too," Sophie reminded her. "And then she would have the Grail right now. I think you did the right thing."

"I know. But . . . they were my family." Nimue felt fat tears rolling down her cheeks. "Maybe not by blood. But they were all I had just the same."

Sophie's eyes softened. "I know how hard it is to lose someone," she said quietly. "I mean, not as many people as you've lost. But my mom . . ."

Nimue looked up at her through her veil of tears. "Your mother? Did she die?"

"No. But everyone thought she did. She vanished without a trace when I was seven. The police searched and searched but they never found her, and eventually everyone assumed she was dead. I still remember the morning I woke up and realized she was gone. That clawing in my stomach." She put a hand to her middle as if it still caused her pain.

Nimue nodded. Her own stomach had tied itself into so many knots she had no idea if she'd ever be able to untangle them all. "Does the feeling ever go away?" she asked tentatively, not sure she wanted to know the answer.

"No," Sophie admitted, giving her a rueful look. "It fades a little with time. The sharp pain becomes a dull ache. But it's always there, lurking. That feeling that something—that someone is missing." She looked up. "Sorry, I'm probably not being very helpful."

Nimue laughed through her tears. "No, you're not," she said. "But I appreciate the honesty."

"My story does have a happy ending," Sophie added. "I finally found my mother. Or she found me, actually. Turns out she's a Companion, traveling through time to help save the world."

"And now you're following in her noble footsteps," Nimue marveled. "I hope someday I can do something important, too."

"I think you already are," Sophie said with a smile. Nimue felt her face heat.

"Maybe so," she agreed. "Or at the very least—"

A crashing in the bushes interrupted her words, quickly followed by a high-pitched whine.

"Wait, is that a dog?" cried Sophie.

Nimue's jaw dropped as, sure enough, a large brown dog burst into the clearing, bounding over and leaping onto her, big fluffy paws on her shoulders, covering her cheeks with exuberant kisses.

"Damara!" she cried, a huge smile breaking out across her tear-streaked face. "Is that really you?" She wrapped her arms around the creature, tears splashing from her eyes. But this time they were tears of joy. "Oh, you big oaf!" she cried. "I thought you were dead, too!"

Damara gave her a reproachful look. As if to scold her for having no faith. She laughed again, hugging the dog with a full heart. Then she gently lowered Damara's paws back to the ground and turned to her friends. "This is Damara," she introduced. "One of our dogs. Don't worry; she may be big, but she's very friendly."

"And very furry," Sophie exclaimed, holding her nose with her hand. Then she sneezed. "I'm allergic to dogs," she explained, backing away and almost bumping right into Stu.

"Oh! Sorry!" she stammered. "I didn't mean to—"

"It's okay," he assured her. He shuffled from foot to foot, not looking Sophie in the eye. Nimue frowned; there seemed to be some kind of weird tension between the two of them since they'd left Vegas. Like they were trying too hard to be polite to each other. She wondered what was going on between them.

She shook her head, turning back to nuzzle Damara, who covered her face with happy kisses and slapped her knees with her fluffy tail. Nimue's heart squeezed.

"Sweet girl," she said. "You don't know how happy I am to have found you."

She realized, suddenly, that the dog was looking behind her. A low growl rippling from her throat. Alarmed, Nimue whirled around to see what was causing the dog's distress. She laughed when she realized it was only Spike, who had hopped up on the giant cooking cauldron and was gingerly walking the perimeter.

"Don't mind him," Nimue assured the growling dog. "He won't hurt you. He's not even a real dragon."

Spike huffed, looking offended at this. Then he fell into the pot. Nimue couldn't help but laugh as Ashley ran over to pluck the dragon out and set him on the ground. Then, before Nimue could stop her, Damara bounded over to the dragon. She sniffed him curiously, then planted a huge slobbery slurp on his face. Spike looked horrified. He squawked loudly and backed away, shaking his body. A healthy amount of dog drool splattered from his scales. Damara grinned goofily, beating her tail against the ground.

"I think she likes you!" Stu teased Spike.

Spike wrinkled his snout. He lifted his chin in the air and

strutted away from the dog. Ashley scooped him up and cuddled him in her arms. "It's okay, Spikey. Everyone knows that dragons rule and dogs drool."

"All right, everyone," Merlin interrupted. "Are we all ready?"

"Yes!" Stu cried, punching his fist in the air. "Let's do *eeeet*!"

Nimue caught Sophie giving him another strange look. As if she wanted to say something, but didn't know where to start. Something was definitely off between the two of them. She just hoped it wouldn't interfere with their mission.

Ashley, on the other hand, seemed oblivious to it all. "Bye, Spikey!" she cried, dropping to her knees in front of the dragon. She kissed the top of his head, then wagged her finger at him. "You be a good dragon, you hear? No burning down the druid village while I'm gone."

Spike burped in response. Ashley groaned and reached into her pocket, tossing a few hair bands in Nimue's direction. "Watch him," she instructed. "He clearly cannot be trusted."

And with that, she, Sophie, Stu, and Merlin hiked into the woods, up the hill, toward the portal to Faerie, leaving Nimue and Emrys alone.

Well, almost alone. Damara wagged her tail expectantly as Spike slurped a black beetle off the ground with his tongue and crunched down on it happily. Nimue sighed. That should be *great* for his digestion.

She turned to Emrys. "Are you ready to head underground?"

"Let's do eeet," he replied, mimicking Stu.

She scooped up Spike and instructed Damara to follow them inside. "You can be our guard dog," she told her. Damara licked her hand, telling her she understood.

They headed into Vivianne's home, closing and locking the door behind them. Nimue handed Spike to Emrys and knelt down on the floor, working to uncover the secret trapdoor that led to the underground temple where the Grail had once been stored. Nimue had only been down there once and hoped they didn't get lost in the twisty passageways beneath the mountain.

"All right," she said as the trapdoor was revealed. "Now I just have to . . ." She pulled on the handle.

It didn't budge.

She frowned. "That's strange."

"Let me try." Emrys set Spike down and wrapped his own hands around the handle. He pulled hard. But the door did not give way. "Is it locked?" he asked, looking up at her.

Nimue sank to her knees, blowing out a frustrated breath. "I think it's sealed by magic," she realized. "I should have known that Vivianne would secure it before we left. There are a lot of treasures buried under the Tor, after all. Priceless relics and powerful magic. Of course she would not leave them lying around for common thieves—or worse."

"Can you open it?"

"If I had my spell book . . ." She looked around the room,

hoping perhaps Vivianne had left a spare lying around, but saw nothing. "What about Merlin's iPad? Did he leave it in Lost Vegas?"

Emrys held up his hands. "No way. Even if he didn't I am not touching that thing. No more magic for this apprentice. Not until I've had proper training."

"Then what are we going to do?"

Emrys rose to his feet. He walked to the door and bolted it shut. "We'll be fine here," he said. "At least until Merlin returns. He's just opening the portal and then he'll be back. He can help us open the trapdoor then."

Nimue pressed her lips together, unsure. "What if someone comes?"

"Then Damara will scare them away," Emrys added. "You trust her, right?"

She sighed. "I guess."

"It'll be fine. I promise," Emrys assured her. Then he reached into his bag. "Now, how about a game of *Mario Kart* to pass the time?"

Nimue cocked her head. "Mario what?"

He pulled out a strange-looking device, then proceeded to break it into three pieces, handing one of the pieces to her. "Stu let me borrow it while I was stuck in bed," he explained. "It's something from the twenty-first century called a video game."

Nimue stared down at the small red device in her hand. It

looked nothing like any game she'd ever seen. "How does it work?" she asked.

"I'll show you." He pressed a button and the screen burst to life. Nimue's eyes bulged from her head as she watched weird-looking creatures in little cabs zoom down the road. Was one of them actually a turtle?

"How did they get those tiny people into the box?" she asked in wonder. "Is it magic?"

"Of a sort, I think," Emrys replied with a grin. "Now pick a character. We're going to race."

"I don't know...."

"Come on. It'll take your mind off things," he said gently. "At least for a bit. And who knows, maybe it will be fun?"

"Fun," she repeated, half to herself, as she reluctantly selected a pink-and-white mushroom with a face—which was strange in and of itself, and stranger still when the mushroom started driving his own cab. "With all that's happened, I hardly know what that word means anymore."

Emrys pressed a few more buttons and the screen flashed. Their characters were on a road, with a countdown on the screen of three, two, one....

"Well, then," he said. "It's high time you remembered."

CHAPTER 27

"A re we almost there?" Sophie called out as she trudged farther up the hill, through the thickening mists. The fog had rolled in not long after they left the druid village and it seemed to get denser the higher they climbed. They were climbing extremely high, too—up a steep, rocky path without any switchbacks, and her thighs, at this point, were burning. Before her next Camelot Code mission, she was so joining the YMCA and getting in better shape.

"Not much farther," Merlin assured them. Which would have been comforting had he not said the exact same thing five minutes before. "And stay close," he added. "For these are no ordinary mists. One could get lost in them and stay lost for a thousand years."

"Then we really would miss our parents' wedding," Ashley declared. As if that would be problem number one in a getting-lost-in-medieval-mists-for-a-thousand-years scenario.

The mists were so thick now she could barely see her hands in front of her face. And when Merlin suddenly stopped short, Sophie slammed into him, almost knocking the two of them right off the mountain. Her heart pounded a little faster in her chest as she struggled to regain her footing. At least she couldn't look down to see how high they were. That would have made her lose it for sure.

"Are you okay?" Stu asked. He knew all too well about her fear of heights, and she was grateful for his concern, especially since things still felt super strained between them. After talking to Ashley, she'd tried to get him alone a couple of times—to demand that he tell her what was going on—but he had somehow managed to thwart each effort, keeping himself practically glued to the group. And every time she'd try to ask him what was wrong, he'd managed to change the subject with a dumb joke or long-winded distraction. At first she thought it was her imagination. But when he started going off on how waffles should always be served with peanut butter rather than syrup for ten minutes for no reason whatsoever? She realized it was intentional.

But what was he hiding? What didn't he want to tell her? She was sure now it wasn't anything to do with Ashley, though

Ashley seemed to know something she didn't. Which was extremely annoying.

Ugh. She shook head. She needed to stay focused. After all, they were on a dangerous mission. She couldn't afford to be distracted. But after this was over, she *would* find a way to get Stu alone and force him to tell her what was going on. Even if she needed to hold him down and make him smell Spike's farts until he confessed.

"Are we here?" Ashley broke in, forcing Sophie to focus back on the current situation. "Is this the entrance to Fairyland?" She looked around. "Doesn't look like much."

"That's because I haven't opened the portal yet," Merlin explained. "But yes, this is the best entrance. For the mists that separate our world from that of the Fey are thinnest in this very spot."

"Cool," Ashley proclaimed. "I've always wanted to go through a real-life portal. Though—do you think it will mess up my hair? Because the security guy at the airport totally stole my shampoo." She tsked. "Even though it was way under three ounces."

"I can make no promises," Merlin said solemnly. "But I assure you my hair has survived many trips."

"So wait. You *have* been to Fairyland before?" Sophie demanded. "Then why can't you come with us now?"

The wizard sighed, stroking his long white beard. "I'm sorry, children. But trust me. You do not want me to come with you."

"But why?" Stu put in. "What's the deal? What aren't you telling us?"

Merlin was silent for a moment, making a big show of pulling off his spectacles and rubbing them against his robe. Then, at last, he cleared his throat. "Let's just say once upon a time I courted the fairy queen. And it did not end well."

"Wait, you mean you were, like, her boyfriend?" Sophie asked, surprised at this information. Of all the reasons he might have given, this she was not expecting. She tried to visualize ancient old Merlin with a girlfriend. A fairy girlfriend. It was hard to imagine.

"It was a long time ago," Merlin explained. "But yes. We were even going to get married. The plan was for me to retire to Faerie and leave the real world behind. We had this wonderful little cottage picked out. Right on a lake. Really beautiful spot. Great fishing."

"So what happened?"

"Things got . . . complicated. The Romans left Britain, saying their army was needed elsewhere, leaving the people helpless to fight the Saxons invading their shores. Civil war broke out in the country, with tribal kings from all corners trying to gain the throne. People were suffering. Dying. And the country was in danger." He sighed. "I couldn't just walk away."

"So . . . you broke up with her?" Sophie asked. "To save England?"

Merlin paused. "Yes?" he said, though he sounded a little uncertain. "Sort of..."

"What does 'sort of' mean?"

"Oh my gosh!" Ashley burst out, her voice thick with indignation. "Did you ghost her? Do not tell me you ghosted the fairy queen."

"Ghosted?" Merlin queried, sounding doubtful.

"You know! Like when some jerk guy stops texting you back for no reason?" Ashley explained. "Or... carrier-pigeoning you back? However you guys send PMs in ye old medieval times."

"She means... did you actually tell her you weren't showing up at the wedding?" Sophie tried to translate. "Or did you just stand her up on her wedding day?"

Merlin let out an indignant huff. "It was a very complicated situation, I'll have you know," he blustered. "Our people were in danger. And if I had gone to see her, she might never have let me leave."

Stu groaned. "Dude, that's cold. No wonder she's mad at you."

"Maybe you *do* need to come to Fairyland with us," Sophie added. "You could, like, apologize or whatever. Explain what happened."

"No," Merlin said firmly. "We can't afford to take such a risk. This mission has to succeed or everything I've sacrificed will have been in vain. In fact, you cannot even let the queen know that you know me. If she finds out I sent you, there will be no way she will make the exchange. She might even exact her vengeance on you."

"Awesome," Stu muttered. "Let's just ramp up the difficulty rating, shall we?"

Merlin cleared his throat. "Now," he said, "if you are quite done lecturing me on my love life, perhaps you wouldn't mind me opening the portal so you can get on with saving the world?"

"Sure," Sophie agreed. "But you are so not off the hook. We are talking about this the second we get back."

Merlin grumbled something that sounded a lot like "Yes, Mom" before beginning his incantation. Sophie rolled her eyes at Stu, even though she knew he couldn't see her.

Merlin's voice rose through the misty air, speaking an incantation in a language Sophie didn't recognize. Fairy, perhaps? Though it could have been French, for all she knew. Or Klingon. In any case, as he chanted, the mists began to swirl and dissolve before her eyes, revealing a glittering golden portal opening up in the ground. Merlin recited a few more strange words and the portal began to swirl in a whirlpool shape.

"Whoa," Stu said with a low whistle. "Cool."

The wizard dropped his hands, finishing his incantation. He looked sweaty and exhausted and his whole body was shaking.

"Are you okay?" Sophie asked, concerned.

"The spell...is intense," he explained. He wiped his brow with his sleeve. "I will regain my strength—but it will take some time." He shook himself, then reached into his pocket. He pulled out a roll of paper and pushed it into Stu's hands. "A map," he explained. "It will lead you to the fairy castle. Do not stray from its path. There are all sorts of terrible dangers in the land of Faerie. Creatures of nightmares, tricky goblins who like nothing more than the taste of human flesh..."

"And you wanted to retire there?" Ashley snorted. "Must have been true love."

He waved her off. "Now hurry," he commanded. "I don't know how long I can keep the portal open."

Sophie gave a vague nod, suddenly a little nervous as she realized what she was about to do: jump into some strange portal—with a hostile land on the other side and no guarantee of return. It had sounded a lot less crazy in the comfort of their Vegas hotel room. But now...

"Geronimo!" Stu cried, leaping into the portal and disappearing into the mists. Okay, then. Guess he was totally fine with it.

"You want to go next?" Ashley asked.

Sophie took a step back. "Go for it. I'll be right behind you."

Ashley nodded. She pinched her nose with two fingers, as if she was diving into a pool, then jumped feetfirst into the portal. A moment later she, too, was consumed by the mists, leaving only Sophie behind.

Merlin leveled his gaze on her. "Are you ready?" he asked.

"Don't worry. It's not a big drop on the other side. And it doesn't hurt nearly as bad as time travel."

"Great. I think...." She stared down at the portal, nausea rising in her throat. And here she'd thought mountain climbing was frightening. But this... this long, long drop—with no sign of a bottom...

"Come on, Sophie. You're a Companion, remember? Your mother trusted you with this role. You don't want to let her down, now, do you?"

"Um, you're one to talk. You won't even face your ex-girlfriend."

"Are we really going back to that again?"

"Okay, okay, I'm going." She sucked in a breath. "Three, two—"

A sudden loud crash in the woods broke her concentration. She hesitated, turning to Merlin with a worried look. To her horror, the wizard's face had turned white.

"What is it?" Sophie asked. Something was wrong. She could tell. "Is someone coming?"

Merlin turned back to her. "No. It's fine. Just go."

Another crash echoed across the valley. She whirled around, squinting to try to figure out what it could be.

"Go, Sophie!" Merlin cried. "Now!"

Sophie's jaw dropped as her eyes fell upon two men on horseback, coming up the mountain. Two very familiar-looking men—though it'd been quite some time since she'd seen them. One was Sir Kay—Arthur's foster brother—and the other Sir Agravaine, the cruelest knight in the land. The last time she'd been in medieval times, they'd captured her and locked her in a tower.

And they didn't look as if they wanted to invite her to tea now, either.

"What are they doing here?" she asked, confused.

"It doesn't matter. You have to go."

"But what about you?"

"I can take care of myself."

"But you're weakened from the portal."

"Yes, and it'll be worse if I have to keep it open for you. Now go! Now!"

And with that, Merlin grabbed her by the shoulders. She tried to fight him, but he was too strong.

"Look! There they are!" she heard one of the men cry. "Get them!"

It was the last thing she heard—before Merlin shoved her down the portal and she spun into blackness.

CHAPTER 28

"**Y**es! I win again!"

Emrys groaned as he watched Nimue's car race over the finish line, beating him for the third time in a row. "I thought you said you never played a video game before," he said. Not that he was all that experienced himself, having only played for about an hour or so back in Vegas when he was stuck in bed. But still...!

"I haven't," she assured him, her eyes twinkling. "I must have natural talent. Or maybe you're just truly terrible."

"Oh, I *know* I'm terrible," he agreed with a laugh.

She set the controller down and lay back on the floor, looking up at the hut's wooden ceiling. "Just another wonderful thing about the twenty-first century," she said with a dreamy sigh. "Why, I could have spent years exploring Lost Vegas alone."

"I don't know." Emrys wrinkled his nose. "It was pretty loud and bright. And the smell of those cabs . . ." He shuddered. "Also, I still don't understand why they would use paper instead of coins." He still had a stack of the paper in his pocket and was not sure what he was supposed to do with it.

"Well, then, next spring break you can stay home and make pea soup," Nimue declared. "While I join Merlin on a new adventure."

"Please. Merlin isn't even going to trust me with making pea soup after what I did," Emrys moaned. "I'll be lucky if he doesn't change his mind and send me home after all this is over."

"Just forget him," Nimue scolded. "You did what you had to do. To me, you are a true hero of Camelot."

He gave a choking laugh. "Very funny."

"I'm not joking," she insisted. "Think about it. You kept the Grail out of Morgana's hands twice now. And you saved my life, too. What else would you call someone who risked his life for another's?"

Emrys felt his face heat. When she put it that way, it *did* sound pretty heroic. Now, if only he could get Merlin to agree. "Well, thank you," he murmured. "You're not so bad yourself." He grinned shyly. "And by not so bad, I mean pretty great."

"You should see me when I have my spell book," Nimue proclaimed. "Then I'm really—"

Her boast was cut off by a sharp bark. Their eyes snapped to the door, where Damara was standing. The dog growled low under her breath. Uh-oh.

Emrys gave Nimue a worried look. A muscle quivered in her jaw.

"Damara," she hissed. "What are you growling at?"

"Maybe she hears a deer," he suggested. "Or a rabbit? You know dogs."

"I know *Damara*," Nimue corrected. "And she's far too well trained to growl at rabbits. She's been training to be a guard dog since she was a pup." She bit her lower lip. "If she's growling, there's something out there. Something . . . or someone."

Her words sent a chill of fear down Emrys's spine. He glanced over at Spike, then down at the trapdoor. If only they'd been able to open it! They would have been so far underground by now no one would ever have found them. But here . . . in this thin-walled hut . . .

He turned off the game to cut the light, then crawled to the window so as to not cast a shadow. He peered outside, holding his breath. At first he saw nothing. Then he gasped as he made out two burly knights approaching on horseback. Two very familiar-looking knights.

"Oh no," he whispered. "They're back."

"Who is?" Nimue scrambled to the window in time to watch the knights dismount and walk over to the fire pit—not twenty paces from the hut. They pulled a few logs from a nearby wood-pile and tossed them into the pit. Nimue shrank back from the window. "The knights from Merlin's cave," she said. "They must have circled back hoping someone would return here with the Grail."

Emrys swallowed hard. "It's worse than that," he whispered, his eyes falling to their horses. Or more precisely the large lump lying astride one of them. "Much worse."

"What do you mean?"

"See for yourself." He pointed to the lump. Nimue gasped.

"Is that...?" She put a hand to her mouth in horror. "Merlin?" She squinted at the wizard. "Wind and Rain! Is he dead?"

Emrys's eyes traveled over Merlin's body, searching for the rise and fall of his chest. "I think he's alive," he assured her. "I can see him breathing. He must be unconscious or something."

"But how is this possible?" Nimue cried. "He's Merlin. No mere knight could ever hope to best Merlin in battle!" Then her face went pale and she sank to her knees. "Oh no."

"What?"

"He opened the portal to Faerie. That would weaken anyone—even those strong in magic. They must have captured him while he was vulnerable."

"What about the rest of them? Do you think they made it through?"

"I hope so," Nimue replied. "Or this quest is truly at an end."

Damara looked over at her, then whined again. Pawing at the door. Emrys watched the red-haired knight lift his head at the sound.

"Did you hear something?" he asked his partner.

"Probably an animal," replied the dark-haired knight, picking his teeth with what looked like a bone.

"Or a demon from the grave, conjured by the witch women who lived here," the other knight shot back. He shivered. "I don't like this place at all."

"Do you think I do? But Morgana will be here soon. We must wait for her return, as promised."

Nimue and Emrys exchanged glances. Oh no. Morgana was coming? Here? This situation was getting worse and worse.

"She's going to be very happy when she sees what we've done to the old man," the redhead crowed, standing up and walking over to Merlin. "Maybe she'll even reward us."

"*Maybe* she'll bring us that chicken she was after. I'd swallow the whole thing in one bite I'm so bloody hungry."

"You can eat later. Help me get Merlin off the horse and tie him up first. The last thing we need is for him to wake up and be able to cast a spell."

"All right, then. I'll grab the rope."

Emrys watched the black-haired knight dig into his saddle-bag and pull out a thick rope. Then he joined his partner in pulling Merlin down off the horse. Emrys winced as the wizard's body hit the ground with a loud thump. Unfortunately, it didn't wake him up.

Nimue backed away from the window. "What are we going to do?" she asked, her eyes wild and frightened. "Morgana is on her way. We can't let her find Spike!" She glanced around the hut. "Perhaps we should sneak out the back door?"

"We can't do that!" Emrys protested. "They have Merlin! We can't just leave him!"

"Merlin can take care of himself. We need to save the Grail."

"The Grail is useless if we don't have Merlin to turn it back into a cup. And if he's dead—"

"Then *you* would have to perform the spell."

Emrys froze. He looked over at Spike. Then back at Merlin. He shook his head.

"No. That would involve magic. I can't do any more magic, remember?"

"You would have to! We would have no choice!"

"But what if I messed up again? What if I turned the Holy Grail into a Holy Turnip or something?"

Nimue raked a hand through her hair. "Then we must rescue Merlin. But how?"

Emrys bit his lower lip. He looked around the hut for

something he could use. But there were no weapons. No magic scrolls or books. Just plain furniture and a stack of logs for the fire. . . .

Suddenly an idea sparked inside him. "The same way we built a fire from sticks," he replied staunchly. "The same way we made a coin turn into a stack of paper."

"I don't understand."

"You said it yourself, remember? Magic is but one branch in the tree of knowledge," Emrys reminded her. "Well, right now that branch is gone. But that doesn't make us powerless."

For a moment, Nimue said nothing and Emrys wondered if she thought him mad. But then, at last, she nodded.

"You are right," she agreed. "We can do this." She squared her shoulders. "We *have* to do this!"

She walked over to the door, but then stopped short. Her face paled once again.

"What is it?" Emrys asked, joining her at the window.

It was then he saw it. Make that—*her.*

"Morgana," they both whispered at the same time, their voices full of fear. "She's back."

CHAPTER 29

Morgana slid off her horse, exhaustion weighing heavy on her shoulders. It had been a long, frustrating trip back home after those horrible children had somehow managed to best her once again, and part of her wanted to crawl back to her castle and sleep for a thousand years.

But she couldn't. Not yet, anyway. Not when she had one last chance to best Arthur while he was still sick and vulnerable. She had a destiny to fulfill, and she couldn't let it slip away. No, she did not have the Grail to help her, which would have been the easiest solution. But there could be another way.

As she'd traveled to Avalon, the plan had formed in her mind. She'd gather up her knights—the knights Arthur still thought loyal to him—and send them to the castle on a recovery mission. If they could steal the scabbard that kept Arthur from being killed, then they could do away with him before the Grail arrived in his kingdom. And when those meddlesome children did show up, Grail in hand? She would be there, on the throne, to greet them.

She grinned to herself, imagining the looks on their faces when they realized she had thwarted them after all. Sure, they'd gotten lucky twice. But the third time she would be the winner.

"Morgana! You're here! At last!"

She nodded to Sir Agravaine, who was running toward her like an excited puppy dog. She assumed Sir Kay was not far behind. Clearing her throat, she clasped her hands in front of her. "My loyal knights," she purred as, sure enough, Sir Kay stumbled from the bushes. "It's so good to see you again."

"You as well!" Sir Kay cried. "We've been waiting forever."

"I ran into a little... trouble," she admitted. "But no matter. I have a plan and—"

"Wait until you see what we have for you!"

She crinkled her forehead, annoyed at the interruption. "What?" she demanded. "If this is another chicken, then I don't really—"

"Come. We'll show you." Sir Kay bounded off in the other direction, Sir Agravaine at his heels. Morgana groaned, but followed them into the druid village. She couldn't help a small smile of pleasure as her eyes roamed the empty buildings. She may have not gotten the Grail, but she'd made great inroads in destroying its protectors. Now it was in the hands of mere children. Soon it would be hers.

"Look!" Agravaine announced, his voice thick with triumph. "The man himself!"

Her gaze followed his pointing finger, and her eyes widened in disbelief at what she saw tied to a tree. Merlin! The great Merlin! Wrapped in thick rope, a cotton gag stuffed in his mouth. Was he asleep? Or...?

"You didn't kill him, did you?" she asked, squinting at the wizard's slumped form. Not that she would have minded him dead. But he was more valuable to her alive. She imagined herself riding into King Arthur's court with his beloved master as her prisoner. Who knew what Arthur would trade in exchange for Merlin's life?

"No. He's just sleeping, I think."

She walked over to the wizard and gave him a swift kick. He stirred, but did not awaken. Her mouth stretched into a smile. "However did you manage this?" she asked her knights. "Why, he should have struck you down like gnats."

"Maybe we're better than you think!" Sir Kay declared, puffing out his chest.

"No." She shook her head. "You're not."

Their faces fell. "Do not misunderstand me," she said. "I'm

most pleased by this. But...Merlin is a very powerful wizard. He wouldn't have gone down without a fight." She eyed the knights curiously. "Where did you find him?"

"He was with some children," Kay explained. "They went up the mountain. We followed them, and they never saw us coming." He grinned gleefully, revealing a mouth full of broken teeth.

Morgana stared down at the wizard, trying to understand. It was then her eyes fell upon the tips of Merlin's fingers—blackened and shriveled like prunes. A sure sign he had just cast a major spell. Realization fell over her like a heavy cloak. "He must have been taking them to Faerie!" she exclaimed.

"Faerie?" the knights repeated doubtfully.

"He probably spent all his energy opening the portal. And you grabbed him before he could go through. Did they have a cup with them?" she asked. "Or a...chicken?"

The two knights exchanged glances. "I don't think so?" Sir Agravaine stammered. "But the mists were very thick. And one of them was carrying quite a large bag...."

Morgana stared down at Merlin. Why would they go to Faerie? Were they giving the cup to her cousin the queen for safekeeping? But no. Her cousin would never help friends of Merlin.

Unless she didn't know they were his friends.

Hmm. Perhaps it was time to pay a little visit to Faerie.

She turned to her knights. "You did well," she said. "Now I need you to do one more thing for me."

"Anything, my queen!"

"Stay here and watch over him until I get back."

Agravaine's face soured. This was clearly not the "anything" he had in mind. "What? I thought we were going back to the castle! To take down Arthur once and for all."

"Yes, yes. We will, I assure you. But there is something I must do first." She turned to leave, then stopped. She stared down at the unconscious wizard, tied up in simple ropes. He looked harmless now, but when he woke, he would have his powers again. And he would easily outwit these fools. If only she could put him on ice for a while. Until she could get back.

Ice...

A laugh bubbled up in her throat. Of course!

She raised her hands, mumbling the spell under her breath. Smoke swirled beneath her feet and her fingers crackled with familiar energy. Out of the corner of her eye she caught Sir Kay giving Sir Agravaine a frightened look. Good. Let them witness her true power. Let them see firsthand why she—and she alone—deserved to be queen of Britain.

"*Glacies*," she chanted loudly, even though it wasn't strictly necessary. "*Glacies, magicae, carcerem!*"

A cold blast shot from her fingers, freezing the great Merlin in a solid block of ice.

"Wind and Rain!" Kay swore under his breath, taking a quick step backward.

Morgana hid a smile, pleased with herself. This was more like it!

"Now," she instructed, "stay here and make camp. I will return shortly."

After a quick quest for the Holy Grail.

CHAPTER 30

"Sophie, Sophie!"

Sophie groaned as rough hands shook her awake. She tried to swat them away.

"Five more minutes, Dad," she begged sleepily, reaching for her pillow to block out the light. It was then that she realized there was no pillow.

Because she was not in bed.

"Finally! The sleeping beauty wakes!" declared Ashley from somewhere nearby. "Without even a kiss from a handsome prince! Which is a good thing for you, because there's no one even remotely good-looking anywhere around this place. No offense, Stu."

"Uh, yeah. Sure," Stu replied dryly.

Sophie forced herself to sit up, rubbing her face. The light was way too bright, stinging her pupils. She dropped her hands, forcing herself to open her eyes.

Her jaw dropped.

The dreary forest, the steep cliffs, the heavy mists of the island of Avalon had vanished completely. And in their place? A candy-colored dreamland ripped straight from the pages of a fantasy book. It was like that moment in the old *Wizard of Oz* movie where everything goes from black-and-white to vivid color... or a new Instagram filter gone wild.

Fairyland. They were actually here.

Her eyes took in the brilliant purples and hot pinks and deep blues all around. And not just from wildflowers—though there were many of these—but entire trees. Their leaves—even their trunks—sported all the colors of the rainbow. Some with stripes, others with swirls. Still others seemed to be coated in glitter. In fact, it was such a wonderland she half expected a Mad Hatter or White Rabbit with a pocketwatch to wander through.

"Pretty amazing, huh?" Ashley said.

Sophie nodded, turning in a circle, trying to take it all in, breathing in fresh, sweet air that smelled vaguely of gingerbread and Christmas spices. A warm breeze riffled through her hair, tickling her earlobes...

...while something else tickled at the back of her brain.

Something odd. Something she was...forgetting.

"Did...something bad happen back there?" she asked suddenly, frowning at her friends. She tried to reach for the thought and pull it back to consciousness. Her head still felt foggy—maybe a side effect from the trip? She wrinkled her forehead. "Is Merlin okay?"

"What?" Stu and Ashley exchanged puzzled glances.

She rubbed her head in her hands, feeling all sorts of confused. "I just...I feel like Merlin might be in trouble." Why couldn't she remember?

Stu shrugged. "He was fine when I left. Ashley?"

"Totally fine," Ashley agreed.

"Right. I guess he was?" Sophie bit her lower lip.

"Are you sure you're okay?" Stu asked, peering at her worriedly. "Did you hit your head on the way down?"

"No. I'm...good." She drew in a breath, the strange sensation fading. She smiled at her friends. "Sorry. That was weird. I don't know."

Stu patted her arm. "Don't worry. Merlin, of all people, can take care of himself. And he's counting on us to find the fairy queen. Now come on. Let's go do it."

Sophie nodded. Her eyes scanned the landscape. It was so beautiful it barely looked real. On the ground were wildflowers with the most intricate petals, and toadstools big enough to sit on. There was a babbling brook to one side, with water flowing frothy cotton-candy pink. And trails led off in all directions, sparkling as if they'd been paved in silver.

Thank goodness Merlin had given them a map. Otherwise there'd be no way to know which direction they should take.

She turned to Stu. "Got the map?"

"Yup." Stu reached into his pocket and pulled out the rolled parchment the wizard had given him. As he started to unfurl it, the air clouded with glitter. He made a face. "Seriously, I can't get rid of this stuff," he muttered, shaking it off.

"Yeah, well, at least it fits in here," Sophie pointed out, gesturing to the trees.

Stu cocked his head. "What do you—"

But his question was suddenly interrupted as, out of nowhere, a large pink bird swept down from the sky. Sophie watched, paralyzed, as the creature dove straight toward Stu, its eyes locked on the glittery map.

Oh no!

"Hey!" Stu cried. "Get lost!"

But the bird didn't listen. Instead it latched on to the map with its sharp talons, plucking it from Stu's hands. He tried to grab it back, but the bird was too quick, rising to the sky and out of his reach. A moment later, it disappeared beyond the thick canopy of trees. Gone forever—with their only way to navigate Fairyland in its claws.

Oh no. No, no, *no!*

"What just happened?" Ashley asked, horrified.

"Your *glitter* happened," Sophie snarled, looking up at the sky in dismay.

"What? How can that—"

Stu groaned. "Birds are attracted to shiny stuff. Like glitter." He shook his hands, trying to get rid of the remaining sparkly specks. "I'm probably lucky it didn't take me with it."

"Oh my gosh!" Ashley cried. "I'm so sorry! I never meant..." She rummaged through her backpack, pulling out her phone. "Ugh. No GPS, either. In fact, I can't even get a signal."

Sophie ran a hand through her hair, walking over to a polka-dotted toadstool and sitting down on it. Part of her wanted to yell at Ashley, but she looked so upset Sophie didn't have the heart to blame her. Besides, what good would it do? It wouldn't bring the map back.

She looked around.

Should they just give up now? Drink the potion and go back home in defeat?

"Come on, Sophie. Don't freak out!" Stu said. "We can still make this work. After all, I was a Boy Scout. And Boy Scouts are always prepared."

"I thought you bailed on Boy Scouts after three meetings."

"Three very informative meetings!"

"Great," she said, though she kind of wanted to scream. "Then which way should we go?"

Stu looked around, tapping his chin with his hand. "Well, there's moss on this side of the tree. Which means that's north? Or south." He scratched his head. "South. Right."

"Do we want to go south?" Ashley asked.

"Was the castle south?"

"What castle?"

"Did anyone even look at the map?" Sophie blurted out.

Stu and Ashley looked at one another, then shrugged guiltily. "I figured we'd look when we got here," Stu said.

Sophie sighed, suddenly feeling a million years old. "This is ridiculous," she said. "We should just drink the potion and go back. Tell Merlin we need to find another way."

"Or maybe we can ask *him* for directions?" Ashley suggested.

Sophie frowned, turning to her. It was then that she realized her future stepsister was looking up, head tilted to the sky. Had the bird returned? But no, backlit by bright sunlight was a person like silhouette, hovering above them. A silhouette with something flickering behind it.

Make that two somethings. As in two large, gossamer wings.

She swallowed hard. "A fairy," she whispered, totally stating the obvious. She glanced around warily, remembering Merlin's many warnings. Fairies were dangerous. Tricky. Not to be trusted. And definitely—

"Super cute!" Ashley cried way too loudly. She gave the fairy boy an approving once-over. "I thought they were going to look like Tinker Bell or something. But this guy is *H-O-T*."

"Please don't let him hear you say that," Stu scolded.

Sophie watched as the fairy began to descend. He was definitely nothing like Tinker Bell. Unless he was Crossfit Master Tinker Bell. In fact, if he didn't have wings, he could have doubled as a male model, with bulging biceps, sparkling blue eyes, full lips, and cheekbones that might have been cut from glass. He wore an emerald-green tunic over a pair of brown leather leggings, and his wings shimmered behind him like sparkling jewels.

"Greetings!" he cried, coming down for a landing in front of them. "Welcome to the land of Faerie!" He pushed a hand in their direction. Ashley ran up to take it, pumping it happily, clearly unconcerned with her own safety when it came to a cute boy.

"Hello!" she chirped. "It's so great to meet you, too. I'm Ashley Jones. But you can call me Ash. Or Lee. Or..." She giggled. "Honestly, I'd answer to 'Hey, you!' if you were the one calling."

"Wow! *Hey you!* What a great name!" the fairy exclaimed,

a big smile crossing his handsome face as his wings fluttered behind him. "This is so exciting. I can't even tell you. We hardly *ever* get visitors here. And it's *so dull*."

Ashley grinned from ear to ear. "Well, allow me to brighten your day!"

"How *amazing* of you to do that for me! I love bright days, don't you?"

"So! Much!"

"He's rather friendly," Stu observed out of the side of his mouth.

"I know, right?" Sophie scratched her head. Puzzled. She thought back to all of Merlin's warnings. How dangerous fairies could be. But this guy seemed so... nice. Was it some kind of trick? Or just another example of Ashley's odd superpowers—able to charm cute boys in a single bound.

Which was annoying, but also possibly useful in this case.

She rose to her feet, and walked over to the fairy. She didn't know if they could trust him, but without their map, they admittedly didn't have a lot of options.

"Excuse me, um, sir," she said cautiously, realizing suddenly that he hadn't given his own name. "Do you know where we might find the castle? We lost our map and need to get to the fairy queen."

"We have a super-cool gift to give her!" Ashley chimed in.

The fairy's eyes lit up. "A gift? Ooh! Our queen *loves* gifts. She just *loves* them. She will be so happy!" He broke out into a little happy dance, as if to prove his point.

"Um...great?" Sophie replied. Seriously, this guy was like ten cans of Red Bull in one gulp. "Then can you...take us to her?"

The fairy stopped dancing. "Absolutely. I totally can! In fact, it would be my pleasure, mortals! Please follow me! This is going to be amazing!" He held out his arm. Ashley took it, still beaming at him. Sophie caught Stu rolling his eyes.

"Lead the way," Ashley declared.

And so they were off, blindly following a random dude they had just met, who still hadn't offered his name, down a glittering path and deep into the woods of Faerie.

What could possibly go wrong?

CHAPTER 31

To say the fairy forest was beautiful would be a complete understatement. It was also completely over-the-top. As if someone was trying too hard. Like, if a tree was already painted with purple polka dots, did you really need to add tinsel and LED lights?

In fact, the farther Sophie and her friends traveled into the forest, the more elaborately the trees seemed to be decorated—with delicate glass-blown orbs, long strings of popcorn and cranberries, and huge golden stars on top. Why, if she didn't know better, she'd think it was . . .

A bird above her started tweeting "Jingle Bells."

"Is it . . . Christmas here?" she blurted out.

The fairy gave her a wink. "Does it *look* like Christmas?"

"Actually it looks like Halloween," Stu declared. "My favorite holiday!"

Sophie snapped her head in his direction. *Halloween?* What was he talking about? It didn't look anything like Halloween. It looked like—

"Fourth of July!" Ashley pronounced. She turned to their fairy guide. "I just love fireworks," she added. "Don't you?"

"Fireworks are the best!" the fairy agreed.

Sophie frowned, something weird tickling at the back of her neck. Fireworks? What was she talking about? There were no fireworks.

The birds started tweeting "Deck the Halls." They passed more Christmas trees. This was getting weirder and weirder. She glanced behind them, wondering if they should have left bread crumbs or something like Hansel and Gretel, in case the fairy was leading them astray.

"Are we almost there?" Stu asked, sounding a little nervous himself.

"Oh yes!" The fairy dipped and swirled in the air. "We are so very close! Follow me! You are going to love this!"

"Love what?" Sophie asked, her skin now prickling with goose bumps. "I thought you were taking us to the castle."

"Of course! The castle! The queen! But first, I thought you might be hungry?"

As if on cue, the trees fell away, revealing a huge Christmas party in the middle of a large meadow, nestled in the candy-colored woods. With tables piled high with food and drink and presents wrapped with bright red and green bows.

But it was the partygoers themselves that caught Sophie's attention. There had to be at least a hundred of them, all as stunningly beautiful as the one who had led them here, and dressed as if they were attending the finest ball. She watched as they laughed and danced and drank, seemingly unaware that mortals had crashed their party.

Sophie turned to their fairy guide. "What are we doing here?" she demanded. "We don't have time for a party!"

"There's always time to eat!" the fairy scolded.

He waved a hand at the huge tables filled with food. Succulent meats and cheeses piled high on one, mouthwatering shiny fruits and vegetables on another. There was an entire table filled with breads that smelled as if they'd come straight from the oven.

And the last table—well, that was all desserts! Spun-sugar dreams, the likes of which Sophie had never seen. Her mouth watering, she took an involuntary step forward, reaching out for a pastel-pink cupcake with at least four inches of icing. Like the fairy had said, there was always time to eat. . . .

"Wait!" Stu grabbed her arm.

"What?" she snapped, a little more harshly than she'd meant to.

"Remember what Merlin said about fairy food? If you eat or drink, you could become their prisoner forever."

Sophie dropped the cupcake like a hot potato. "Oh my gosh," she cried. "I totally forgot!" Which was really weird, she thought, seeing as she totally remembered at the same time. What was wrong with her head? Why couldn't she seem to clear it?

She spotted Ashley a few feet away, reaching for a crusty roll. She ran over and batted the pastry out of her hand.

"I know," Ashley moaned. "Totally filled with carbs. It just looks so good!"

"It's not the carbohydrates I'm worried about! It's—" Sophie clammed up when their guide approached.

"What's wrong?" he asked, looking grouchy for the first time. "Don't you like the food?"

"We're actually not that hungry," Stu confessed. "And we're in kind of a hurry?"

"Of course! Of course! We'll be on our way in just a moment! You may not be hungry, but I am starving. Haven't eaten a thing all day! Just let me grab a quick bite!" He reached out for a shiny apple and crunched down on it. The juice ran down his chin. And even though that was admittedly a little gross, Sophie felt her mouth water again.

"Just going to grab a little nectar," the fairy added. "Be right back!"

He danced off to another table. Sophie watched him go, then

turned back to the sparkling Christmas trees. "So weird that it's Christmas here, don't you think?" she asked Stu. "I mean, are they just behind? Or do they celebrate all year long? 'Cause that would be kind of awesome. All-year-round Christmas." Christmas had always been her favorite holiday. Every year she begged her dad to keep the tree up long past New Year's Day.

"Dude, what are you talking about?" Stu asked, sounding confused.

She gestured with her hand. "The trees? The presents? This is obviously a Christmas party."

"Christmas? Are you blind? Do you not see all the costumes? And the pumpkins? They're clearly celebrating Halloween."

"Halloween? There's nothing here that even remotely looks like..."

She trailed off, a feeling of dread washing over her. She looked at Stu. His face was as pale as hers felt.

"We need to get out of here," he said in a low voice. "Like, right now."

CHAPTER 32

An awful dread rose inside Sophie. On the surface nothing had changed. The fairies were still dancing and drinking and eating without a care in the world. The presents were still piled high on the tables and the trees were still glittering with globes of light. But somehow it no longer felt festive. Instead, an almost-sinister vibe seemed to fill the air, and her skin started to crawl with unease. Her mind flashed back to Merlin's warnings. Fairies were tricky. Dangerous. They could not be trusted.

"Where did Ashley go?" she asked, realizing her future stepsister was no longer standing near the bread table. "We need to grab her before that fairy comes back."

"There she is!" Stu pointed to the other side of the clearing, where the fairies had set up a makeshift dance floor. There was a small band with flutes and drums and violins playing a lively tune while the other fairies danced. Sophie could just catch a glimpse of Ashley, hand in hand with a fairy boy, twirling and laughing.

"Of course. Five minutes in Fairyland and she's already got herself a new boyfriend," she groaned.

"Do you want me to go get her?" Stu asked.

"No. I'll do it," she replied. "Just be ready to go when we get back. This place is seriously giving me the creeps."

And so she started toward Ashley, pushing past throngs of fairies who somehow kept getting in her way. They seemed to have multiplied since she and Stu and Ashley arrived. The party was really getting packed. As she wove through the crowd, trying to get to Ashley, the fairies smiled happily and greeted her cheerfully—some even offering up elaborately frosted cupcakes and sweet-smelling milkshakes with extra sprinkles on top.

"Just try one!" a pretty young fairy with long blond hair and sapphire-colored wings begged, holding out the most amazing-looking donut Sophie had ever seen. (And Sophie had seen a lot of donuts in her day.) It had chocolate crumbs and gummy worms and was dripping with rainbow frosting. It was all Sophie could do not to snatch it from her hands and take a huge bite.

It's a trick, she reminded herself, keeping her hands glued to her sides instead. *Don't fall for their tricks.*

"No thank you," she said, even as her stomach growled in

protest. She pushed her way past the fairy and kept walking toward Ashley. Who still seemed so very far away . . .

"Do you want to dance?" a handsome fairy boy asked, stepping in front of her and blocking her path. He gave a low bow, holding out his hand, palm up, as if begging Sophie to take it. "Please, please say you'll dance with me!"

Sophie shook her head, surprised at how much effort it took to do so. The band broke out into a new song, with high, sweet notes trilling from a piccolo.

"No thank you," she managed to spit out, holding her hand over her eyes to try to see through the lights, which were getting kind of hazy. Where was Ashley? She had to be close now. This meadow was not that big. . . .

It was then she spotted her across the dance floor. Still dancing. Still laughing.

Still so far away.

The pace of the music picked up. She started dance-walking, hoping that would get her there faster and avoid more interruptions. A few fairies clapped as she did a little spin move she'd learned long ago when she used to take hip-hop dance classes. She repeated the move, trying to remember some of the others she used to know. If only she hadn't stopped taking dance lessons at age eight.

"Sophie! There you are!"

Ashley ran over and grabbed Sophie by the hands, twirling

her around. Sophie laughed in delight as her head spun with the lights on the trees, creating a delicious blur of sound and sight.

The music soared, picking up tempo again. The fairies cheered; their dance steps becoming faster and more intense. Sophie and Ashley tried to keep up, laughing as they tried the complicated steps.

"This is the best!" Sophie exclaimed as she somehow managed to execute a perfect break-dance move. "Why did I ever quit dance classes? Dancing is amazing!" In fact, she couldn't remember the last time she had had so much fun. Maybe Stu had been right—since the mission had started, she had been acting like the fun police. But no more! From now on, she was determined to enjoy herself. To have a good time—no matter what.

"No, *you're* the best!" Ashley replied, hugging Sophie with wild exuberance. "I am so excited you're going to be my sister!"

"I know, right?" Sophie cried, dance-hugging her back. Mostly because she didn't want to stop dancing. "I love you *so much*."

Wait, what? Something in the back of her brain started to tickle. And not like a funny tickle. But the tickle that kind of hurt. Like something wasn't right about this at all.

But that was ridiculous. She was having fun! Having fun with her friend. Who was almost her sister. And the music was so wild. Such a driving beat, she could barely keep up!

Why, she could stay here and dance forever and ever and—

"Sophie! We need to get out of here. NOW!"

Sophie whirled around, her eyes lighting up as she found Stu standing beside her. For some reason he was wearing his Beats headphones over his ears. She grinned at him, reaching up to try to pry them free.

"You have to hear the music!" she begged. "And dance with us."

But Stu only shook his head, keeping his hands on his headphones. The speed of the music picked up again, the beat faster and faster, and the dancers once again increased their pace. Sophie vaguely realized she was starting to get tired. In fact, she could barely breathe she was panting so hard. But how could she stop? The music was so good! The dancing so great. Her sister so fun.

"Sophie! Listen to me!" Stu cried, poking her hard in the arm. She scowled, poking him back.

"Do you mind? I'm trying to dance!"

"Yes. I can see that. But do you know *why* you're dancing?"

"'Cause I love dancing?"

"Do you, though?"

"Of course!" she retorted.

But then something niggled at the back of her brain again. *Did* she love dancing? If so, why had she quit hip-hop? Why did she never go to school dances, choosing to stay home and play video games instead? And hadn't her dad tried to get her to sign up for ballroom lessons so they could dance at the wedding? What was it she had said to him? *When pigs fly, I'll dance?* Well, pigs weren't flying. But fairies were.

Stu met her eyes with his own. "You're under a fairy spell," he insisted, his voice dark and serious. "I've read about this in books. You'll dance until your legs give out. Until your heart stops." He grabbed her by the shoulders, shaking her hard. "Sophie, you're going to dance yourself to death!"

"No! That's not true! I can stop anytime. I can—"

Stu grabbed his headphones and placed them over her ears, muffling the music.

And the fairy spell.

Sophie stopped dancing. She stared at Stu in horror. What had she been doing?

"Come on," he said, covering his ears with his hands. "We need to grab Ashley and go."

Sophie nodded. She could still hear the music slightly and her legs ached, begging to keep moving. But she planted her feet firmly on the ground, then stalked over to Ashley. Her future stepsister was still dancing to a horrifying beat that was so fast the movement of her legs looked blurred. Sweat poured down her face and her eyes were bulging, while a manic smile stretched across her mouth. Sophie grabbed her arm, trying to pull her away from the fairy she was dancing with.

"What are you doing?" Ashley demanded, fury slashing across her face. "I'm dancing!"

Sophie clamped her hands over Ashley's ears; then Stu started dragging her away from the dance floor. At first Ashley struggled, trying to break free, but she was too exhausted, too weak to put up much of a fight, and when they finally got outside the circle, she practically collapsed on the ground, panting hard.

"Oh my gosh," she said. "That was...awful. I couldn't stop! Why couldn't I stop?"

"You were under a fairy spell," Sophie said, sinking down beside her. Her future stepsister's eyes were wide and terrified. On impulse, she reached out and gave her a hug. Ashley collapsed in her arms, shaking. Sophie felt a little shaky, too. Her heart was still beating a mile a minute.

"It's okay," she assured Ashley, stroking her hair. "It's going to be okay."

But was it?

As if in answer, their fairy guide suddenly reappeared, pushing through the crowd with deliberate steps. He looked down at them, his arms crossed over his chest. He made a tsking sound.

"What's wrong?" he asked in a sulky voice. "Don't you like the party? Aren't you having *so much fun*?" He held out a hand in Ashley's direction. "Come on! One more dance? It'll be so amazing!"

"No!" Ashley declared, struggling to her feet. She planted her hands on her hips, staring the fairy down. "I'm not falling for your tricks again. We're done here."

An amused smile floated across the fairy's face. "Are you, now? I guess we'll see about that, won't we?"

Suddenly, just like that, the color seemed to leach from the sky. The festive landscape crumbled away, the bright and shiny trees morphing into dead copses of twisty branches and dried-up gray leaves. The tables that had been piled with cakes and breads were now filled with rotten meat and moldy fruit, covered in cobwebs. And those gummy-worm donuts? Real worms slithered through them now. The music, once so lively, now screeched with the sound of a requiem fit for a funeral.

But it wasn't the trees or the food or the music that truly terrified Sophie. Rather, it was the fairies themselves. Or, more precisely, the creatures who had been pretending to be fairies. Now their ethereal facades had been ripped away, revealing their true nature. The once beautiful, lithe creatures with candy-colored hair and gossamer wings had transformed into ancient hags with hunchbacks, green skin, bulging eyes and noses, and mouths filled with broken teeth.

Not fairies at all.

Goblins.

And their guide was the most hideous of all. With red-glowing eyes and sharp fangs and long twisted claws instead of finger-nails. He raised one of those claws in their direction, his lips rising to a sneer.

"Get them!" he commanded.

Sophie turned to Stu and Ashley. "Run!"

CHAPTER 33

Stu's heart raced as they ran through the woods, the goblins hot on their heels. From behind, he could hear their angry shouts. Their stomping feet. Were those awful creatures gaining on them? What would they do if they caught them? His mind flashed back to their guide's razor-sharp fangs and he shuddered.

As they ran, the landscape seemed to shift before his eyes. What was once bright, shiny— even glittery—was quickly turning into the set of a horror movie: dark trees loomed above them, gnarled branches stretched out like claws, and ground tangled with twisted roots, ready to reach up and trip them. Even the beautiful babbling brook—once a perfect pumpkin orange— now raged with molten lava.

Merlin was right. Fairyland was dangerous!

"What are we going to do?" Sophie cried, gasping for breath. "We can't keep running. They'll catch us for sure."

Stu looked around, desperate. His eyes caught something to his left—the entrance to what looked like a small cave, cut into the hillside and half-hidden by vines. "Look." He pointed. "Maybe we can hide in there until they pass."

"But we don't know what's in there!" Ashley protested. "What if it's dangerous?"

"More dangerous than murderous goblins?"

"Good point."

They cut left, ducking into the cave, which was dark and weirdly moist—but at least out of the path of danger. Once they were inside, Ashley pulled her phone from her backpack to use as a flashlight. Stu peeked out to make sure no one had seen them come in. Thankfully, the goblins were still some distance away. He let out a breath of relief and dropped the vines he was holding to better cover the entrance.

"Come on," he said. "Let's go deeper in. We don't want them to see Ashley's light."

They stepped farther into the cave, Ashley leading the way with her phone. To their surprise, after a few yards, the low-ceilinged tunnel ended, opening up into a massive cavern with a ceiling so far above them it disappeared into the darkness. The ground was made of bumpy crystal, and phosphorescent little worms crawled along the walls, casting an eerie green-tinged illumination around the space. Gross, but effective, Stu decided.

Ashley put her cell back in her bag, no longer needing the flashlight, and let out a low whistle. "This place is huge," she cried. "We must be inside some big mountain or something."

"But there was no mountain," Sophie argued. "The cave was just under a small hill."

"Things in Fairyland are clearly not what they seem," Stu remarked wryly. His ears pricked up as they caught a high-pitched twittering sound echoing through the cave. He looked up to see a few rainbow-colored bats flutter above them before disappearing into the darkness.

"Bats and bugs," Ashley mumbled, half to herself. "There just better not be any snakes."

Stu looked in the direction the bats had flown. His eyes caught a sliver of light shining in the distance. Wait, was that where they'd just come from? Had they already walked this far? Or was this some kind of weird magic, too?

"We need to be careful," he warned. "We don't know what could be in here."

As if in answer, a gust of wind howled through the cave. The hairs on the back of Stu's neck stood on end. He forced himself to keep walking, trying to ignore the screeching sounds from above, which, unfortunately, sounded like more bats. Like *a lot* more bats.

"Look!" Ashley suddenly cried. She started dancing with excitement. "Look! Look! Look!"

"Please no more dancing," Sophie protested, holding up her hands.

Stu looked up to see what had gotten Ashley so excited. To his surprise, there was something resembling a road sign above them, cut into the rock.

MORGAN LE FAY'S CASTLE—400 METERS AHEAD

Yes! Finally! They were getting somewhere. Maybe this mission wouldn't be a failure after all.

"Come on. What are we waiting for?" he exclaimed, jogging ahead.

But Ashley hedged. "You think it's safe to go there now? What if they're friends with the goblins? What if they turn us over to them as their prisoners? Or take us captive themselves?"

"It's possible," Sophie agreed. "But what else can we do? We need that flower or Merlin can't create his potion. We can't go back without it."

Ashley made a face. "I had a feeling you were going to say that."

They hurried down the twisty passageway. Stu's heart fluttered with a mixture of excitement and unease at every step. Ashley wasn't wrong. They *could* be walking into a trap. But Sophie wasn't wrong, either—they literally had no choice.

Suddenly Ashley screamed, and stopped so abruptly that Stu

almost ran into her. He looked down and his eyes widened in horror.

The cavern had opened up again.

But this time there was no ground.

At least not anywhere near their feet.

CHAPTER 34

S tu gaped into the abyss below them, so deep he could barely see the bottom. There must have been a cave-in or an earthquake or something that had caused the ground to collapse, leaving a chasm behind. It was too steep to climb down and back up again, he realized with dismay. And there was no way he could see to walk around it. His eyes traveled to the far end, meeting up again with the passageway they'd been following. A sign that read MORGAN LE FAY'S CASTLE— 200 METERS AHEAD hung above it, as if mocking them.

"Oh no!" Sophie shook her head. "No, no, no!"

Ashley put a hand to her mouth, staring down into the pit. "What are we going to do?" she asked. "Do you think we need to turn around?"

"No way. If we go back out there, the goblins will spot us." Stu rubbed his chin with one hand. If only there was some sort of bridge . . .

A loud groaning sound interrupted his troubled thoughts. He looked up, shocked to see a long rope bridge—exactly like the one he had just been imagining—unfurling across the canyon, stretching all the way to the other side.

"What on earth?" he whispered. Had it been there all along and he hadn't been able to see it? Or had it only appeared once he'd wished for it?

"Did you do that?" he asked Sophie. Maybe she'd used some magic?

She shook her head, her eyes never leaving the bridge. "No," she said in a small voice. "Definitely not."

"Well, whatever. Let's just go," he said, deciding not to look a gift bridge in the mouth.

He made a move toward the ropes, but Sophie grabbed his arm. Her face was stark white and her hands were shaking. "No. No freaking way."

It was then that Stu remembered her paralyzing fear of heights. There was no way she was going to be okay walking across some random magical bridge that hadn't been there five seconds before. She wouldn't even ride the Ferris wheel at the Topsfield Fair.

He racked his brain for a solution. "Can you fly over it?" he asked. "You know, turn into a bird like you did in Vegas?" After all, she seemed to do better with heights while in winged form.

Sure enough, Sophie looked visibly relieved. "Oh. Right. Good idea." She reached into her pocket for her spell book. Then her eyes widened with panic. "Oh no!"

"What's wrong?" Stu asked worriedly.

"My mom's spell book. I must have lost it when I was dancing." Her eyes welled with tears and Stu's heart ached at the devastation he saw on her face. He knew how much that book meant to her. Not only for practical purposes, but because her mom had given it to her....

"You know, you should really make a backup of those spells," Ashley broke in. "I mean, at least take photos of them with your phone? Then you'd always have them and—"

Stu shot Ashley a warning look. "Not. Helping."

"Sorry," Ashley mouthed.

Stu placed his hands on Sophie's shoulders. "It's okay," he tried to assure her. "We'll deal with that later. Right now I need you to close your eyes and hold on to me. I'll lead you across."

Sophie's jaw quivered. He could tell she thought this was the worst idea ever. And hey, maybe it was. But at last she gave a shaky nod.

"Fine. But I'm *really* hoping this isn't one of those cases where I have to tell you 'I told you so.' Because that's going to be difficult to do when I'm dead at the bottom of a Fairyland ditch."

She choked out a laugh. But Stu knew it was only half joking. Which he supposed was fair, given the circumstances. He walked over to the bridge, stepping on it and testing its weight.

"It feels sturdy," he assured Sophie. Well, as sturdy as a magical rope bridge leading across a fairy abyss could possibly feel, but he didn't think it was necessary to add that out loud. While he stepped aside, waiting for Sophie to make her way over, Ashley practically leaped onto the bridge and began skipping across it. Evidently, she had no fear of heights whatsoever. Stu watched, feeling a little nauseous as the bridge swayed wildly under her steps.

"Slow down," he scolded her. "You're making the whole thing shake."

Thankfully, Ashley obeyed and the bridge eventually settled. "See? It's fine," Stu told Sophie. "Look! Ashley's already halfway across."

Sophie looked as if she wanted to debate his definition of "fine," but instead she just clutched his arm, white-faced. Stu shot her a valiant smile, then steeled his nerves and stepped onto the bridge, trying not to look down as it shifted again under his weight. The last thing he needed was to catch a glimpse of how far they had to fall if they lost their footing. Sophie was counting on him. He couldn't let her know he was scared, too.

He took another step. Sophie followed, her whole body shaking like a bobblehead figure in an earthquake. He had to steady himself to prevent her from accidentally knocking him off-balance.

"Don't think about it," he instructed her.

"Um, what else can I possibly think about?"

He considered this, racking his brain for the memory of a good day. A day when they had both been happy. A day when there had been nothing to be afraid of. Which actually wasn't that hard to do. After all, there'd been so many good days since they'd become best friends. Days, he realized, he hadn't fully appreciated at the time. Mostly because he had no idea they were numbered.

At last he settled on one. "Remember that amazing snow day back in December?" he asked. "The one after the big nor'easter?"

"The day they told us not to go outside? And yet you waded through three feet of snow to get to my house before the plows did?"

"Yeah, well, we were out of hot chocolate at my house. So, you know."

"And I had it waiting for you when you stepped through the door."

"With extra, extra marshmallows. Just how I like it."

Stu took another step across the bridge, a warm feeling washing over him. "And then we ran up to your room and locked the door and did nothing but play video games the whole day."

"And I finally hit level eighty on *Camelot's Honor.*" Sophie's grip on his shoulder loosened as she took another step. "Remember that silly dance we made up to celebrate?"

"That was a terrible dance!"

Sophie smiled. "But a great day."

"Come on, slowpokes!" Ashley cried, some ways ahead. Stu watched as she grabbed the rope railings and swung her legs back and forth, as if performing a gymnastics stunt. *Show-off.*

"We're coming!" He took a few more steps, realizing he and Sophie had almost made it to the center of the bridge. And Sophie didn't look half as panicked as she had at the beginning. Maybe they'd make it after all.

"I hope we get lots of snow days next year," Sophie declared. "We could do that every time. Maybe even swap houses sometimes. Though you'd better stock up on hot chocolate. And marshmallows. Maybe even some whipped cream."

"Um, yeah," Stu stammered, reality suddenly smacking him hard across the jaw and ruining the moment. "I, uh, love whipped cream."

But there would be no more whipped cream, his mind taunted him as icy-cold air whipped across the bridge. No more snow days, either. No more walks to Sophie's house. No more lazy days of video gaming. When they got back from this trip, everything was going to change.

And Sophie had no idea.

He had to tell her. As soon as they crossed the bridge he would. No matter what.

"Come on," he said. "We're almost there."

"This bridge is so insane!" Ashley called out, her voice echoing over the chasm. She'd reached the other side and was leaning against a wall, examining her fingernails. "Totally reminds me of this swinging bridge I crossed in California once. It was the coolest thing." She walked over to one of the end posts and leaned on it casually. "Oh my gosh, Stu!" she exclaimed, as if the greatest idea ever had just occurred to her. "You should totally check it out when you move there!"

Stu froze in his tracks.

Oh no.

Sophie fell into him, letting out a startled cry. She fumbled for the railings for support. He turned to try to help her regain her balance . . . but she yanked her hands away.

"What did she just say?" she whispered, somehow managing to look alarmed and horrified and confused all at the same time. Which gave Stu a pretty good idea that she had heard Ashley just fine.

"I, um . . . I . . ." he stammered, unable to form words. Unable to do anything but stare at her. To watch her face go from pale white to bright red as his heart slammed against his chest like a jackhammer.

"Nothing!" Ashley shouted at them with way-over-the-top cheerfulness. "I didn't say anything! Boy, this bridge is super cool, isn't it? Now hurry up so we can find the fairy queen! I think I see a light at the end of the tunnel. Like, literally!"

Stu clenched his teeth. His heart pounded in his chest as his mind raced to find options. His first thought was to deny Ashley's words. Or tell her she misheard Ashley somehow—or at least misunderstood what she meant. But that would only make things worse in the end. After all, she was going to have to find out at some point.

He just *really* wished it wasn't in the middle of a creaky rope bridge high above a fairy abyss. Like, pretty much *anywhere* else would be better.

This is all your fault, he scolded himself miserably. *If you had just told her from the beginning...*

He swallowed hard. "Come on," he said, beckoning. "Let's just get off this thing." He reached out for her hand. But she clamped it down on the railing. Hard.

"No," she ground out.

"But —"

"But nothing. I'm not budging until you tell me what's going on. Are you moving to California?" Her voice cracked on the words.

"Well, um, I don't..." He raked a hand through his hair, glancing down at the pit below them. There was no escape.

"Oh my gosh, you are! You're moving? To California?" Her voice was high-pitched, squeaky. "How long have you known? Why didn't you tell me?"

"I wanted to!" he blurted out. "I was just...waiting for the right moment."

This, however, was not the right moment. In fact, this was pretty much the worst moment ever.

Her lower lip wobbled. "But you told Ashley?"

"No! She already knew. Lucas told her." His stomach felt like tossed salad. He wanted to vomit.

"So this is why you've been acting so weird," Sophie said woodenly. "I knew something was wrong! Why wouldn't you just tell me? I thought I was your best friend."

This was bad. So, so bad. If only they were somewhere else. If only they weren't on this stupid bridge.

A loud creaking noise interrupted his thoughts. He looked up, just in time to see the bridge—which he possibly had willed into appearing—now *disappearing* before his very eyes.

With them still on it.

He shoved Sophie in front of him. "Run!" he cried. *"Run now!"*

She looked past him. Her face went white. Then she turned and ran across the bridge as fast as her legs could carry her. Stu dove after her, his heart in his throat. When he dared look back, he saw the bridge dissolving only a few feet behind him, as if it were being eaten by an invisible monster. If they didn't get off quick—

Sophie hurtled off the bridge, landing hard on the ground on the other side, her hands skidding across the rocky ledge. Stu let out a breath of relief. At least she was safe. That was something. Considering this was likely his fault and—

"Stu!" Sophie screamed. "Jump! Now!"

He leaped, the bridge disappearing completely under his feet seconds after he left the ground. His arms shot out, clawing at the edge of the ravine. His body slammed into the rocky cliff face—so hard it knocked the breath from his lungs. He tried to pull himself up, but he was losing traction, his grip slipping fast. The ravine below seemed to weave in and out of focus— stalagmites grinning razor-sharp smiles as if inviting him into a deadly embrace.

Tears slipped from his eyes. Was this it? Was it game over for good?

"Help!" he squeaked. "Please! Help me!"

Suddenly strong hands gripped his own. He looked up to see both girls—each one holding one of his hands with both of theirs. They yanked him hard and the momentum helped him scramble up to safe ground. Once there, he collapsed, struggling to breathe.

"Are you okay?" Sophie asked, tears streaming down her cheeks. She was shaking like a leaf.

"I . . . think so. . . ." With effort, he pushed himself up to his feet, brushing himself off. His heart was still racing a thousand miles a minute, but he didn't think anything was broken. Just really bruised. He pulled air into his lungs. "Okay. I take it back. You were right to be afraid of that bridge."

Sophie nodded grimly, but didn't look him in the eyes. "I'm glad you're okay," she mumbled.

"I'm glad *you* are," he said honestly. He reached out to put a hand on her shoulder, but she stepped out of his reach, staring at the rocky wall so hard he wondered if she would burn a hole in it. Stu swallowed hard, watching her not watch him, feeling as if his heart would shatter with fear—and this time not from a near-death experience.

"Sophie, I'm so sorry," he tried. "I am so, so—"

"Guys! Guys! Come quick!" Ashley shouted over him. "You've got to see this!"

Sophie and Stu ran down the passageway toward the mouth of the cave. Sunlight streamed in, almost blinding Stu with its intensity. He blinked a few times, trying to adjust his eyes.

Then everything came into focus.

"We're here," Ashley whispered. "We made it to the castle of the fairy queen."

CHAPTER 35

Back at the druid village, Nimue and Emrys watched the knights clink their cups in a toast as Merlin sat motionless, trapped in his block of ice. Fear crawled down Nimue's spine. Was he still alive in there? Was it even worth trying to set him free? And if so, how were they going to do it?

She broke from the window, stalking around the small hut, her steps eating up the distance between walls. "This is terrible," she moaned. "What are we to do?"

"At least Morgana's gone," Emrys reminded her. "It could be worse."

She stopped pacing. "It *is* worse! She's on her way to Faerie. What if she finds the others and freezes them, too? Or kills them outright?" She thought back to the screams of her sisters and bit down hard on her lower lip. Sophie, at least, was a Companion, and surely knew the risks of her role. But her friends shouldn't even have been involved.

It had been all she could do to stop herself from following Morgana after she left the druid village. But she knew it would be a fool's mission. And dead, she was no good to the Grail. As long as she lived, she could still hold out the hope of saving it.

She looked down at the dragon. A small hope, anyway.

As if hearing her thoughts, Spike blinked at her. Then he belched a small ball of flame, which shot out and set the hem of her robe on fire.

"Argh!" she cried. "Emrys, help!"

Emrys grabbed a pitcher of water from a nearby table and poured it down Nimue's front side. Thankfully, it doused the fire. Though she was left with a gaping black hole at the bottom of her robe. And she was soaking wet.

She scrambled to the window to peek outside to make sure her cry hadn't alerted the knights. Thankfully, one of them had pulled out a lute and the other was singing tunelessly to a bawdy tavern song. She turned back to Spike, trying to wring out the water from her gown.

"Is it not enough for you to destroy the world?" she grumped at him. "You have to destroy my clothes, too?" She reached for Ashley's hair bands. "That's it. Your fire-breathing days are over."

Suddenly Emrys jerked to attention. "Wait," he cried.

"For what? For him to burn down the entire hut?"

"No." Emrys shook his head. "It's just—Merlin. He's trapped in ice."

Nimue's heart quickened as she realized what he was saying. "You think Spike could melt it with his fire?"

"I don't see why not."

"Hmm." Nimue mulled this idea over. "But what about the guards?"

"I could distract them," Emrys replied. "I could steal one of their horses. They would have to come after me."

"At least one of them would. Though I could probably find a way to deal with the second." Nimue considered. "But then... I don't know."

"What?"

"Well, Spike isn't exactly a trained dragon. We could tell him to free Merlin while we're both distracting the guards, but who knows if he'll understand? What if he flies away once we set him free? We might never find him again."

"That would be bad," Emrys conceded.

"It would be end-of-the-world catastrophic." She gave him a rueful look. "I'm sorry. Truly, it was a good idea. If he were a trained dog like Damara, I'd definitely give it a try."

Then an idea hit her. "Although..."

"What?"

She turned to Emrys. "Damara could help."

"Um, dogs can't breathe fire."

"No. But they can be awfully distracting," Nimue said with a smile. "If she and I can lure both knights away, you could take Spike to Merlin."

A spark of hope lit Emrys's face. "That could work. At least it has a chance to."

"Then what are we waiting for?" Nimue asked, lifting her chin. "Let's melt Merlin."

Emrys's heart was pounding hard in his chest as they snuck out the back door and around the hut, tiptoeing so as not to be overheard by the knights. Thankfully, the men were making quite a bit of noise themselves, still singing tunelessly as they slugged their tankards of mead and argued about whether or not they should make a fire. The redheaded knight, known as Sir Kay, believed it would be fine. The black-haired knight, Sir Agravaine, worried that any heat source would melt Merlin's block of ice. Emrys's eyes caught their swords, lying on the ground, a few feet away. Too far to grab them, unfortunately. At least they had taken off their armor. That was something, he supposed.

"Are you ready?" he whispered to Nimue. In the darkness, he could just see her nod. She held Damara by the scruff of her neck. And Spike sat on Emrys's shoulder, his mouth wrapped tightly in the hair band to prevent him from firing off too soon. Emrys drew in a breath. Would they really be able to do this?

Nimue gave him a serious look. "If this doesn't work," she said softly, "I want you to know, I'm still glad we tried."

He smiled at her, feeling a warmth rise in his stomach, displacing a little of his fear. "Me too," he replied, daring to reach out to squeeze her hand. She squeezed his in return.

"All right," she said. "Let's do this."

He watched as she dropped to her knees before the dog, whispering something in her ear. Damara's ears perked up as she listened, and a moment later she was off, bounding through the woods. Soon Emrys could hear loud barking in the near distance.

Sir Agravaine set down his bottle. "What was that?"

"Sounds like a dog." Sir Kay yawned, clearly not impressed.

"What would a dog be doing out here?"

"How am I supposed to know?"

"What if he's with someone?"

Sir Kay groaned. "Go check it out if you're so concerned." He tipped back his drink and gulped it down.

"Maybe I will. Nothing else to do, anyway," Sir Agravaine huffed, then grabbed his sword and stalked off into the woods.

Damara kept barking. *Good dog.*

Emrys turned to Nimue. "Now's your chance," he whispered.

She nodded, stepping out from behind the shadows of the

hut and into the center of the village. She walked confidently to the remaining knight and cleared her throat. He looked up from his drink, his eyes widening.

"You!" he cried, stumbling to his feet. "You're that girl. That cook from Merlin's cave."

Nimue smiled prettily. "Aye," she agreed. She fluttered her eyelashes at him. "And thank goodness I've found you, my brave knight in shining armor! I've been looking for you *everywhere*!"

"What? Why's that?" Sir Kay cocked his head, clearly confused.

"That... artifact you were looking for? Why, I think I have found it!"

"You have?" Sir Kay squinted at her. "How is that possible? And..." He scratched his head. "How did you find me here?"

Emrys snorted. Not exactly the sharpest sword in the armory, that was for sure. Which would hopefully work to their benefit.

Nimue's smile dipped to a frown. She made a tsking sound with her tongue. "So many questions," she scolded. "If you're not interested, I can give it to someone else."

"No!" Sir Kay protested. Then his lips curled greedily. "Bring it to me. If it is what I seek, then I promise you will be rewarded handsomely."

Nimue shrugged. "I am sorry, but I cannot bring it to you. However, if you were to come with me..." She beckoned him with her hand. "I promise, it is not far."

She turned and walked off into the woods. The knight watched her for a moment, not moving, and Emrys could almost see the smoke emanating from his ears as he tried to work out what to do. Emrys held his breath, praying the man would follow—that this risk had not been for nothing.

At last the knight sighed. He took one last glance at Merlin, seemingly satisfied that the wizard was still immobile, and then stalked off after Nimue. And bonus? He left his sword behind.

"Slow down!" he called out as he disappeared into the trees. "Wait for me!"

Emrys squared his shoulders. It was now or never. Pulling Spike down off his shoulder, he ran the dragon to the block of ice.

"All right," he said once they reached it. "Time to save Merlin, Spike." He reached down and pulled the band off the dragon's mouth, then set him in front of the ice. He stepped back a few feet, readying himself for the blast. "Do it! Now!"

But Spike did not do it. Instead he slurped up another beetle off the ground and crunched it between his teeth. Emrys groaned.

"Come on!" he begged. He shot a nervous glance into the woods. It wouldn't be long before one or both of the knights returned. "Breathe fire! Burp! Anything!"

But the dragon only fluttered his wings. Then he started picking at his teeth with his claw. Panic rose inside Emrys. This was their one chance. If they didn't save Merlin now...

"Spike, please!" he cried. "Blow fire."

But it wasn't happening. And they were quickly running out of time. Emrys looked around the camp, desperate for another option. It was then that his eyes fell upon the piece of flint lying next to the fire pit. His mind flashed back to Nimue sparking her own fire. No magic or dragon necessary.

Emrys dove for the flint, then reached into his pocket to find the wad of cash paper he'd gotten in Vegas. It looked like it would prove useful after all. He arranged the paper in a small pile, then struck the flint against a rock.

Nothing happened.

He gritted his teeth and tried again. And then a third time. Finally, on the fifth try, he got a small spark to ignite.

Which went out immediately, before igniting the paper.

No! Emrys dropped to the ground in frustration, squeezing his hands into fists. He should have known he couldn't do it. He couldn't even start a bloody fire—that's how useless he was. No wonder Merlin wanted to send him home. The wizard *should* send him home. That's where he belonged. He should just walk away from all of this and never look back. He would be doing everyone a favor.

But just as he started to rise, his mind flashed to Nimue. She was still out in the woods, risking her life for this. She was counting on him. She'd trusted him with everything.

To me, you are a true hero of Camelot.

He squared his shoulders and lifted his chin. Nimue wouldn't quit. She would fight until there was no breath left in her body.

And Emrys wouldn't let her down.

He reached for the flint again. But to his surprise, Spike stepped into his path, blocking his reach.

"Move," he scolded the dragon. "You good-for-nothing—"

Spike squawked. Then, to Emrys's surprise, he opened his mouth and directed a small stream of fire at the ground, easily igniting the pile of paper. Emrys stared at the small fire in shock, then up at the dragon, hope rising in his chest.

"Yes!" he cried. "Good boy! That's how you do it!" He patted the dragon on the top of the head. "But we need more! We need to thaw Merlin!" He pointed to the block of ice. Then to the fire Spike had started.

Spike cocked his head, as if not quite understanding. Emrys pointed to the fire again. Then at the dragon. Then at the ice. Then he repeated the gestures all over again.

Finally, Spike's eyes brightened. As Emrys watched, breath caught in his throat, the dragon slowly turned to the block of ice. He pulled back his head...

And blasted Merlin with fire.

CHAPTER 36

Emrys expected the ice to melt. He didn't expect it to explode at the first lick of flame. But this was magical ice, and explode it did, the force of the blow sending him flying. He hit the ground with a painful thump, icicles raining down on top of him.

"Ow!" he cried, rubbing his back. Then he sat up, heart in his throat. With trembling hands he looked over to where the ice block had been.

It was gone. Only Merlin remained, on the ground, gasping for breath.

"Merlin!" he cried, scrambling to his feet and stomping out the rest of the fire, which thankfully wasn't large. He scooped

Spike up with one hand and grabbed the wizard's arm in the other, dragging him in the direction of the hut. "Come. Quick!"

Merlin stumbled, still dazed, but managed to follow Emrys across the clearing and back into the hut where they'd been hiding. Once they were inside, Emrys slammed the door shut and pulled a table in front of it. Then he dropped to his knees to see to Merlin. The wizard was shaking with cold and dripping wet. But he was alive. That was all that mattered.

"By the gods," Merlin exclaimed, his voice still a little froggy. "That blasted witch! I thought I'd be stuck in there forever." He looked around. "Where's Nimue? Why aren't you two hiding underground like you're supposed to?"

"You should be very happy we aren't," Emrys shot back. "You'd still be stuck in a block of ice if we were."

"Oh," Merlin began to bluster, wringing water out of his beard. "Well, yes, I suppose—"

Emrys gave him an apologetic look. "Sorry, Merlin. You can scold me later. Right now Nimue's still out there. I have to make sure she's all right." He made a move toward the back door. But before he could open it, he heard a scream.

A scream that sounded a lot like Nimue.

He stumbled over to the window, peering outside. His eyes caught movement in the bushes. A moment later Sir Kay emerged, a struggling Nimue in his grip. He threw her to the ground in front of the fire pit, shaking a fist at her. "You vile wench! You try to trick me—"

"Where's Merlin?"

Sir Agravaine stomped out from the bushes, joining his friend. Thankfully, Damara was nowhere to be found—hopefully she at least had gotten away. The knight stared down at the puddle of water—all that was left of Merlin's icy prison—his arms crossed over his chest. Then his eyes snapped to Nimue.

"You!" he spit out. "You're that girl from Merlin's cave. What did you do with him?"

"Please. As if I would tell you!" Nimue replied, shooting daggers with her eyes in his direction. Sir Agravaine kicked her in the stomach and she fell backward with a groan. It was all Emrys could do not to dive out of the house and tackle him. But he forced himself back. He had to play this right if he were to have any chance of saving her.

"What are we going to do?" Sir Kay moaned, looking down at her in disgust. "Morgana will have our heads if she returns to find Merlin gone."

"Do not fear. He will come back," Sir Agravaine insisted. "After all, we have his cook." He grabbed Nimue by the scruff of the neck. "Merlin!" he shouted into the woods. "We have the wench! Show yourself or I will slit her throat." He yanked a knife from his belt, as if to prove his point.

"No!" Emrys whispered hoarsely. He turned to Merlin. "You have to do something. Please!"

"I'm sorry." Merlin rose shakily to his feet. "But I cannot."

Emrys stared at him, horrified. "What? What do you mean you cannot? You're Merlin. You can do anything."

"Not at the moment. I am weakened and unable to access my magic."

"Then what are we to do? We can't let her die!" He turned back to Nimue. His eyes locking on the knife Agravaine held to her throat. "You have to save her!"

"Actually, *you* do," Merlin replied in a quiet voice.

"What?"

"You said you wanted to learn magic, Emrys. Now is your chance."

A chill tripped down Emrys's spine. "But I can't—I mean, remember the last time?"

Merlin held up a hand. "A wizard does not dwell on the past. Only the present."

"Right." That was easy for him to say. Emrys stared out at Nimue. She was scowling at the knights, not showing a hint of fear, even though he knew she must be terrified. She was so brave.

He needed to be brave, too.

"All right," he rasped out. "Tell me what I need to do."

Merlin nodded solemnly. "Just repeat after me."

Emrys drew in a breath and did just that, repeating the magic words Merlin fed to him. He was careful to pronounce them exactly right—in the exact right order. Which wasn't easy to do with his lips trembling so hard. But he couldn't make any mistakes. Nimue's life depended on it.

As he repeated the last words, there was a puff of smoke. A flash of fire. A scream that turned into . . .

A squawk?

Oh dear. Had he done it right? He could barely breathe, waiting for the smoke to clear. When it finally did, his eyes fell on Nimue, who was standing alone in the clearing, looking bewildered beyond belief.

Well, alone, that is, except for two very angry-looking chickens.

"Wha—?" Emrys cried. "Oh no! Not again. Not more chickens!"

Merlin broke out in a laugh. He slapped Emrys on the back. "Sorry!" he cried. "I couldn't resist."

Emrys stared at him, his mouth open. "So . . . wait," he stammered. "I did it? I performed the spell correctly?"

"You performed it *perfectly*," Merlin assured him, patting him on the shoulder in a fatherly way. "Good work, my young apprentice. Perhaps you have the makings of a fine wizard after all."

"Oh, Merlin!" Emrys cried, throwing his arms around the magician before he could stop himself. "Thank you! Thank you so much!"

"Stop squeezing me! I'm fragile still, remember?" Merlin humphed, untangling himself from the hug. But he didn't sound angry. In fact, he sounded rather proud, which made Emrys's heart soar with joy.

"Now," Merlin instructed, "go get that girl and bring her back inside. And try to stay out of trouble until I get back." He chuckled. "Not that you two can't handle yourselves, I suppose."

"Where are you going?" Emrys asked, cocking his head.

Merlin looked up. "First I am going to the sacred well to get my magic back. Then I will go to where I should have gone from the start," he declared. "The land of Faerie."

CHAPTER 37

Sophie stared up at the fairy castle, her heart thumping hard in her chest. She knew she should be thrilled to see it—especially after all they'd gone through to get here. But at the moment it was difficult to stay focused on the task at hand, especially after everything that had just happened in the cave.

If only she could call a time-out—put the quest on pause—like a video game. Then she and Stu could talk it out. And clear the air before moving on to the next level. Her mind flashed back to him hanging off the cliff, his fingernails slipping, *this close* to plunging into the abyss. Game over—forever.

At the time, his moving to California didn't seem as big a deal.

But now that they were safe on solid ground, it all came rushing back to her. Like a dodgeball straight to the gut. Stu was moving. Stu—who had lived down the street from her her entire life—was now going to be three thousand miles away. Which meant no more 7-Eleven Slurpee runs after school. No more lazy snow days with hot chocolate and marshmallows. If they wanted to hang out, they'd have to board an airplane and cross the entire country to do it.

She felt like she was going to be sick.

Maybe it wasn't definite, she told herself. Maybe this was just something his mother was suggesting. Or maybe Stu would figure out a way to stay with his dad. Maybe...maybe...

"Sophie? Earth to Sophie!" Ashley waved her hands in front of Sophie's face, snapping her back to reality. "Are you just going to stand there? Or do you want to go hit up the fairy queen?"

"Sorry," she said. "I'm coming." She glanced longingly at Stu, who, she realized, was watching her with worried eyes. She wanted so desperately to go over and give him a hug. There were so many questions buzzing around inside her head. When was he leaving? Was he ever coming back? But she knew if they started talking about it now, she might fall apart, and they still had their mission to complete. She'd hold it together just a little longer.

Sophie forced her feet to move toward the castle. Or what stood for a castle in Fairyland, which was very unlike the castles she'd seen in the real world. For one thing, instead of being built of stone, it was carved into a gigantic living tree, stretching high in the sky—at least eleven stories tall—with thick, strong branches adorned with emerald-colored leaves. Little windows had been carved into the wood and fitted with colorful stained-glass patterns.

But the coolest part of all was the carvings. Etched everywhere into the tree's trunk were elaborate depictions of great battles and highly detailed portraits of mythical forest creatures: unicorns, winged Pegasus-like horses, griffins—and some Sophie didn't recognize.

It was impressive, that was for sure. And also . . . well guarded, Sophie noticed as they got closer. The main entrance, a huge set of double doors that stretched twenty feet high, was flanked by at least ten guards, dressed in uniform, and sporting large wings. She wondered why they needed such security. Were they at war with the goblins, perhaps?

As they approached, the guards stepped into their path. The tallest one slipped from the pack and met Sophie and her friends. He had blue eyes and a trim green beard. Also, a sharp-looking spear.

"Who are you?" he demanded. "State your names and business or begone from this place."

Sophie swallowed hard. Here went nothing.

"Um, I'm Sophie? And these are my friends Stu and Ashley,"

she replied, trying not to trip over her tongue. "And we're here to see the fairy queen?" She paused, then added, "Is she home right now?" It would be just their luck, she realized suddenly, if the fairy queen were on spring break as well.

The guard looked her up and down. "You're mortal," he noted. It wasn't a question.

"Yes? That's not a problem, is it?"

"It depends," he replied. But did not elaborate. Which was so not helpful. Sophie shot a glance at Ashley. *Use your talking powers*, she tried to project.

Thankfully, Ashley seemed to get the message. "Look! We're cool, I promise!" she piped in. "The fairy queen will love us! We even brought her the most amazing present!"

The guard frowned. "A present? You can just leave that with us. We will make sure she gets it."

Ugh. These guys were impossible.

"You don't understand," Sophie argued. "We need to see her. To talk to her."

The guard sniffed. "The queen does not simply *talk* to mortals," he said with a huff. Then he narrowed his eyes, as if something had just occurred to him. "Who sent you, anyway? And how did you get here? No mortal can open up a fairy portal and just walk right through."

Sophie felt her forehead break out in a cold sweat. She was afraid they were going to ask something like that. What were they supposed to say? They couldn't name-drop Merlin, or they'd never get an audience with the queen. But who else? Who did they know that the fairy queen would recognize? The Companions? Sophie's mom? But no, the Companions might not be friends of the fairies. They couldn't take that risk.

Then it hit her with the force of a ten-ton truck.

"Morgana!" she cried. Stu and Ashley gaped at her in horror, but she ignored them, pushing on. "The queen's cousin. She was the one who opened the portal for us. And gave us the gift to offer to your queen. She told us we must deliver it in person, too." She shot the guard a knowing look. "Trust me, I'd much rather just drop it off and be on my way! But you know how Morgana can be."

The guards exchanged glances. Sophie held her breath, praying this would work. At last, to her relief, the fairies nodded.

"Very well," the lead guard replied. "Come with us."

One might assume that, since it was located inside a giant tree, a fairy castle would be earthy on the inside, with low ceilings and small cozy rooms, hollowed out from wood. It turned out, however, to be the exact opposite. In fact, the throne room was a cavernous space, with vaulted ceilings dripping with crystal chandeliers. The floors appeared to be made of some sort of glass-like material and were partially covered by colorful throw rugs and pillows. Elaborately dressed fairies lounged here and there, eating delicacies off low tables piled high with food and drink.

At the very end of the long hall there was a small stage. On it sat a magnificent throne, also made out of glass. On the top of the throne were several spires, capped by multicolored gems: emeralds, rubies, sapphires. The lights from the chandeliers hit these gems just right, casting prismatic rainbows across the room.

As they walked down the hall, escorted by the guards, they could feel the court fairies staring at them curiously. But no one said anything or tried to stop them. Finally, they reached the stage. They glanced at one another, then at the empty throne. Now what?

Suddenly trumpets sounded. Everyone in the place stood up. A male fairy with long blond hair pulled back into a ponytail flew out onto the stage. He cleared his throat. "Ladies and gentlemen," he called out, his voice echoing through the chamber. "May I present to you, Her Royal Majesty, the greatest queen of our time, maker of all things good, the moonbeam maven, whisperer of the butterflies, defender of all things fluffy..."

He kept going. Evidently the fairy queen had a lot of titles to her name. And as her list of rather odd accomplishments stretched on and on, Sophie started to get a little nervous again. What if the queen refused the gift? What if she didn't buy their story of working for Morgana? What if she just took the skin-care products and didn't give them the Agrimony they needed in return?

What if, after all this work, they failed?

"...exhuberant hugger of baby goats, dignified defender of mud pies, tireless troubadour for tarantulas..."

She shook her head. No. She couldn't think like that. She was a Companion. Her mother had endowed her with this title, and she would prove herself worthy. She would not let her mother down. Or the rest of the world, for that matter. They'd gotten this far. They would see this through.

"...slayer of chocolate cake, queen of afternoon naps, glit-terer of the glamourati—your queen, ladies and gentlefairies, *Morgan le Fay!*"

The assembled guests gave a round of rowdy applause, though it wasn't entirely clear whether the courtiers were cheering for their queen or were just happy to have the announcer finally stop speaking. In any case, the trumpets sounded again and there was a large poof of smoke. When it cleared, Queen Morgan le Fay stood in front of the throne, as if she'd appeared out of thin air.

Titles aside, Sophie thought, the lady sure knew how to make an entrance.

Morgan le Fay definitely resembled her cousin. She had the same long black hair and violet-colored eyes. But whereas Morgana always had her mouth turned down in a frown, le Fay was smiling widely and had a sparkle of excitement in her eyes as she lowered herself onto her throne.

She wore a simple tunic dress with no jewelry, and if it wasn't for the crown of woven branches on her head, she could have been mistaken for a peasant rather than a queen. A far cry from Morgana's elaborate purple gowns. She also had wings, of course, tucked daintily behind her.

The queen smiled at her subjects, waving genially into the great hall. For a moment, it didn't appear she'd even noticed the outsiders. But when their escort cleared his throat, she stopped waving. Her gaze locked on Sophie and her friends.

"And who might you be?" she exclaimed in a high-pitched voice that tinkled like Christmas bells. "For I'm sure I've not seen you before. I'm certain if I had I would remember your charming faces." She smiled sweetly at them and then gave them an expectant look.

"They say they are messengers from your cousin," one of the guards explained before Sophie could open her mouth. "Here to present you with a gift."

The queen's smile faltered a bit at the mention of Morgana. Sophie's heart pounded. Was she wrong to have name-dropped her? Did the cousins not exactly . . . get along?

She dropped to her knees in a respectful bow, yanking Stu and Ashley down with her.

"Your Majesty," she said, keeping her head bowed, "it is so

good to meet you at last. I am Sophie and these are my companions, Stuart and Ashley."

"Rise," the queen instructed. "And tell me why you have come here. You say my cousin sent you?" Sophie heard something skeptical in her tone.

She scrambled to her feet. "Yes," she stammered. "You see, she needs a special ingredient for a spell she's working on and—"

"And she cannot come and ask for it herself?" the queen interjected, sounding a little hurt. "She sends mortal children instead? Doesn't she know how dangerous Faerie can be for mortals? I mean, the goblins alone!"

"Yeah, we know all about them," Stu muttered.

"Then you are lucky to be alive," the queen replied somberly. Sophie saw the nods of the others around her, agreeing. A shiver tripped down her spine and her legs ached as they remembered the endless dancing.

"Morgana *totally* wanted to come," she assured the queen. "But she's super busy trying to get the Holy Grail back from that nasty Merlin guy." She rolled her eyes. "You know how *he* is. . . ."

The queen's mouth dipped into a frown at the mention of Merlin. She leaned back in her throne. "That wizard." She cursed under her breath. "Always trifling in matters that do not concern him. Why I ought to—"

"Open your gift?" Ashley suggested. She stepped forward, reaching into her backpack. "Spoiler: It's an amazing new skin-care line from Dr. Brandt. Cleanser, toner, a mask." She squinted down at the mask. "No, wait. Not this one. You don't want the iron one." She rummaged through her bag again. "Aha! The best night cream ever. Use this for a month and you'll feel like a new fairy."

The queen eyed the products greedily. She poked her guard, demanding he go retrieve them for her. He did so, then placed the goods in her hands. She examined each one carefully, a delighted look on her face.

"I remember this brand," she exclaimed, holding up a bottle. "The last time I time traveled with Merlin we went to this amazing store. Sephora, I think they called it."

"Oh my gosh, I know! Sephora is to die for," Ashley agreed. "And trust me—I bought out half the store for you." She pulled another bottle from her bag. "Like this great exfoliator. It'll totally slough away all those dead skin cells. And a blemish zapper. No one wants a fairy queen with zits, am I right?"

Stu snorted. Sophie shot him a warning look.

But the queen only rubbed her hands together with glee. "This is wonderful!" she cried. "I cannot wait to try all of these amazing products you have brought for me."

"And you can!" Sophie broke in quickly. "All we need in exchange is a teeny, tiny bouquet of Agrimony. I'm sure that won't be a problem, right?"

To her surpise, the queen froze. She turned to Sophie, cocking her head. "Agrimony? Why would my cousin want Agrimony?"

"Uh, for a spell she's trying to do?" Sophie tried, worry rising inside her all over again. Why was the queen looking at her so strangely?

"But what about her garden?" the queen pressed. "The one in the courtyard of her castle? Does Agrimony not grow there? I planted it myself, the last time I visited."

Uh-oh.

Sophie shot a look at Stu. He winced, giving her a helpless half shrug.

Thankfully, Ashley stepped in. "Oh! You know Morgana!" she groaned. "Worst green thumb ever. Am I right?"

The queen looked baffled. "Green thumb? But she is not a goblin! Only goblins have green—"

"She means she's not a good gardener," Sophie corrected quickly.

"Oh. Right." To Sophie's relief, the fairy queen chuckled. "She gets that from her mortal side." The courtiers around her laughed. Her eyes leveled on Sophie. "Do not tell me she already killed those plants."

"Half the garden is gone, Your Majesty," Sophie replied soberly. She was starting to get the hang of this now. "It's a travesty. Really."

The queen sat a little straighter on her throne. "Well, then," she said. "Though I would definitely love to teach my cousin a lesson, I'm sure her spell is important. I'm happy to help. Especially after such fine gifts!" She turned to the serving woman on her left. "Violet! Will you escort these children into the royal garden? Let them take whatever they need!"

Sophie's shoulders slumped in relief. They'd done it! Somehow they'd done it! They'd talked the fairy queen into giving them what they needed. Now they just had to gather it up and drink the potion and get back to Merlin. This was almost too good to be true!

The serving woman stepped down off the stage, heading in their direction. "Come, children," she instructed. "And I will get you—"

But she never got to finish that sentence. Because at that moment, the back door to the fairy court flew open and a new voice rang through the hall.

"There they are! You wretched beasts! You will not escape me this time!"

With shaking hands, Sophie turned slowly. There, standing silhouetted in the doorway, stood none other than Morgana herself.

CHAPTER 38

Stu watched as the fairy queen rose from her throne to greet her new visitor. Her face was a mask of confusion. "Cousin?" she queried. "What are you doing here? I thought you were chasing Merlin down. These children said—"

"Do not trust these children, cousin," Morgana spit out, stomping toward them with heavy steps. She must have done a bit of shopping while in Vegas, and now wore a pair of patterned leggings and a blinged-out T-shirt that read, *What Happens in Vegas Stays in Vegas.*

If only that were true.

The fairy queen crossed her arms over her chest. "But they said they were working for you. To help you take down Merlin!"

Morgana tsked. "You poor naive creature. Do you not know

that mortals lie? They are not working to take down Merlin! They are *friends* of Merlin's!"

The queen gasped. She stared at Sophie, Stu, and Ashley, a look of horror clouding her face. "Is this true?" she demanded. "Are you working for that ... that ... horrible man?"

"He's really a good guy!" Ashley tried. "I know he kind of left you hanging. But he had a really good reason and—"

"Silence!" Morgana's voice sliced through the air like a knife. She grabbed Sophie by the chin, tilting her head up until Sophie was forced to meet the evil villainess's eyes with her own. "Now, where is the Grail?"

"You're too late," Sophie rasped, her voice strangled by Morgana's grip. "Merlin's taken it to Arthur."

Good save, Stu thought. Until Morgana started laughing. A cold, dark laugh that made his skin crawl. "Merlin?" she cackled. "Please. Your dear Merlin is not taking *anything* to Arthur. He's trapped in a block of ice back in Avalon. Guarded by my own knights."

"Oh no!" Sophie's face went white. "I knew something was wrong! That's what I couldn't remember earlier! Those knights were coming for us just before I went through the portal!"

"Don't feel bad," Morgana cooed. "The land of Faerie can play tricks on your memories. It's one of its many charms, really. You stay here long enough, you'll soon forget you ever lived anywhere else. That's why I only visit twice a year." Her grip tightened on

Sophie's neck. "Now. Where. Is. My. Grail? I'm running out of patience here."

Stu watched, helpless, as Sophie's face started to turn purple. He turned to Ashley, hoping for more of her quick wit.

But to his surprise, Ashley was no longer standing beside him. Had they grabbed her and taken her away when he wasn't looking? But if so, wouldn't he have heard her scream? Maybe she'd slipped away on her own somehow. She had the go-home potion in her bag, after all. He hoped she'd hidden herself somewhere so she could drink it and go for help.

In the meantime, it was up to him.

He stepped forward, locking his gaze on Morgana. "Why do you want the Grail so badly, anyway?" he demanded. "You're not sick, are you? What else is it good for, other than curing illnesses?"

The sorceress's eyes narrowed into slits. She shoved Sophie away and stalked over to him. Sophie crumpled to the ground, hands on her neck. But at least she was still breathing.

His breathing days, on the other hand, might be numbered, judging from the furious look in Morgana's eyes. "You again!" she cried. "Why, I should strike you down where you stand."

Stu forced a bored groan from his lips. "Are we really back to this again? Like I said at the tournament, if you kill me, I can't tell you where the Grail is." He met her eyes with his own steely gaze. "Now. Why do you want it, again?"

Morgana's face twisted in frustration. "To make Arthur pay for all he has done, of course."

"Right." Stu tapped his forehead. "You mean like that whole pesky 'bring peace to the land' thing? That was brutal. Oh, and the 'feeding hungry people' mission?" He shook his head. "That jerk. And let's not forget that whole 'everyone deserves health care' decree." He beamed at the sorceress. "That was my idea, by the way."

Morgana turned and began stalking down the fairy hall. "Peace?" she spit out. "Peace? He's a Pendragon! They know nothing of peace." She whirled back to face Stu. "Did you know his father murdered my father so he could marry my mother? Then forced my mother to banish me from the only home I ever knew?" Stu was surprised to hear her voice cracking on the last part. As if it still upset her.

He walked over to her, placing a hand on her shoulder. "Dude, I get it. That's rough," he said kindly. "But you can't blame Arthur for that, can you? I mean, parents do messed-up things all the time. You should have seen my parents' divorce. Not pretty. And now my mom thinks it's a good idea to drag me all the way across the country to California. Which is basically just like banishing me from the only home I ever knew. Not to mention my best friend."

He could feel Sophie's eyes on him, but refused to look in her direction. His hands were shaking as he watched Morgana's face. She seemed to be listening, at least. And she wasn't actively trying to kill them, so there was that.

"Anyway," he stumbled on, "you can't judge a dude by his parents. And sometimes things are out of control. Arthur was just a baby when all this happened. He had nothing to do with any of it. Maybe he deserves a second chance?"

Morgana was silent. Her eyes roved the fairy court—everyone was still as stone statues, waiting for her response. Stu held his breath, not daring to move. Would his words reach her somehow? Would she have a change of heart? It seemed crazy. But maybe—

"Ahhhhh!"

Morgana's scream rang out through the chamber. She clutched her face in her hands, tears streaming down her cheeks. She was clearly in pain—but from what, Stu couldn't figure out. No one was touching her. No one was anywhere near her!

"Get it off me!" Morgana begged, clawing at her face. "It burns!"

The throne room erupted in chaos. Guards drew their swords, circling their queen. Others tried to grab Sophie and Stu. But Stu whirled around, shoving his attacker square in the chest. The fairy stumbled back, tripping over a low table, sending food and drinks flying. Stu dove on top of him, grabbing his sword from his hand.

He ran to Sophie, who was fighting her own guard. The

fairy had an arm around her neck and was choking her from behind. Stu raised his sword, desperate for an opening. He didn't want to cut Sophie by accident. His mind raced. What should he do?

Suddenly the guard screamed. As loud as Morgana had. He dropped Sophie like a hot potato, hands to his face. Stu watched in horror as smoke started pluming off his skin, as if acid were burning his flesh. Sophie scrambled away from him, running to Stu. Her face was pale and frantic.

"What's going on?" she asked.

Stu shook his head. "I have no idea."

"Psst!" A voice from behind caused them to whirl around. But to Stu's confusion, no one was there. Just a weird tub of face cream, seeming to hover in midair.

A tub of face cream... and a really stuffed pink backpack.

"Are you guys just going to stand there?" Ashley demanded. "Or are we going to make our grand escape?"

Stu's jaw dropped. "What? Where—?"

"I'm invisible, you idiot!"

"Invisible?"

"Yes! Don't you remember? I took a picture of Sophie's spell book back at the hotel? I was going to use it to spy on the Celts' cheer team before regionals, but this seemed a much better time to try it."

"Wow." Stu didn't know what else to say.

"Now come on! I'm running out of my secret weapon."

It was then that Stu realized what she was talking about. The face mask she'd bought in Vegas—the one Merlin had warned against giving to the fairy queen because the iron ingredients would burn her skin! And since Morgana was a fairy, it did the same to her.

"Ashley, you're a genius!" he exclaimed.

"Duh. Now let's get out of here!"

Stu didn't need a second invitation. He ran out of the chamber, Sophie, and presumably an invisible Ashley, hot on his heels. From behind him, he could hear Morgana screaming bloody murder and vowing to come after them. Stu picked up the pace, his lungs burning in protest as he raced down the hall, through the front gates... and back into the woods.

Once they were outside the castle, Sophie stopped, hands on her knees, panting for breath. "I can't run anymore," she begged. Her neck was bright red where Morgana had choked her, likely not helping matters.

"We have to go! They're going to be here in a second!" Stu pleaded.

"We can drink Merlin's potion," Ashley suggested. The invisibility spell had begun to wear off and she was eerily ghostlike in front of them.

"But what about the Agrimony?" Sophie protested. "We came all this way and we still don't have it!"

"We won't have our lives, either, if we stay," Stu shot back. "I vote for the potion."

"Fine," Sophie said. "Where is it?"

"I have it!" Ashley replied, coming more and more into focus. "It's in my bag somewhere...."

Ashley started digging through her bag. Stu's heart thudded in his chest. With all that she had in there, this could take a while, and they really didn't have a while to spare.

"There you are! You think you can escape me?"

Stu whirled around, just in time to see Morgana practically flying out of the castle, her face blackened from where Ashley had struck her with the iron cream. She also looked ready to murder someone, and he was pretty sure the three of them topped her list.

"Hurry!" he begged Ashley.

She lifted her face from her bag. "Here we are!" she crowed, raising the potion triumphantly in the air. Then she frowned. "I guess we just chug it? He didn't leave any instructions—"

Morgana raised her hands. Sparks danced on her fingers. Stu gulped hard. He tried to grab the potion from Ashley, but his fingers fumbled it and it fell to the ground, rolling away from his grasp.

"No!" he cried, diving after it, heart now in his throat. He knew he had just moments before Morgana would let her fire fly, striking him square in the back. And then—

WHOOSH!

A huge gust of wind whipped up out of nowhere, dousing the flames. Morgana screamed, knocked backward by the force of the gale and giving Stu enough time to grab the potion.

"Got it!" he cried. Then he turned back to Morgana. "What happened? Did one of you do that?"

But the two girls only shook their heads, appearing as mystified as he was. Then Sophie's eyes widened. "Look!" she cried, pointing behind him.

Stu whirled around. To his shock and amazement, he saw Merlin stepping out from the forest, his whole body crackling with energy. He looked fierce and furious and, well, kind of amazing. And as he raised his hands, he mumbled something under his breath.

There was an earsplitting screech, then a big poof of smoke.

And when the smoke cleared?

Morgana was frozen in a block of ice.

Yes!!!

"Now you know how it feels," Merlin muttered, stalking up to the ice block and kicking it with his boot. But, of course, Morgana didn't answer. Couldn't answer, Stu realized, what with her face frozen mid-scream and all. Which was completely grotesque, but also amazingly cool.

"Merlin!" Sophie cried, running over to the wizard. She threw her arms around him. "Thank goodness you came!"

He hugged her in return. "Yes, well, looks like I arrived just in time."

"You can say that again. We were about to be fairy flambé."

"Yes, well, I did warn you that Fairyland was dangerous," he grumbled. "Did you at least get the Agrimony?"

The three of them hung their heads. "Not exactly," Sophie confessed.

"Things got a little messed up," Stu added.

"And now the fairy queen is super mad," Ashley finished. "There's no way she's going to give us the stuff. Even though she kept all the skin cream."

Merlin nodded solemnly, stroking his beard with his fingers. For a moment, he said nothing. Then, at last, he let out a long, deep sigh.

"Let me go talk to her," he said.

A spark of hope ignited in Stu. "Really?" he asked. "But I thought..."

Merlin gave him a rueful look. "I know, I know. But you were right. I've been behaving like a coward. And most unbecoming to a grand wizard like myself. I think it's high time I face the music." He took off his glasses and cleaned them on his robe. "Let's just hope it's not a goblin dance party. I hate those things."

"Though they are a great cardio workout," Ashley piped in. "Just saying."

"Do you want us to go with you?" Stu asked Merlin. "Like, for moral support?"

Merlin shook his head. "Thank you, but no. This is something I need to do on my own. You three should drink my potion and head back to the real world. Find Nimue and Emrys and the dragon and head to King Arthur's court. Tell Arthur to hang on—that I will get him what he needs…somehow." He tried to smile, but it didn't quite meet his eyes. He was worried, Stu realized. Probably for good reason.

For Morgana might be gone. But their mission was far from over.

CHAPTER 39

Sophie opened her eyes. At first she had no idea where she was. She was lying in a small bed, in some kind of crude wooden hut with simple furniture and wood-shuttered windows. A peek outside revealed normal-looking trees with normal-looking brown bark and green leaves—and no glitter to speak of.

She let out a groan of relief. She was back in Avalon. Merlin's potion must have worked.

She struggled to sit up, reaching her hand to her neck, which was still sore from where Morgana had grabbed it. But thankfully that seemed to be the extent of her injuries. She rubbed her eyes . . . and felt something wet and rough lick the back of her hand.

She pulled her hands away, shocked to find none other than

Spike himself hovering in midair in front of her like some kind of dragon-shaped hummingbird. He gave her an enthusiastic grin, his black tongue lolling from the side of his mouth. When he made a move to lick her again, she laughed, playfully shoving him away.

"Not that I'm not thrilled to see you," she assured him. "But dragon slobber. Ew!"

Thankfully, the dragon didn't seem offended. He swam through the air, performing a barrel roll. Which would have been impressive had he not smacked headfirst into a chair at the end of it, crashing to the floor like a cartoon character.

"Worst dragon ever," Sophie groaned, sliding her feet out of bed. She picked up the dragon—who looked a bit dizzy from his adventure—and cradled him in her arms. He nuzzled against her hand, causing her to smile. "Okay, maybe not the *worst*. In fact, you're actually not that bad."

Spike farted happily. She screeched, almost dropping him as she reached to pinch her nose. "I take it back!" she scolded him. "I take it all back!"

"Hey! She's awake!"

Sophie looked up to see Stu and Ashley barging into the hut, their faces lit up with excitement. Which made her wonder how long she'd been out.

"How are you feeling?" Stu asked, looking her up and down.

"Like I've been run over by a truck," she confessed. "Seriously, before we get the next Camelot Code mission? I'm hitting the gym, hard. I'm not in shape for this much questing."

"Ooh! Maybe you can start taking my mom's Zumba class!" Ashley cried. "Then when the bad guys come? We can totally dance-battle them to death!" She leaped into a wild pose, then started dancing and kicking her legs in a crazy dance-karate combo that looked utterly ridiculous.

Sophie laughed. "Let's not get carried away." Next thing you knew Ashley would be suggesting she try out for cheerleading. She scrambled to her feet. "Thanks for that awesome rescue, by the way," she said. "The iron cream thing was genius. Though I still don't understand how you made yourself invisible."

"Um, yeah. Don't get mad at me for using your mom's spell, okay? I figured invisibility could be super useful in many situations and—"

"Yeah, but…" Sophie scratched her head. "You did magic. Not everyone can do magic."

"Oh. I didn't even think of that." Ashley's face brightened. "Do you think I have magic powers, too? That would be so amazing! I could totally change my history grade! Or what about that hair-changing spell Mal had in *Descendants*? I could *definitely* put that to good use. Especially on poor Tanya Cooper. I'm not sure she even owns a brush—"

"Anyway!" Sophie interrupted, resisting the urge to face-palm. "You did great. We couldn't have done this without you."

She threw her arm around Ashley's shoulder. "I'm really glad you came along."

Ashley's face reddened. "You don't have to say that."

"I know. But I want to. And I mean it, too."

Ashley had more than proven her worth to their team and she'd proved to be a decent friend as well. And while maybe the two of them would never run in the same circles or braid each other's hair, neither did Lucas and Stu. And somehow they found a way to get along as stepbrothers.

She swallowed hard.

Stu...

She turned to him. He stared down at the ground, not meeting her eyes.

Ashley caught the look. "So, I'm going to go join Nimue and Emrys, okay?" she told them. "They're still looking for Damara. I'll be right back. I mean, not *right* right back. You guys will have tons of time. Maybe you can use it? To talk?" She gave them a meaningful look, then dashed out of the hut, slamming the door behind her.

Once she was gone, Sophie opened her mouth. "Look, I—" she started.

"I didn't—" Stu said at the same time.

They both stopped, laughing awkwardly. Then they lapsed into a heavy silence. In the distance, they could hear Nimue,

Emrys, and Ashley yelling for Damara. But they sounded another world away. Here, it was just the two of them, as if they were the only two people on earth.

Sophie's stomach burned with anguish as she struggled to figure out what to say. *This is Stu*, she scolded herself. Her best friend. She should be able to speak her mind. But her thoughts were so tangled up inside, she didn't know where to begin.

Thankfully, Stu took the lead. "Please don't be mad at me," he begged. "I know not telling you was wrong. And I'm really sorry. But I swear I was trying to do the right thing. I knew if I told you you'd be all upset, and it might distract you from your mission. I knew how long you'd been waiting for a Camelot Code quest. I didn't want to mess it all up with my own stupid drama." His voice caught on the words.

"It's not stupid, Stu," Sophie corrected, setting Spike on the bed and walking over to a chair. "This is a big deal. And I'm glad you want to be there for me, but—well, I want to be there for you, too." She sank into the chair and sighed. "I'm sorry I freaked out on the bridge. It was just...a shock. And the fact that Ashley knew and I didn't..."

Stu groaned, banging his fist against a post. "I blame loudmouth Lucas for that," he said. "Though it was kind of good she knew, actually. I mean, I know that sounds weird, but I was totally freaking out. And she gave me some good advice."

"What, like the proper footwear to wear for moving to California?" Sophie couldn't help but joke.

Stu made a face. "She's not that bad, Soph."

"I know. I was just kidding. She's all right. Except for the glitter thing." She shivered. "If I never see another speck of glitter in my life, it will be too soon."

"Yeah, well, I'm pretty sure I'm still going to be finding specks of it in my hair till I turn eighty," Stu joked.

"Probably. In fact, I think I see a few pieces right now...." She stood up to try to pluck them from his hair. He swatted her away and they both burst into laughter.

But the laughter soon faded into silence. Stu caught her eyes with his own. "I'm going to miss you," he said simply. "A lot."

Sophie's stomach twisted into knots all over again. She felt tears well in her eyes. "I'm going to miss you, too," she said, her voice cracking a little on the words. "You've lived down the street from me my entire life. If anything bad happened, I knew I could reach you in five minutes and you'd make everything okay."

"Yeah." Stu shuffled his feet. "It's going to be really weird. Though we can at least still hang out online. Play *Camelot's Honor* over voice chat. I know it's not the same. But it's better than nothing."

"That's true," Sophie agreed.

"Also, I'll be home all summer long. We won't have school then or soccer or anything. So we can hang out every day.

Honestly, you'll probably be sick of me by the end of summer. You'll be begging me to fly back to California."

Sophie laughed, tears leaking from her eyes. "Never," she swore. Then she reached over and gave Stu a hug. He hugged her back and a warm feeling rose inside her. The future would be different, she knew, and it wouldn't be all sunshine and roses. But they would get through it somehow. And they would stay best friends forever—no matter what.

"Now," she said, pulling away from the hug, swiping the tears from her eyes. "It's time to get to Camelot. We need to finish this thing and go home."

"Absolutely. After all, you have a lot of avocados to glitter!"

She punched him in the arm, laughing. "And you are so helping me do it!"

CHAPTER 40

Ｉt was a long journey by foot. But at last they reached Camelot Castle, Arthur and Guinevere's new home. As they stepped across the moat and into the courtyard, Sophie couldn't help but admire the sweeping white-stone walls of the mythical manor, complete with tall towers topped with majestic spires, stretching high into the sky. A total fairy-tale castle like the ones you'd find in a fantasy novel, and a far cry from the crumbling old fortress Arthur had lived in with his foster father, Sir Ector, before pulling the sword from the stone.

"Wind and Rain! My guards spoke true! You're actually here!"

Sophie looked up and saw none other than Princess Guinevere—*Queen* Guinevere—rushing toward her, arms outstretched. The queen looked more beautiful than ever, her formerly long blond hair now sheared into an adorable pixie cut—a twenty-first-century influence?—and adorned with a simple circlet around her head. She wore a soft blue gown and silver slippers. Only her eyes, shadowed and dark, hinted that times had been rough.

The two girls hugged; then Guin turned to Stu, putting out her hand. He took it in his own and brought it to his lips, bowing his head and kissing it respectfully. Guess all those medieval manners he'd learned playing king had stuck with him over the last few months. Sophie hid a laugh, not wanting to embarrass him.

"And this is Nimue, Emrys, and Ashley," she said, introducing the rest of the group.

"I remember you," Guinevere said, pointing at Ashley. "From the twenty-first century. You're Sophie's best friend!"

Ashley screwed up her face. "I am?"

"It's a long story," Sophie said quickly. She'd almost forgotten that Guin had come to the twenty-first century when history had been all out of whack. When the head cheerleader had somehow become a gamer geek's best friend and pepperoni pizza didn't exist. She still wasn't sure which had been weirder. "Ashley is going to be my sister," she explained. "Our parents are getting married."

"Oh, how lovely!" Guinevere declared. "I always wanted a sister." Then her smile faded. "But I must ask. Why are you here?

Not that I am not delighted to see you! But this is rather a bad time. Arthur is sick, you see."

"We know," Sophie assured her. "That's why we came." She quickly explained all that had happened. The Grail, the dragon, the works.

Guin listened carefully, her face draining of color at each twist of the tale. "So you do not have the Grail?" she asked, her voice cracking. "You cannot cure Arthur?"

"We have it. It's just . . . dragon-shaped," Nimue explained apologetically. "But Merlin is going to fix that. Just as soon as he gets back from Faerie with the Agrimony."

Guinevere brought a shaky hand to her forehead. "I am afraid that will be too late. Arthur worsens every day. He will not live much longer if he does not receive the healing medicine from the Grail."

Sophie's heart sank. Were they truly too late to save him?

"There must be something we can do," she said. "To help him hang on until Merlin gets back." She rubbed her chin, thinking back to times she'd been sick herself. "Have you been giving him lots of fluids? Do you have vitamins?"

Guinevere stared at her blankly. "Vita-mints?"

"If only we could time-travel him," Stu mused. "We could get him to a hospital or something. I'm sure twenty-first-century medicine could help."

"Nay. He's far too sick to travel," Guinevere replied. "He'd never survive the trip."

"And you don't have *any* medicine here?" Sophie asked, reaching for straws. "Like herbs or whatever?"

"We have already tried everything. Eye of newt. Scale of snake. All the usual remedies."

"Eye of newt? Ew. Thank goodness I live in the land of antibiotics," Ashley muttered. "Swallow a pill. Get better."

"You know those are made of mold," Stu pointed out.

"What? Oh my gosh. That's so—"

"Perfect!" Sophie exclaimed, her heart leaping in her chest as she remembered.

Everyone turned to look at her.

"What's perfect?" Ashley demanded. "Mold?"

"*Antibiotics,*" Sophie clarified. "Don't you have some in your bag?"

Her heart pounded in her chest as her mind flashed back to the scene at the airport. The security agents digging through Ashley's bag. Taking out the shampoo.

And the bottle of her mother's pills.

"Oh! Right. Of course. Why didn't I think of that?" Ashley unzipped her backpack and started rummaging through. After what seemed an eternity—seriously, what else was in that thing?—she triumphantly yanked a bottle of pills from the sack.

"Ta-da!" she proclaimed, waving it in the air. She gave Sophie a smug look. "And here you thought I overpacked."

"What is that?" Guinevere asked, peering curiously at the bottle.

Stu grabbed it out of Ashley's hands and held it out to the queen. "May I present penicillin, my lady," he said grandly. "The moldy magic that will save us all."

CHAPTER 41

Three Days Later

Nimue had had her doubts about this whole "modern medicine" idea, but in the end, it worked out extraordinarily well. Looking at Arthur now, sitting on his throne, the color back in his cheeks, she could hardly tell that he'd ever been sick.

Thank you, twenty-first century.

"It's a true miracle," she remarked to Emrys, who stood by her side at the back of the great hall along with half of King Arthur's court. Her apprentice friend was dressed in a brand-new robe—this one tailored to fit him—and he actually looked like a wizard rather than a boy playing dress-up.

She also had a new gown, plucked straight from Guinevere's

closet and made of the softest silk she'd ever felt in her life. It would be hard to go back to her stiff, coarse druid robes after this. But she would enjoy it while it lasted. Tonight, she would dance at a royal ball. Just as she'd always dreamed of doing.

"If only we had more of those magic pills," Emrys replied. "Can you imagine how many lives we could save?"

Nimue considered this for a moment. "Who says we cannot get more?" she asked, her eyes twinkling. "Perhaps we could take another trip to Lost Vegas to buy some."

He grinned at her. "You just want to play more video games."

"And you don't?"

The court trumpets blew, calling everyone to attention. They turned to the dais to see Arthur rise from his throne. He was still a little unsteady on his feet, but his queen stood by his side, allowing him to lean on her.

Arthur smiled at Guinevere, then his gaze shifted to his guests. "Lords and ladies of the court," he called out, his voice ringing through the hall. "Today we gather to honor some very special members of my court. Who risked their lives to save my own." He beckoned to Nimue and Emrys and the twenty-first-century visitors. "Will you step forward?" he asked.

Emrys dipped his head to Nimue and held out his hand. She took it with trembling fingers and together they walked to the center of the room. The court erupted in cheers and applause. Nimue felt her face heat with pleasure.

"Look, everyone! That's my boy up there!" shouted a gruff male voice from the back of the room.

Emrys stopped short. "Is that my father?" he cried in disbelief, standing on tiptoes to try to see over the crowd. "Is my father actually here?"

"I think your whole family is," Nimue said with a smile, catching sight of the overly enthusiastic group of very tall people at the other side of the room, cheering and whooping in excitement. "And I have to say, they look quite proud."

"They should be proud," Arthur declared from his throne. "You, Emrys the Excellent, have proven yourself a true hero of Camelot."

"Uh..." Emrys stammered. "I really didn't—"

"Shush," Nimue scolded, poking him in the ribs. "Heroes don't argue with their kings."

Emrys's cheeks turned bright red, but a grin stretched over his face.

"And you, Nimue," Arthur added, a fond look in his eyes. "You risked your life to save the Grail. And you kept it safe—in whatever form it might take."

As if on cue, Spike burped loudly from his perch on Ashley's shoulder. Everyone laughed.

Nimue dropped to her knees in a bow before her king. "And I shall continue to do so," she vowed. "For the rest of my life, if need be." And she meant it, too. As long as the Grail existed, she had a purpose. Even if she had to carry it out alone.

Well, not totally alone. A wet nose nudged at her hand. She smiled down at Damara and scratched her behind the ears. "You and me, girl," she whispered. "We'll do it together."

"Actually, that won't be necessary."

The crowd gasped as the back door to the great hall suddenly swung open and none other than Merlin the Great stepped into the throne room. He looked a bit ragged, especially among all the well-dressed guests. And—to Nimue's shock—he was clean-shaven. No beard to be seen!

"Merlin!" exclaimed Arthur. "I was so worried!"

In a blink, he and Guinevere dove off the dais, pushing through the crowds until they reached the wizard, throwing their arms around him and hugging him with wild abandon.

"Now, now!" Merlin huffed, trying to untangle himself from their enthusiasm. "Take it easy on an old man!"

"Did you get the Agrimony?" Nimue asked after Arthur and Guinevere stepped out of Merlin's way. "Are you able to turn the Grail back into a cup?"

It was funny, she realized as she asked the question, she wasn't actually sure what she wanted him to say. Sure, she knew the Grail should, by all rights, be turned back to its proper form. But at the same time, she was going to miss the little dragon if it was. Digestive issues and all.

Merlin nodded solemnly. "I did. And I can," he told her. "It took a bit of groveling. And much apologizing, too."

"And... a trip to the fairy barber?" Stu asked, raising an eyebrow.

Merlin blushed, automatically reaching up to stroke his no-longer-there beard. "Don't ask," he grumbled. "In any case, in the end we came to an understanding."

"So... does that mean you're dating again?" Ashley asked with a wicked smile.

"Not that it's any of your business," the wizard huffed. "But we shall see how it goes. For now, I have agreed to winter in Faerie—the weather is much better there, anyway. No blasted snow! And then, each spring, I will return to check on the human race." He shrugged, giving a sheepish smile. "I think that's what you call a win-win?"

"Nice!" Stu declared, slapping Merlin on the back. "Our work here is done. So if you could just zap us home? That would be awesome. Let's just say we've got a lot on our plates back in the good old twenty-first century."

Merlin waved them off. "Do not worry," he assured them. "I will get you back where you belong very soon. And none of your parents will have even noticed you were gone."

"And my history test?" Ashley asked hopefully.

Merlin rolled his eyes. "Fine, fine. But next time you *really* need to study!"

Ashley planted a big smooch on his clean-shaven cheek. "Thanks, Merl! You're the best!"

"But wait," Nimue interjected. "What of Morgana? You have not mentioned what happened to her."

"She is still in the custody of the Fey court," Merlin replied. "I made it a condition of our new deal. After all, there will be less need for my help here in the real world if she's not running around mucking things up all the time. Which means I will get to spend more time in Faerie." His eyes twinkled. "Win-win, as I said."

"Sounds like quite the happily-ever-after indeed," remarked a new voice.

Everyone whirled around. There, at the back of the room, stood a tall woman dressed in a long white gown cinched with a silver cord. Nimue's eyes widened. A Companion! She dropped to her kness, bowing her head. The others around her quickly followed suit.

Except for Sophie.

"Mom!" she cried, rushing toward the woman. "Oh my gosh, Mom! You're here!"

The woman wrapped her arms around her daughter, squeezing her tight and nuzzling her face against her hair. Nimue's heart ached a little at the love she saw between them. She had never known her own mother. And now the woman who had raised her was dead. Still, it was nice to see Sophie with her own happily-ever-after.

"Darling daughter," Sophie's mother said, pulling away from

the hug. "You have done so well. On your first assignment, too!"
She looked around at the group. "You all have," she added. "I
am very proud of you."

"Thanks," Sophie said, beaming. "It was nothing." Stu gave
her a sharp look. "Okay, almost nothing," she amended with a
laugh.

"And you," the Companion said, turning to Nimue. "You
have fulfilled your sacred vow as a druid. You kept the Grail
safe, even at the risk of your own life."

Nimue squared her shoulders. "And I will continue to do
so," she declared. "Once it's changed back to a cup, I will take
it back to Avalon and return it to its resting spot and guard it
until it's needed again."

The Companion smiled. "That is very generous of you," she
said. "But you are only one girl. It would be unfair to put such
a burden on your shoulders."

"But…" Nimue faltered, suddenly worried all over again.
"I really don't mind!" She knew the Companion was right—it
would be a tough task to accomplish on her own. But if she didn't
look after the Grail, what else would she do? She didn't have
anywhere else to go. Any other calling…

"That is not true," Sophie's mother said sternly, as if she could
read Nimue's thoughts. "In truth, you have a very important
destiny, my dear."

Nimue gawked at her. "I … do?"

"It will be clear in time. For now, I want you to go with Merlin to his Crystal Cave. He has agreed to take you on as an apprentice along with Emrys. Together, you will learn magic and become powerful sorcerers in your own right. We will need as many as possible for the dark years ahead."

Nimue stared at the Companion, her face aglow with a mix of fear and wonder. "Me? A sorceress?" she breathed. "How can that be? I am only an orphan girl of no importance!"

"You may have been told that. But nothing could be further from the truth," Sophie's mother assured her.

Nimue's heart skipped a beat. "Do you . . . know where I came from, then?" she asked, her voice squeaking on the words. "Who my parents were?"

"I promise you, dear one, all will be made clear in time," Sophie's mother said. "But for now, tell me: Will you accept your destiny? Will you agree to train under Lord Merlin?"

"Why yes! Of course, yes! I would like nothing more in the world!" Nimue burst out, ecstatic. Then she glanced over at Emrys. "You don't mind, do you? Being stuck with the most bothersome girl in the world a little longer?"

Emrys grinned at her. "I can think of nothing I'd like more."

"Excellent," Sophie's mother pronounced. "Then let it be so."

She turned to her daughter, Ashley, and Stu. "Now," she said, "if you three are ready? I think it's time to go home."

EPILOGUE

The wedding venue was beautiful. Situated in the backyard of an old Victorian mansion on the shore of a quiet lake, it glittered like a true fairy forest—with sparkling lights strung from tree to tree. Small, circular tables were scattered across the lawn, each adorned with pale peach tablecloths that matched the bridesmaid dresses perfectly and mason-jar centerpieces that Sophie and Ashley had filled with glow-in-the-dark stones. After the amount of glitter they'd endured during their adventure, they'd decided to skip the avocados.

Ashley had wanted more decor, of course. But by the time Sophie's mom zapped them home, they barely had time to do the centerpieces. Sophie had felt a bit awkward informing her mom that her dad was getting remarried. But her mother had been totally cool with it, in the end. She still loved Sophie's father, she told Sophie, but she could never be with him. And since she couldn't be there to make him happy, she was thankful he'd found someone who could.

"There you are!"

Sophie looked up. Ashley was on approach. She hadn't seen her now stepsister since the church ceremony, as Ashley had been busy helping her mom get changed into her reception dress. Ashley surveyed the scene now, smiling widely.

"It looks amazing out here, doesn't it?" she asked, letting out a low whistle. She turned to Sophie. "Thank you for all your help. I mean, we had zero time to do this. But somehow we pulled it off!"

"We totally pulled it off," Sophie agreed with a smile of her own. "Everyone's going on and on about how beautiful it all looks." She smirked. "Of course, they all said that I looked beautiful, too. So maybe they're a bit nearsighted."

"Please. You look amazing," Ashley assured her. "Despite the dress."

Sophie raised her eyebrows. "I thought you loved these dresses!"

"Are you kidding me? They're orange chiffon. That pretty much makes them hideous by any standard."

"But I thought . . ." Sophie shook her head. "Why didn't you say something before?"

Ashley gave her a sheepish look. "Because they mean a lot to my mom," she confessed. "They remind her of this Barbie she really wanted as a little girl."

"A Barbie?" Sophie had to admit, now that she thought of it, the dresses did seem rather Barbie-like.

"The Peaches and Cream Barbie," Ashley explained. "My mom wanted it so badly. But her mom couldn't afford it." She shrugged. "My mom grew up really poor."

"Oh," Sophie said, suddenly feeling terrible. "I had no idea. Did she ever get the doll?"

Ashley nodded, her eyes lighting up. "Yes!" she told her. "From your dad!"

"What?"

"Didn't he tell you? That was how he proposed to my mom! He brought her out to this nice restaurant. And he gave her a box. She opened it up and it was the Peaches and Cream Barbie. He'd found it on eBay or something and paid a fortune for it. And on the box he stuck a little sticky note asking 'Will you marry me?'" Ashley beamed. "Of course she had to say yes! I mean, how romantic is that?"

Sophie nodded. She had no idea her dad had it in him.

"Anyway, it was like the nicest, sweetest thing ever!" Ashley continued. "And my mom wanted him to know how much it meant to her. So she found these awful dresses that look just like the doll's. Super ugly and out of fashion, I know. But they mean the world to her. So how could I say no?"

"Wow," Sophie whispered. She looked at Ashley's dress now, and then at her own. "You know," she said, "they're not *that* bad...."

Ashley laughed. "Yes they are, but they're also pretty great in their own way."

"Yeah." Sophie nodded. "Wow. I can't believe they actually did it. We're actually sisters."

"Crazy." Ashley snorted. "But also ... pretty great, too?" Her voice held a hint of uncertainty.

Sophie reached out and gave her a hug. "Pretty great," she agreed. And she was surprised, she kind of meant it. Sure, this wasn't the happily-ever-after she'd imagined as a child—with her parents magically getting back together—but it could be a pretty decent alternative.

And hey, she and Ashley had just teamed up to save the world. How hard could this sister thing really be?

"By the way! I have amazing plans for our bathroom," Ashley chirped, her eyes shining excitedly.

"Wait, what?"

"Total makeover! It's going to be spectacular. I have this whole Pinterest board dedicated to ideas. We'll start with taking everything off the walls...."

Sophie sighed. Well, she'd wanted an adventure....

"Sophie!"

She turned to see Stu running across the lawn, dressed in

a suit that looked two sizes too big. He'd spent the afternoon with his mom, talking things out, and must have just arrived at the reception. She excused herself from Ashley and ran over to him. "How'd it go?"

Stu drew in a breath. "Well, I told her I'd go," he said hesitantly. "I mean, not like I really had a choice. But I wanted her to know I was cool with it." He shrugged. "And this way I get to help pick out the apartment. I'm holding out for something near the beach."

"Near the beach would be amazing," Sophie cried. "Maybe you can learn to surf!"

Stu snorted. "Let's not get carried away. This is still me we're talking about. King of the geeks."

"You'll never know unless you try."

"True." He wrung his hands together. "I'm also going to check out my new school. It's really a cool place, actually. They'll teach me how to code and do game design and it goes all the way through high school. A lot of their students even end up at Caltech, where all the best game designers go to college."

"Nice," Sophie said. And she meant it, too, even though her heart ached at the idea of losing her best friend. At least he was going somewhere cool. "Maybe I can visit you sometime?"

"You'd better. Maybe you can even figure out a way to teleport from time to time? You did get a new spell book from your mom, right?"

"Oh my gosh, I didn't even think of that! What a great savings that will be on airfare!"

Stu nodded. "And, of course, we'll always have the Camelot Code. Who knows what crazy quest we'll be called on to do next?"

"I can't wait to find out."

"Look, look!" Ashley cried, rushing over to them. "The bride and groom!"

Sophie looked up. There, standing on the porch, were her dad and Ashley's mom, looking radiant and happy as they waved to their guests. Her heart swelled in her chest. And as she watched them step down the stairs and onto the dance floor to start their first dance, she and Stu and Ashley clapped and cheered.

"Look at them!" Sophie heard her father say, glancing in their direction. "They actually look like they're getting along."

"Sometimes dreams do come true," her new stepmother said with a smile.

Sophie felt herself smiling, too. She looked over at Ashley and then at Stu, her heart suddenly feeling very full. Their adventure in Camelot may have ended. But in many ways, this was a new beginning. Who knew what was in store for them next?

And then, as if on cue, her cell phone chimed.